EMBDEDDED

STONEWALL SERIES
BOOK 2

J.L. DRAKE

To Paul,
Sorry, man, but it was time to shake shit up.

CAST OF CHARACTERS

A Friendly Reminder

- **Daniel:** Cole's father, first generation Blackstone. Married to **Sue,** Cole's mother.
- **Abigail/Abby:** Mark's adopted mother, Cole's childhood nanny, house aide. Sister to **June.**
- **Dr. Roberts:** House psychologist. Dating **Abigail**.
- **Frank:** Blackstone contact for the Army. First generation Blackstone member.
- **Zack:** First generation Blackstone member. Restaurant owner.
- **Chili:** Undercover Agent
- **Grim Gates:** Mafia King [Havoc of Sins Trilogy]

- **Trigger:** MC President of [Devil's Reach Trilogy]

FAMILIES

- **Cole:** Owner of the Shadows safe house. Leader of the Blackstone special ops team. Married to **Savannah**. They have two kids, **Olivia** and **Easton**.
- **John:** Blackstone member. Married to **Sloane.**
- **Mike:** Blackstone member. Married to **Catalina.** Daughter **Gabriella.**
- **Keith:** Member of Blackstone. Was married to **Lexi.** They have two kids, **Brandon and Reagan.**
- **Mark:** Blackstone member. Married to **Mia.** They have a set of twins, **Liam** and **Ethan,** and a daughter, **Tabby.**
- **Paul:** Blackstone member. Deceased. *Well…I won't ruin this one for you.*
- **Dell:** North Rock member. Dusk Safe house in North Carolina.

- **Davie:** North Rock member. Dusk Safe house in North Carolina.
- **Steve Chamness:** North Rock member. Dusk Safe house in North Carolina.
- **Denton Barlow:** The American. Deceased.

ANIMALS/PETS

- **Goats:** Friendly reminders of home
- **Chickens:** Annoying and always in the way
- **Scoot:** A-hole house cat
- **Butters:** Mark and Mia's husky
- **Tripper:** John and Sloane's German shepherd

CARTEL PLAYERS

- **Martin Castillo** – Dead (From Dark Water Series)
- **Eric Noah** – Martin Castillo's right-hand man, "Dead"
- **Talya Canos** – Eric Noah's ex-girlfriend (Dead)
- **Jerry and Elva Canos** – Talya's parents who have now taken over Martin Castillo's operation
- **Esmeralda Perez** - Bruno's Mother

ONE

Mexico/Texas Border

BRUNO

I swung my arm as hard as I could and jammed the knife into my security guard's neck. His body jerked from the impact. His eyes widened as the pain registered, then he struggled to breathe as he grasped his neck and dropped to the marble floor. "You see him?" I screamed at my staff in English. "That's what happens when you don't follow orders!"

"*Sí*—" Another man started to speak, and I glared at him. "Yes," he quickly corrected himself. "The woman used the restroom to do her live video. We did not know she was on the other side of the wall from where we watched for her."

"Well, now you won't know anything." I shot him in the head, and the rest of the men stayed silent.

"*¡Mierda!*" The bullet wound in my foot throbbed and switched between hot and cold pain.

"Bruno?" Sully Sanchez appeared. He stood in the doorway of the house I owned, less than ten minutes from the border. "Bruno," he repeated, "you need to see a doctor."

"No, I need all of you to do your jobs," I snarled at him, happy to have someone new to lash out at. Sweat clung to my forehead and dripped down the back of my neck. The loss of Nicole and that child fueled me.

"I explained from the very start that Nicole was up to the task of finding that child for you. As a war correspondent for the *Washington Post*, she has resources I can't even come close to. I couldn't get within ten feet of Rafael Cruz, in spite of the fact it was my own damn party." Sully dropped his hands to his sides and opened his mouth to say something, then stopped.

"What?" I fought the urge to pass out from the pain in my foot and cursed that damn woman who'd caused it. I took a deep breath. "Say it."

"Okay." He stepped farther into the small room. The click of his heels echoed off the plastered green walls. He stopped and looked around, no doubt for an exit, then said, "You came on too strong with Nicole again. I warned you." He held up a hand as if to say *hear me out*. "Remember what we talked about before all this happened." His voice stayed even, and I watched him closely. He was within minutes of death.

"Go on," I dared him, "but tread lightly." I saw his neck contract.

"Bruno, you went too dark too fast when you first met her. Remember, you sent me in to do damage control, and we agreed you'd back off and keep your distance until I gained her trust. I did, and things were working in our favor. She had no idea you were spinning the press from behind the scenes. You're a smart man, Bruno. We both know that."

"Don't patronize me, Sully. You are dangerously close to having your throat cut."

"I'm only trying to help you." He licked his lips. "That day you had her brought here and demanded she find that child and bring him to you, you set our progress back about three years. You should've sent Nando. You could have been with her instead of having her run off on her own. You lost an opportunity to get her back into your life." He held his hands up. "And, well, here we are."

The nerve. "So, this is all my fault?" I hoped he'd say yes, so I could drive a bullet into his head.

"Bruno, my friend," he sighed. "What I'm saying is that you need to take a breath and give me a chance to fix this for you. Please, let me see what I can do."

"He's right." My mother strolled into the room, sidestepping around the pool of blood next to my guard.

Sully stood straighter and cleared his throat as he addressed her. "Hello again, Esmeralda."

"Mother, what are you doing here?" How did she always know how to find me?

"You're not answering your phone."

I patted my pockets and wondered where I left my phone. "I must have left it in the car." I brushed it off and asked my question again. "What are you doing here?"

"Do you imagine even for a moment that I don't always know what you are up to?" Her movements were graceful, and she oozed power as she lowered onto a chair. Rio, her right-hand man, went directly to the bar to make her a drink. She kicked her crossed legs out and leaned back like she was in control. The men in the room stood straighter and looked nervous. "You need to let Sully help you figure this out. That damn American reporter has caused too much trouble already."

"But she hasn't crossed the border yet," I wanted to shout, but didn't dare, so my voice stayed even. "I have men at every lane. They will find her. What I need is to wait this out, and when she reveals herself, I will deal with her and that damn child myself."

"No, you won't." Her tone had an edge to it. "You didn't listen to me all those years ago. You should have killed the little bitch when you had a chance. We're in this situation because of you." She reached for the drink Rio held out and took her time as she sipped. "Now, besides sending Sully out to do what he can, what are you going to do about this, son?"

My insides shook as I shifted my weight off my

burning foot. My shoes were sticky with blood, and it reminded me of what I'd like to do to Nicole.

"I awoke the sleepers."

My mother's brows went up, and her face was intrigued. "About time."

"Yes, well, these things take time, Mother." I gave in and lowered myself onto the couch to ease the pain. It did nothing. I felt my clothes stick to my sweaty skin. "I will get you what you want—what I promised you I would deliver. Things just went a little sideways."

"It's because you think with your *verga*," she pointed to my crotch, "especially around that Nicole woman." I looked away because I knew she was right. "Everyone out." She flicked her wrist, and within seconds, the room was empty.

I heard the leather on her chair hiss as she leaned forward and took my hand. "*Cariño*, I need you to fix this. Do whatever is necessary to get me that Canos baby and kill that reporter."

"I will, I promise." I had no intention of killing Nicole, at least not right away. She would be mine to enjoy, until I was done with her. No woman would walk away from me without repercussions.

"She's smart, Bruno." Her gaze went cold, and the temperature in the room dropped. My foot throbbed even more as my blood pressure went up. "So, I need to know you understand what will happen if that woman discovers even a fraction of what we're up to. She has a reputation. She's like a dog with a bone and will be relentless until she discovers the truth." Her phone rang, and she glanced down at it. "He can wait," she murmured and silenced it. I knew it was Papa. He wouldn't like that, but Mama was not a woman who backed down from anyone. She was the one who was changing the Cartel game, and Papa would have to wait for her to call him back. "Do you hear me, son?"

"Yes." I hated how small I felt.

"I need to hear you say it."

I licked my dry mouth and swallowed my pride. "I wouldn't jeopardize our empire. Especially not after the death of Uncle Martin." I hoped the mention of the death of her brother, Martin Castillo, would turn her anger elsewhere.

Mama studied my face again with her eyes in slits. I felt her effort to instill in me that her position in the family was way above me. "Get that looked at." She pointed to my foot. "I won't have you getting an infection. We have enough eyes and ears out there, so you can take a few hours to go see a doctor." She stood, and Rio popped out of nowhere as she crossed the room. She stopped at the door and said over her shoulder, "I want them all dead, Bruno, every last one of them. There is no room to spare a single soul this time around."

"Understood."

PRESS

TWO

Mexico/Texas Border

NICOLE

"Nicole Winter?" The man who looked like Rip from *Yellowstone* loomed over me with his eyes shaded behind a pair of dark sunglasses. He didn't smile or show any warmth as his head lifted to look over mine. I knew he'd be looking for any trouble I might have brought to the border. If I was about to get into a stranger's car, I was glad that Jack, my best friend at the *Washington Post*, knew what was going on. I looked over my shoulder and spotted a Canos soldier getting closer. Rip was my only hope.

"Yes."

"Put this on." He handed me an oversized coat.

"Up over your head too." I followed his instructions, as I knew it was my only option.

"Thank you so much, Lucy, all of you." I beamed at the ladies.

"Only too happy to help, dear. Be safe, now." Lucy smiled back. "Look after these two." She gave the stranger a stern look, but he didn't react.

"You ready?" He looked at me, and I nodded. "Good. Now, follow me and keep your head down." I did but scanned the area like it was my next breath, maybe because it kind of was. We weaved through the sea of people, and I had to use my arms to create a protective shield around Chase and hoped to God he wouldn't start to cry again. The man kept a few paces in front of me with his head constantly on a swivel.

He took me around a corner away from the hustle of the car lanes. Then he stopped at a blue eighteen-wheeler. He opened the huge rolling door at the back and nodded. "I can get you across if you hide in here."

"There?" I repeated and looked inside the long, dark box as I lowered the coat from my head.

"Yes."

"Okay. Wait! Can I at least know your name since you know mine?"

Suddenly, something moved inside the box, and I locked eyes with… My heart dropped straight to the ground, and I turned back to him with my mouth open. *What the hell?*

"My name's Chili." He waited for me to weigh

my options. He saw the fear that had taken hold of me and tilted his head to one side then offered me a hand to help me step up inside. "You either get in, or you both will die waiting for another ride." He pointed to poor little Chase, whose flushed face could just be seen from where he lay in the makeshift sling.

"Are you really going to help us?" I pleaded as I looked into the dark container. The young woman I had locked eyes with gave me a slow nod as if to say it was okay.

"Yeah." I took his hand and let him help us both up into the massive truck. Once my eyes adjusted, I could see there were boxes and boxes filled with avocados. "Chili?" I turned to look at him as I felt a sense of panic rip through me. "I don't care what happens to me, but can you promise to get this little guy to safety?"

He didn't say anything as he studied me with a face like granite, but I thought I caught a small nod as he reached up and pulled the giant door closed to leave us in total darkness.

Oh, my God.

"Put your hands out and come toward me." The woman's voice made me jump right out of my skin. At least I wasn't completely alone. "Move toward the sound of my voice," she called again.

"Yeah, okay." My voice outed my nerves, and I felt my way around the crates until I found her hands.

"Good," she coached me. "Now, there's a fake

wall here, you need to take a step to your right to get around it. Feel the side of it here." She moved my hand, and I felt what she referred to as Chase gave a nasty cough that vibrated through me. I instinctively rubbed his back and talked to him in a soothing voice. "We're okay, buddy. I got you." I could feel the heat from his fever through my shirt and knew the poor little guy needed a doctor desperately.

"Okay," the young woman whispered when she came to a stop, "don't freak out…" She pulled back a metal cover on the roof and revealed a skylight that let some of the warm sun in. It lit up the tiny space, and I blinked to let my eyes adjust then drew in a sharp breath as I looked around. "It's okay. We're not going to hurt you." I saw at least seven girls huddled together who looked to have been through war and back. The angle of the light deepened the dark circles under the eyes. Their hair was wild, and I noticed none of them had shoes on. As a girl reached up to brush her hair back, I saw her hands, the nails bitten into stubs and bleeding. One girl was hunched over as if in pain. Her ankle looked purple and swollen.

"What's going on?" My panic returned full force. "Were we just sold?" I hugged Chase a little tighter and felt the walls of the tiny tin room close in on me.

"We were hoping you could tell us that answer." The young woman who had helped guide me behind the panel pushed back her long auburn hair and offered me her hand. "I'm Crystal."

"You're American?" Damn, they were barely out of high school.

"We all are." She nodded at the others.

"I'm Nicole," I told her.

Crystal handed me a bottle of water, and I wondered where she got it. "Please have a seat." She offered me a pillow that, to my surprise, looked clean. I downed some water and tried to drip a little into Chase's mouth, but it only made him cough.

"Thank you." I tipped my head back and felt how sore my body was.

"Your baby's sick?" one of the young girls asked. She had bangs cut super short straight across her forehead.

"Yes. I'm worried about him." I kissed Chase's feverish head and felt extremely protective over him. "He needs a doctor." I tucked a bit of fabric over his face as I wondered how much trouble we were in. There was no way this could be good. We were all jammed in a hidden space at the back of a truck behind crates of fruit that Cartel killed farmers over.

"What's your story?" Crystal asked.

"I'd like yours first." I smiled at her. She seemed to have taken the lead among the group, as the others looked at her to speak first.

"She and I," she pointed to another girl whose face was as pale as her hair, "were at a party in LA. One moment we were dancing and having fun, and the next we were grabbed by some guys. They injected us with some kind of drug and tied us up." She swallowed and looked at the pale blonde. "That's Cindy. She hasn't been the same since."

"Hi, Cindy," I said softly and smiled at the girl but got no response. Her eyes were swollen like she had just had a breakdown. I would have done the same.

"We woke up inside some kind of trunk. They didn't even give us food or water for like two days. We woke up in a truck." She looked around. "It was smaller than this one. Then a couple of guys brought us to a tunnel where we met the rest of these girls."

"It was in Yuma," the girl with the bangs added. "I heard them say that. I'm Alexi."

"Hi, Alexi. Did you hear anything else?"

"Yeah, a guy told me we were going to Mexico because we were now owned by someone else. Like we'd been sold or something." Her eyes were wide and frightened. "We walked for what seemed like a day through that tunnel, and there wasn't much light in there." She shivered.

"When we came out the other side," Crystal took over again, "there was this man who looked at us. He just nodded, and we were loaded into a really fancy car. They put bags over our heads so we couldn't see, and after that, we drove forever."

"Yeah, we switched cars at least three times, before being handed over to this guy," Alexi added as she pointed in the direction of the cab of the truck. "He said he was going to take us back to the US and that his name is Charley." I squinted as I repeated the name in my head. He'd told me his name was Chili. I decided not to question it; either way, we were now all in this together.

"They never said anything else to you?" I wondered why, with all I'd heard, they would find themselves headed back across the border. What the hell was going on here?

She shrugged her thin shoulders. "No," she sniffed.

"Do you know anything at all?" Crystal begged. "It's been the longest and scariest days of my life—of all of our lives." She reached for her checked-out friend's hand and gave it a squeeze. The girl barely registered her touch. "Then there's you and a baby with us now, and we're even more confused." She gave a half laugh, half cry.

"I wish I had an answer for you, but my story is very different than yours." I decided to share a little of my story so if one of them got away, maybe they could say I was with them. "I'm a war correspondent for the *Washington Post*. I do stories on the drug war between the US and Mexico. For the Cartel, to be more specific. I try to shed light on what the country and its people are going through." My voice shook as I heard the truck's engine start. The noise scared Chase, as he jumped and started to whimper.

"Mama, Mama." He rubbed his fists into his eyes. His bottom lip stuck out, and my heart broke all over again for the poor little guy.

"It's okay, sweetheart." I lifted him a little and

tucked his head under my neck the way I now knew he loved and rubbed gentle circles on his back. "Um," I fought to remember where I'd left off. "Long story short, this little guy's in trouble, and I need to get him over this border and into the hands of someone who can protect him." A strange coldness tightened inside my chest and made it hard to breathe. I had been so focused on getting Chase to safety that I hadn't thought about how I'd have to hand him off to a stranger. What if they didn't know he loved to be sung to? Or that he felt safe when tucked under my chin? Or that he only loved to rub his bunny's left ear and not the right?

"Wait, he's not your baby?" Crystal squinted at him, but she would have had a hard time seeing his features in the dim light. Besides, his little face was deeply tucked inside Paul's hoodie. "But he called you Mama."

"His mother was killed," I pulled back my chin and kissed his little head again through the fabric, "and I don't think he's calling me Mama. I think he's calling out for her."

"I'm from a big family." She reached out and rubbed his bare leg, "I'm the oldest and helped raise my little brother after my mom got ill. I know he thought I was his mother because I held him all the time. He called me Momma and our actual mom Nana." She smiled warmly, and I wondered how a family like that would feel about Crystal being taken.

My anger bubbled to the surface. "I can confidently say he thinks you're his mama."

I struggled over her comment. I knew I shouldn't get attached to Chase, but it was practically impossible not to. He was the sweetest little thing and so helpless. I already knew I'd fight to the death for him.

"My job doesn't allow me to have a family. He'll be confused when I have to give him to someone else, but it's for the best." I felt the pain of saying that out loud, and my arms tightened around him.

The truck's engine turned off, and we were once again at a standstill. "How long have you guys been here in this truck?"

Crystal looked at one of the other girls then turned to look back at me. "Since last night, but we were parked at a truck stop for a long while. Charley brought us food and explained that we would be crossing in the morning. Then this morning he said we had to wait for one more person."

"Me?"

"I guess so. No one else showed up."

That was odd. I didn't know I'd be getting this ride until I arrived at the border and reached out on that live feed from the restroom. I couldn't believe my luck that someone offered to help. *Wait.* But that Chili guy knew my name, so he had to have seen my video. The timeline of Crystal's story was confusing, and it simply didn't work.

Suddenly, the engine started, and we were on the move. It seemed as if we were changing lanes. Maybe border patrol waved for him to go through a faster line, or maybe they saw me get in? Whatever was happening, it sent an extra dose of fear through me, and I was maxed out on fear.

"It's okay, ladies," Crystal assured the girls when one of them began to cry softly. "He said we we're heading back to the US, and that's a good thing, right? We just have to be smart, and the first chance we get, we run." They all murmured their agreement, but these poor kids were all in bare feet and tight outfits. I couldn't imagine how they'd ever run, especially in their current mental state.

I leaned my head back against the wall and closed my eyes. My head hurt with trying to piece the *what the hell is happening* puzzle together. I needed to focus on something else. Paul popped into my head, and I couldn't help but feel sick that he might not be all right. *He has his team. They'll get him.* I pushed Paul's handsome face away and tried to focus on something a little less hard on the heart. Bruno took his place, and I flinched when I thought about how far I pushed him at the border. I used that fear and gave myself a mental high five when I thought about how I shot him in the foot. I hoped it left him with a permanent limp. Maybe the women and men he hurt in the future would have a fighting chance of getting away.

"We're at the border booth," Crystal whispered, and it brought me back to the present. I saw her peek through a tiny crack between the truck's wall panels. I looked down at Chase and hoped to hell the little guy wouldn't cry. "He just waved us through!" Her excitement spread across to the other girls.

"Aren't trucks supposed to be scanned?" The words flew out of my mouth without me meaning too.

Crystal's face fell and she looked around. "I-I don't know."

With wide eyes and open ears, we listened for the truck's engine to slow to say we were being pulled over to secondary, but it never did. Crystal was glued to the little peep hole and relayed what she could see. "Still just open road. There's a family in a car next to us." She leaned back, and I could see her tears. "Crazy, isn't it?" She looked at me. "How many trucks and cars have you driven past in your lifetime. You never know what's really going on inside."

I thought about Bruno's phone in my bag and wondered if I should offer it to them to call their families. I'd turned it off before I left the bathroom at the border. I hadn't wanted to take any chances. I knew the second I turned it on, he'd see my location. I felt guilty that these girls needed to get to their families, but I had to get Chase and myself to safety. I was his only hope. Chase shifted, and I watched as his fingers played with the GoPro camera that was attached to my shoulder and was still recording.

"Crystal," I pointed to my camera, "you said the first chance we get to run and get help, right?" She nodded. "Why don't each of you speak to my camera, and if I get away, I can use my contacts in the media to get this to go viral."

"Yeah," she sat up straighter, "yes, Nicole that's a great idea!" She brushed her hair away from her face and took a deep breath. "My name is Crystal Bleak. I'm twenty-one and from Malibu, California. Mom," she started to cry, "I'm so sorry we went to the party." I watched as each girl introduced themselves and quickly told their version of what had happened to them. If anything, it gave us something to focus on. It gave the girls hope.

I squeezed the arm of the checked-out girl named Cindy and slowly pointed my camera at her. She just stared straight ahead with empty eyes. I wondered if she was screaming for help inside. It crossed my mind that even if she was rescued, would she ever really escape her battled mental state? "It's okay," I tried to reassure her, "it's okay, Cindy. Even if we just show your family your face and that you're alive, it might be enough." Her eyes remained deep, blank pools, and I could only hope my words got through. I smiled warmly and hoped they did. "There you go, that was perfect."

Afterward, we all sank into a terrible silence, their earlier desperate smiles of hope forgotten.

My head flopped around as sleep begged me to give in. The truck was hot, but Chase was hotter. I wasn't a doctor, but I'd been around my fair share of sick children, thanks to growing up in an orphanage, and my guess would be that his fever shouldn't have stayed this long. I was so afraid for him.

Hours later, the sun began to set, and the truck went dark. I settled against the wall and let the weight of Chase's tiny body rest on my lap. Finally, my body gave in, and I felt my mind let go as I fell into a restless sleep.

I glanced at myself in the mirror in the hotel lobby and fixed the collar of my dress. I had borrowed it from my good friend Mari. The soft white fabric of the skirt billowed out as I walked, and I felt so good in it. I had met Mari through my friend Jack's wife, Emily. She'd spent a year abroad here in Mexico City and had connected the two of us. Mari hadn't hesitated when I called to ask if I could stay with them, and so began a solid friendship. I'd visited her and her husband a few times over that year.

My phone rang, and I twisted to grab it from the table. "Hey, Jack."

"Nicole, I was thinking," he said in a low voice. He was probably in the computer room. "I don't think this is a good idea. Mari was telling Emily these guys are ruthless. She's worried."

I laughed. "Well, of course. They're Cartel. I've been in these situations before. Don't worry."

"Right, but I've got a really bad feeling about this one." He paused. "You know I've always got

your back, but when have I ever said I don't think you should do this meet and greet?"

I dropped into a chair and glanced around as I contemplated his words. He was right. Jack let me run with just about everything but had never warned me off before. It was just that this was such a huge opportunity. "I hear ya, I do, but Sully will be here with me."

"Sully?" Jack cursed under his breath. "Nicole, Sully is one of them. I know you think he's sweet and different than the rest, but he's still Cartel. Don't lose sight of that."

"Oh, I haven't." I wasn't that stupid. "Sully is trouble, but he can get me an in with Martin Castillo and his sister." I knew Esmeralda Perez was even harder to connect with. "I know they're up to something, and I can feel it in my bones it's something big."

"I know, I know, you've told me that but, jeez, rubbing elbows with Castillo's nephew and his sister is a whole new level. The fact that Bruno is friends with the Tunnel to Hell Devil, as you call him, is damn scary in itself."

I remembered the first time I'd seen Eric Noah and how he snapped a man's neck without a second thought. I shivered at the thought and knew Jack's worry was justified. "I'll be careful, I promise."

"Nicole, I'm telling you, where there's Bruno, there's Eric." He went on. "Just know you're

setting yourself up to meet that guy at some point. It's just a matter of time."

A call pushed through, and I saw it was Glen calling.

"Sorry, Jack, but I need to take this."

"Nicole, wait. Think about this. You're only two years into the job, and you've turned up some major threads that've led you to bigger things. You don't need to be on Bruno Perez's radar."

The call that pushed through ended and started to ring again. "I promise I got this. I'll call you when it's over. I'm sorry. I have to go."

"Just stay alive."

"I will."

I hung up and had to admit to myself I felt off. Jack never gave his personal feelings about things. The fact that he had put me on edge. The phone rang again, and I pressed the button and tensed as the call connected.

"When I call, you answer," he snapped at me.

"I was working."

"Need I remind you, you work for me too?" I rolled my eyes; he was such a dick. If I didn't feel working for him was for a higher purpose, I'd ditch the guy so fast. "When's this meeting?" My stomach twisted with a sudden burst of panic. What if Jack was right? "I'm second guessing my idea. Maybe having Sully introduce me to Bruno isn't a smart move." Maybe, but what a fantastic opportunity. I couldn't give up

the idea I could potentially get into the inner circle of the Cartel. What a source that would be.

He laughed. "I ask again, when is the meeting? You've got a lead that points directly to the Perez family. I need to know the inside players, and you made a deal with me to get those names and find out what their next move is. I pay you good money to get me what I want." No, your boss pays me, but I won't point that out. *"Now, are you wearing what he likes?"* I swallowed down the lump in my throat and looked down at my outfit.

"Yes, it's a white cotton dress with brown sandals. Hair down, no makeup, with a few thin gold bracelets."

"Good, now quit stalling and do your damn job." The line went dead.

I lowered the phone and took a deep breath. Was I doing the right thing? Should I let a man like Bruno Perez into my world? Everything inside of me screamed no, but my head told me it was now or never to make the play.

I saw movement as Sully came into view. He walked toward my table with a smile.

"Don't you look pretty." He grinned at me. "Ready?"

No.

"Yeah." I stood and snagged my purse off the chair and joined him.

I jolted awake at the feeling of dread inside and blinked away the awful memories. How I wished I'd never gone with him that day. Sunlight beamed through the cracks of the truck, and I wondered what time it was. I didn't feel like I'd slept through the night, but I must have. The girls were all still in their almost zombie-like state with far-off stares or closed eyes. Chase lay still; he'd barely stirred, but perhaps I'd never noticed. His diaper felt full when I patted his bottom through the fabric. I took the opportunity to lay him down and pulled back the hoodie to check his little body. I hated how he simply lay there, red-faced and quiet. A wave of fresh worry washed over me again.

Crystal leaned over to help as I pulled out a diaper. We didn't speak, just made quick work of getting him cleaned up. She wiped his little face with a bit of fabric and murmured something as she shook her head. The excitement of us joining them and getting across the border had now faded and reality had set back in. We had no idea if we were safe. I gathered up Chase and got him tucked back in the hoodie. I was constantly afraid something would happen, and I'd need to move fast. I pulled my things close and settled myself again.

Hours later, the truck pulled over and the door opened.

"Bathroom break." Chili pointed at an old port-a-potty next to what looked like an abandoned truck stop. One by one, the girls stumbled from the back of the truck and stood on wobbly legs. They squinted at the sunlight, but I knew it must feel like heaven to them.

I climbed down and was thankful for the chance to get out but eyed the portable toilet like the germ-infested thing it surely was. I'd die first. I quickly did what I had to behind a nearby tree, ignoring the fact that I knew I wasn't completely hidden from sight.

I walked back toward Chili where he stood by the truck, and we waited for the girls to help each other to do whatever they needed.

"How's the kid?"

"He's really sick. I'm really worried about him."

Chili looked down and pulled out his phone, but as he read something, his face fell. He looked over my head and then down the opposite way. The hair on the back of my neck stood at attention at his sudden change in behavior.

"All right, ladies, back inside. Quickly, now." They didn't argue maybe because they were shoeless, starving, and terrified of what the next step might be for them. I, on the other hand, wondered why I got to keep my shoes.

I stopped at the step and turned to face him head on. "We need food, Chili. It's inhuman to keep us without food and water."

"I agree." He walked around the truck trailer and opened the door of the cab then came back with two big grocery bags. "Here's food and water, best I could do. There should be something in there the kid can eat," he growled. "Now, get in." He slung the bags up into the back of the truck.

"What did your text say?" I blurted and blinked at my question. *Where did that come from?*

"It said get in." He picked me and Chase up and hefted us into the back of the truck without even a warning. "We need to leave." He closed the door, and I felt Crystal pick up the bags and tug on my arm.

"Help me get this stuff back to the girls."

The truck took off before I could even sit. Something was wrong, and I wondered what it was. Who were we running from? How long were we going to be driving?

Crystal and I quickly passed out the food and bottled water to the girls. They tore at the wrappers and gulped down the water in a frenzy of activity. "There was a time I wouldn't dream of putting a premade truck stop sandwich in my mouth," Crystal said loudly with a mouth full, "but here I am. Turns out two-week-old baloney tastes damn fine." A few of the girls chuckled, and for a hair of a moment they seemed normal.

Chase wouldn't eat, but he did take a few sips of water, and I hoped that would help him. I coaxed him to open his eyes and was rewarded briefly with a little complaint sound. I was happy with that tiny tidbit. He was lethargic but alert enough that I felt a little easier.

We settled back into silence, and some of the girls drifted off to sleep because it was better than being awake. I was too keyed up and tuned in to the engine whenever we would speed up or change lanes. I couldn't see anything through the little hole. As the hours passed, it was dark again, and as nothing had happened since the truck stop, I began to relax enough to nod off a few times.

After a bit, I must have fallen asleep again, because I was jolted awake by the vibration of the truck as the brakes were suddenly applied. My eyes flew open, and I saw beams of sunlight.

Something was wrong. I felt fear deep in my stomach.

Then everything happened so fast that even if I had been ready for it, I couldn't have prepared myself. The truck's brakes went on hard, and we were all thrown forward. Then it came to a sudden stop. We could hear shouts, and I thought I heard gunfire. Then the door was pulled open, and sunlight broke around the makeshift wall we hid behind.

"Come out with your hands up!" someone shouted, and Crystal fought to stand on shaky legs.

"It might be a trap!" one of the girls cried out.

"Maybe, but they should be Americans, so I'm taking a chance." She pushed by the other girls and squinted at the light as she stepped around the wall. "Please don't shoot."

Heavy footsteps rushed inside the container, and Crystal was pulled forward with a yelp.

"You're okay," a man called. "Are there any more of you?"

"Yes," Alexi called, and the girls began to step out. I waited for a beat before I joined them. A SWAT team with covered faces started to help the girls out of the back.

Hope flooded me, and I wanted to cry. I was so incredibly thankful the nightmare might be over. I carefully climbed from the back with my arms around Chase and walked toward an officer.

"My name is Nicole Winter." My voice was raspy and low. "I'm a war correspondent based in Mexico. I need your help." The officer moved around me to take the arm of one of the girls. "Would I be able to use your phone?"

Again, the officer ignored me. So, I repeated it in Spanish just to see if he would pay attention. Nothing. "Sir?" I grabbed his arm, but he jerked it away. I looked at another soldier who wouldn't even glance in my direction. They loaded up the girls in several vehicles. Panicked glances were thrown at me by the girls, and I heard their gasps of fear.

"Nicole!" Crystal screamed as she fought the officer who was trying to get her inside the black vehicle. "No, wait, please! She's with us! She has a baby!" The man just gave her one last hard push then slammed the door behind her.

"Crystal!" I cried as I awkwardly reached out my arm.

As fast as they came, they left. My head couldn't catch up as the cars peeled away with the only friends I had left inside. I raced toward Chili as he stepped into view and stopped hard enough to make Chase whimper. A cold, low prickle started at the base of my spine and inched itself up to the back of my neck. It left me with a warning to tread carefully.

"What happened to the girls? What's going on?"

"They're fine." He checked the time on his watch, then something passed over his face. A moment of concern? As quickly as I saw it, it was gone. "You want the front seat or stay back there?"

My brows pinched at such a strange request. *Stay calm. Figure out the situation before you panic.*

"What I need is children's Tylenol."

"When we can, we'll stop for some."

"Where are we going?"

"It's not in me to ask twice."

I gave him a look and figured I'd be safer in the back, so I climbed up into the container again.

"Suit yourself." He shrugged and shut the door in my face. Once again, I was left in the dark. I was afraid to put Chase down, so I sat with him in my arms, ready to move quickly if I had to.

The girls' faces flickered in front of me. I tried so hard to believe they'd be okay. I hated that they were gone, but I was glad I was the one stuck in the back of the truck, and not them. Maybe, just maybe, they were heading back to their families. As the truck took off again, I closed my eyes while I stroked Chase on the back and imagined them being reunited with their families. I needed something to keep my mind busy.

The last thing I remembered were tears streaming down my face as I drifted back to sleep once the sun faded away for the third time since I'd been put in that steel trap.

I jerked awake at a bump in the road and felt around for my bag. I cupped Bruno's phone and licked my lips. I didn't have Cole's number anymore, but I knew Jack's number at the *Washington Post* by heart. I hovered my fingers above the *on* button and fought a battle inside.

"Fuck it." Just as I went to press the button, the truck came to another hard stop. I managed to support myself against the wall, but I dropped the phone. "Shit." I carefully shifted Chase so I could see out the crack. We were at another truck stop, and I could see a few cars in parking spaces. I quickly rescued the phone and dropped it back into my bag, silently wishing I'd had a chance to power it on and make that call. The door rolled up, and I grabbed my things. I'd leave nothing behind if I was being transported elsewhere.

"Time to rest." Chili offered me a hand, but I used the handle on the side instead and carefully hopped down so as not to jostle Chase. "You don't need that." He pointed to my bag, but I held it tight against me. "Whatever." He used his chin to point to a table. "Let's get a place to sit. I'll bring you something to eat."

"Please get some children's Tylenol," I begged, and he nodded.

We crossed the parking lot and stepped onto the dry Texas grass where he chose a table that was shaded by a tree. I untied the arms of Paul's hoodie from around my waist then lay Chase on top of it. His eyes fluttered open, but the glazed look that filled them let me know he needed care, and soon. His breathing sounded wheezy, and it had my worry factor at a full ten. I decided to change his diaper and pulled a clean one from the bag.

"What can I do?" Chili asked but remained a few feet back.

"You can start by letting me go."

"I'm not keeping you captive, Nicole. I just can't let you out of my sight yet."

Yet? Such an interesting choice of words, given that he'd had us for three days.

"Why wasn't your truck scanned at the border? Do you have people working for you?"

He moved his head around like he was watching for someone. "Don't worry about it."

Oh, sure, I'll just add that to the growing hype of anxiety I'm 'not supposed to worry about.'

"Are you going to hurt us?"

His brows pinched behind his sunglasses. "I don't make it a habit to hurt people."

"No," I rolled my eyes, "you just traffic young women."

"Just because things look one way doesn't make it so." He checked his phone, and his jaw tightened. His lips thinned out into a straight line.

"So, those girls are okay?"

He looked away. "Yes."

I didn't know if I should believe him or not, so I went back to dealing with Chase. Once he was changed, I gently sat him up on the picnic table in front of me while I sat down. My back ached from carrying him so long.

"Mama, Mama." He held out his little arms, and I leaned in to give him some love. "*Arriba.*"

I smiled at him. "Oh, you want up. You do know more than one word, you smart little cookie." I pulled him onto my lap, and he immediately snuggled against my chest in his favorite spot. I noticed Chili's interest as I interacted with Chase, and I hoped maybe if he saw how sad the situation was, he'd help me get to Cole.

"He likes you."

"I hope he does," I confessed. "Look, you said you'd try to get him some Tylenol. He really needs it. I'm worried…" My words trailed off as three government issued vehicles stopped right next to Chili's big rig. He immediately stepped close to me and placed a hand on my shoulder. I tried not to flinch.

"Nicole, be very careful with these men. They're not people to fuck around with." We watched as they approached us. His hand stayed heavy on my shoulder, weighing me down as a secondary warning to mind my next move.

They were all dressed in flashy suits, shoes polished to the point where they caught the sun, and their skinny, trendy ties were outdated by a decade. They looked important but ridiculous. "I wasn't planning on fucking around with them, believe me. They look like they work for James Franco's security team," I snapped, and he hid his amusement with a light cough.

"You must be Nicole Winter." The guy who spoke was quite handsome in his suit and tie. He held out a hand. "I'm Cooper Colin. Nice to meet you."

"I'll be the judge of whether it's nice or not." I set the tone that I wasn't one to be fucked with. I'd been through enough.

"I heard you were a pistol."

"Then you know you should get right to the point." Chase pushed his feet into my thighs and let out a cry.

"So, you're the famous little boy who has all of America in tears. I watched your video, little fella, and that's why I'm here."

Boy? I never once said he was a boy.

"You watched my video and have swooped in to save this little one?" I couldn't keep the sarcasm from my voice.

He grinned, but it felt off, almost like a cat grinning at a mouse before it attacked. "That's right."

I shook my head, tired of playing these games. "And you just happened to know we were in this very spot?"

"It's part of my job to know where you are."

"Is that so?"

"Yes, I'm FBI." He pulled back his jacket and showed me his badge. No way. These guys weren't in the usual black FBI garb. Even his sunglasses were Gucci. No way the FBI would have the money to dress like this fool.

"And I was the Easter bunny a few years ago, and before that I was an astronaut." Sarcasm dripped from my lips again. Chili chuckled and Agent Colin cast him a nasty glance. "Am I being arrested for something?"

"No."

"Then why not identify that you're FBI when you introduced yourself?"

"Didn't my suit give me away?" He huffed in an attempt to be funny, but I wasn't amused. The guy rubbed me the wrong way. Something about him felt off.

"Actually, no. It comes off more like you're giving information to *TMZ* about some B-list celebrity." More like A-list, but I didn't want him to take it as a compliment. His brows went up as I stood with Chase in my arms and began to head for the truck. Chili moved with me, right on my heels. "We're done here."

"Okay, so we got off on a bad foot. I apologize." He moved to block my path. "What can I do to make it right?"

"Get me some children's Tylenol." I pointed to Chase. "He's sick. If you do that, I'll give you five more minutes of my time." He nodded over his shoulder, and one of his men approached. He spoke to him, and he raced off toward his car.

"Please, Nicole, take a seat." I studied him for a minute then went back to the table and lowered myself onto the bench.

Chili moved to lean against the trunk of the tree. He seemed relaxed, but his gaze was fixed on Colin. It was interesting that he hadn't said a single word since the man introduced himself.

Colin's phone must have vibrated because he pulled it free and held up a finger, then turned to answer it. I looked at Chili again and saw he kept one hand close to his gun. *Who the hell are these people?* The last I checked this wasn't how the US conducted business, especially with missing people in trouble.

The agent who left to get the Tylenol returned in record time with an unopened bottle of medicine. He set it down then stepped back as Colin hung up.

"Good news," he said as I made quick work getting the medication into Chase. He didn't like it and cried as he swallowed it. "I've been instructed to bring the kid into custody."

The panic flooded inside me as I tucked the medicine away and my arms tightened around Chase. "Under whose orders?"

"My boss's."

"And who might your boss be? Because I too have orders."

His smug smirk only pissed me off further. "My

orders trump yours." Agent Colin took a step toward me, and Chili did the same.

There is no way Chase is going with any of these guys.

I instantly slipped into work-slash-survival mode and flashed him a massive smile. "Smile, Agent Cooper Colin." He froze. "You're on live camera." I pointed to the GoPro on my shoulder and circled my finger around the little red light to show it was recording. "You don't really think I'd stop filming until I got this little one to safety, do you?"

I grinned when I saw him shake his head at his men.

"There is no way this baby is going with you, especially without me. I made a promise to my boss and to him." I patted Chase's back. "He needs to know not everyone in this world is bad. So, you can decide if you want all of America to see you rip an innocent baby from a woman's arms. I'm going to finish my job of returning this baby to the safety of the US military." I figured I'd toss in a little American pride since the FBI, CIA, DEA, and military were all supposed to be one working wheel with the same goal in mind. Protect the people and our land.

Chili held up his phone as he stood next to me. "Eighty-six thousand people are currently watching your every move, Agent Colin." I could have hugged him for playing along, even if I still wasn't sure what his own motives were. At least Chili wasn't trying to separate Chase and me.

Agent Colin rubbed his lips as he thought. "Christ." He huffed. "I wasn't looking for a war here, Ms. Winter, I just want to make sure the boy gets into the right hands."

"And that's all I'm doing as well, sir." I kept my on-air voice.

"At least let me drive you somewhere safe."

"She's good," Chili said before I could. "I've got my orders, too."

So many orders and so many lies.

Colin slid his card across the table. "In case you change your mind."

"I won't, but I'll still take it."

He got up and began to walk back toward their vehicles. I saw him say something to one of the men before he slammed the door and disappeared behind a blacked-out window. I tucked the card away. I planned on discussing that little encounter with Paul and Cole. FBI Agent Colin gave off the same kind of darkness Bruno did.

"We should go." Chili grabbed my bag, but I held up a hand to stop him.

"I'm putting my trust in you. I'm not sure why, but I am. Please, don't make me regret it."

"He said you were a good judge of character." He gave a quick smile then turned and began to walk toward his rig, and I rushed to follow.

"Who?"

"The guy who hired me to get you to safety." I rolled my eyes, and his brows raised at my reaction. "You don't believe me?" He put a hand on his hip.

"I'll believe it when I see it." I walked past him. "Also, I'll take the front seat now." It wasn't easy, but I finally managed to get up into the cab while I held on to Chase for dear life.

Chili rounded the front and hopped inside the truck like it was a tiny Ford Focus. He eyed Chase and seemed to think for a moment. "I can rig something for the boy to sit in."

"He's fine on my lap," I assured him as I looked down at the little guy. His eyes were closed again, and I prayed the Tylenol was working. "Let's get moving before the FBI realizes I just lied to them, and they come after me again."

He started the beast of an engine and checked his mirrors. "They won't leave. They'll be following us until our next stop."

"Next stop?"

"Mmhm." He changed gears, and we were off.

I swallowed hard and hoped the next stop would be somewhere safe.

Another night came around, and I started to imagine he was just taking me on some crazy road trip. At least being in the front, I had a sense of where we were in New Mexico, but over time, we entered Texas. I desperately wanted to ask why we jumped states, but I didn't want him to realize how much I was watching. So, I steered our little conversations away from anything location-wise.

Chili opened up a little, and he made a bit of small talk, but for the most part, I was left alone with my thoughts. Occasionally, I comforted Chase and even sang to him when he got restless as the miles went by.

"You a Tyler Childers fan?" He glanced over at me when I ended the song *Nose on the Grindstone*.

"I wasn't until…" I felt emotion get stuck in my throat when I thought of my old team and knew at some point I'd need to deal with their deaths, "until some friends of mine introduced me." *Friends.* I smiled at that word. I didn't have many, and they'd all been so kind.

"Country, huh?"

"It's a great genre."

His hand covered his mouth as he smiled. "You *would* fit in."

"Fit in?" I hated how cryptic he was. "Care to elaborate?" He kept his eyes on the road. "Okay, so, we're going back to the silence again." I rolled my eyes. "Got it."

He chuckled but didn't elaborate.

I had so many questions about the girls and why they'd been taken then ended up going back over the border. I wondered who the masked men were who had come for them once we got back into the US. Why had they ignored me so completely? Was Chili really in the human trafficking business? Was he really a monster?

"I'm not." Chili's voice found me, and I rewound my thoughts and wondered what I had said out loud.

"What?"

"I'm not what you think I am. I'm not a monster."

I stared out the windshield and thought about my words. "No offense, Chili, but so far, things are not leaning in your favor. I mean, those girls, are they really okay? They told me about what they'd been through. They were so terrified by the whole ordeal."

"That's the idea." He didn't miss a beat as he rubbed his face. I could see he wanted to say more but maybe couldn't. "They're fine, though."

"Oh, well, if you say so," I scoffed, and he shook his head in amusement, and it pissed me off further.

"They are."

"You sure about that? Because those men, whoever they are, wouldn't give me a second glance, and I had a baby strapped to me."

"They were under orders not to engage with you."

I tossed my hands in the air with an exasperated sigh. "Orders from who?" Once again, he gave me nothing. "You obviously want to tell me what you know, so why don't you?"

"I will," he nodded, "but not yet."

"Why?"

"Because," he huffed. "If we get stopped, I need you to still be scared of me."

"Just so it's said, none of this is comforting in any way." I shook my head.

His cell phone rang, and he hit the button that pushed the call through to his earpiece. I thought about what he'd said and tuned out his one-word answers he gave to someone else.

"Fuck, all right. Yeah, I got it." He nearly slammed his fist into the phone to hang it up. I felt the anger that poured off him. Shit, I hoped I'd never get Chili mad. Not that he'd been easygoing, but I didn't plan to let my guard down. He squeezed the steering wheel, and he cleared his throat several times. I couldn't take the angry silence anymore.

"Anyone ever tell you that you look exactly like Rip from *Yellowstone* in that outfit?" I tried to lighten his mood. To my surprise, the stress seemed to fade from his face, and I watched his mouth morph into a small smile. My guess would be yes, he had.

"My buddy Eric used to say that all the time."

My stomach plummeted as icy sweat broke out on the back of my neck. "You don't mean Eric Noah?"

He removed his glasses and stared straight into my eyes, and I felt like I was under some kind of hold. "Eric was a good man."

Great, this is the cherry on top of the shit cake I've been served.

"No, Eric was a monster," I shot back, and he pushed his sunglasses back on. "No worries, though, Chili. Your concern about me not acting scared if we run into anyone shouldn't be a concern. Sharing that you and Eric Noah were friends is enough to keep the fear at a level ten." I hugged Chase a little tighter.

"Funny you're scared of a monster, but you love his child like he's your own."

I felt anger replace my fear. "How could you make such a comparison? He's just a baby."

"So, you believe in nature versus nurture?"

He was really trying to push my buttons. "Of course, I don't. When I look at him, I see a scared, sick baby who only wants to be loved. You don't come out of the womb corrupt. That's something you're taught. He might carry the blood of a monster, but this little guy is as innocent as they come." I kissed his head. "And I'm determined to make sure he gets into the right hands so he's nurtured to be a sweet boy so he can get the life he deserves."

I caught his smile as I watched him out of the corner of my eye. God, he was a hard man to figure out. He went silent again. *Good, stay that way.*

I settled back and drifted in and out of sleep. If Chase moved, I'd wake with a jump. Holy shit, I was tired. No, I was way past tired. I was bone-deep exhausted. I bounced awake as I felt the engine pull back and we made a quick turn, and I hit the door with my shoulder. "Ouch."

"Sorry," he grunted as I rubbed the sting from my muscle, "but we're here, and I don't need a tail coming in behind me."

"Behind you where?" I tried to fight the fog from my head, but it was proving to be a task. "Where are we?" I blinked and read the giant sign as we drove under it.

Fort Echo United States Military Base. That removed the fog like a jet engine clearing a runway.

I leaned forward and scanned area. "Are we? Are you? Do you know?"

We pulled up to a gate, and a man stepped out as Chili lowered his window. "ID." He reached for the small folder Chili handed him. I couldn't see it and was more than curious to know what his full name was and what he really did for a living. "You alone?"

"No, we got company, but they're staying out of view."

"Suits or rifles?"

"Suits."

"Copy that." The man stepped back, lowered his head, and said something quietly into his radio. "You're clear to enter the hangar."

"Copy that." Chili used the same lingo as the soldiers, and it sent my head into another tailspin as we continued through the massive base.

"So, you're a soldier?" *There's a lot more to this man than I imagined.* He gave a little shrug. "Look, Chili, you clearly saved me from a bad situation at the border, and for that, I'm grateful. You said someone hired you to get me to safety, but you won't tell me who. You didn't let the FBI take him." I tilted my head to indicate Chase. "Now you've taken me to a base and gotten past the security check point and used military language. I think it's only fair that you tell me who you really are and what we're doing here. Don't I at least get that?"

He refused to answer me, and I saw we were headed inside an airplane hangar. The big rig slowed as we entered, and the hairs on my arms stood straight up as I became hyperaware that something big was about to happen. Once inside, the doors shut behind us, and I lost it.

"I have money." I jumped into panic mode. "Holy shit, what's happening?" My breathing picked up, and my head went light. I grabbed the handle above the seat and contemplated how I was going to escape.

"Nicole." His voice held a warning.

"Please, Chili, you don't have to do this. Please, take me instead. Trust me, Bruno will pay good money to have my life destroyed. Use me as a bargaining chip. Or better, let me tell you what I know, and you can go after him. He's evil. Trust me, I've seen things that would make a grown man fall to his knees." Tears burned paths down my cheeks and my heartbeat thumped wildly against my throat. "There's something bigger happening within their family, something I think I'm close to discovering." My mouth ran away with me. "If I just had another few weeks of digging, I could—" Everything started to hit me at once. "I've gone through so much just to make sure this little one had what I didn't. A family and hope. Please," I repeated.

He turned off the engine and shifted in his seat to

look at me. "Nicole, stop," he shouted. "Damn it, I'm not here to hurt you two. I'll tell you everything, but you have to turn off your camera first."

I hesitated and forced my breathing back to normal. "Sorry, I don't know why I panicked. I mean, I don't usually…" I reached over and turned off the GoPro.

"Thank you. Now let's get out of this truck and we'll talk."

"Okay." I took a deep breath and gathered my things. The door opened, and Chili helped me down then shut the heavy door. Chase didn't react, but I sure did. My body shook so hard that my vision was blurry.

"All right," Chili smiled, "I was under orders to keep my identity from you in case we ran into trouble. Which we did. I needed you to fear me so my own position wasn't compromised, but now that we're safe, I can tell you this. My name is Chili, and I work with a military group that helps those human trafficked to Mexico get back home. The men who took the girls from the truck are part of the same organization, but they were instructed not to engage with you in case we were being followed."

"Why?" I tried to follow along, but my ears were ringing.

"Because I merged two missions together in order to get you out."

Something clicked. "Is that who you told the girls you were waiting for? Was it me?"

"Yes," he glanced at the door we just came through, "I got word that you were in trouble and might need some help to get across since your ride was compromised at the border."

"The car in the parking lot?" He nodded as I tried to make sense of everything. "But who gave you those orders?"

His mouth pulled up on one side. "Him." He nodded over my shoulder, and I turned to see both John and Cole walking toward me. My heartbeat drained from my ears as relief spread through me. I'd never been happier to see anyone in my life. He smiled. "Go ahead."

I turned to run but stopped myself. "Sorry if I was hard on you. It's just…"

"You played your part well. Never be sorry for protecting a child. You're a good person, Nicole. Feisty as hell, but a good person."

"Thanks." I reached under Chase and hefted him a little higher on my chest and reached out to shake his hand then decided on a side hug and was rewarded with a grin.

I turned and hurried toward the guys while tears flowed freely down my face.

THREE

PAUL

I fought my way out of sedation. It wasn't the first time I'd forced my way out of that darkness, but this time I had a reason to come back from the other side.

My fingers moved first. *Good. They work.* My toes were next, then I shifted my knees. *Okay, that's a plus. I'm not paralyzed.* I swallowed hard in relief. I tried to open my eyes. That took a lot more brain power, but after a few tries, I managed it. I let out a groan as the light found my pupils and quickly shut them again.

I dared blink again, and my vision slowly cleared. A familiar face stared at me from above.

"How bad?" I whispered.

"Better than we expected."

I slowly raised a hand and felt around my chest. There were only bandages but no pain. "Feels numb.

John said something about stab wounds?" He took his glasses off and looked away. "Daniel, please, give it to me straight." I needed to know.

"You got knifed a couple times, yes, but they didn't hit any organs or major arteries. You were beaten up pretty bad, but nothing that you haven't been through before. It'll heal in a week or so. They drugged you pretty good too."

"That's explains the throbbing head."

"That and a mild concussion."

"My son?" I flinched as I tried to sit up and the pain ignited like a match. Daniel clicked something on my IV, and before I could register what he'd done, my eyes grew heavy.

"He's on his way back to you," he promised as I fought back the darkness and lost.

Time was just a word when you were healing from an injury. It came and went like breathing. You simply lost track of it. I didn't even have to speak when the pain became too bad. I'd simply move a little, and someone would click my IV. I'd barely registered the light smell of salt and vinegar chips as the pain faded again. John.

One moment of clarity, I heard his words. "It's been two days, buddy. Don't worry. They're on the way." He was my brother; he knew what I needed to hear. I slipped back down. I may have been oblivious to the world, but my brain flashed from one memory to the next, until Talya's face drifted up and everything went soft as I heard her.

"Hi," she whispered from where she sat on my balcony with a cup of something dark between her fingers. Dressed in only a t-shirt and panties, she looked good enough to eat. "I wondered if you were ever going to wake up."

I grinned. "After the night I just spent with you, I'm shocked I can still walk."

"Well," she pulled back her long dark hair as she stood in front of me, "walking is overrated." She kissed my lips gently, and I wrapped my arms around her waist so I could feel more of her body against mine. "I love you, Eric." My grip on her suddenly fell away. It should have been one of the best moments of my life, but it wasn't. She was in love with an illusion. Someone I didn't want to be but was forced to. She didn't love the real me; she loved the monster I pretended to be. She turned into liquid as I reached for her again, then she flowed like water through my hands.

"What is it? Paul, open your eyes." His voice came to me on the wind like I was caught in a storm.

My eyes popped open, and the room came into focus immediately. Frank and Daniel both appeared at my bedside.

"Welcome back." Daniel smiled, and when I tried to sit up, he leaned down to press the button on the side of the bed to raise it. Thank God the meds seemed to be subsiding. My head felt almost normal.

"How long have I been here?"

"Rounding on four days." Daniel beeped for the

nurse. "And before you ask, Nicole and Chase are about four hours out."

"You think you can get up?" Frank interrupted and ignored Daniel's expression.

I pushed back the blanket. "Don't know 'til we try."

"I don't think that's a wise idea, son," Daniel warned. "Let's not forget you've been stabbed twice."

I tried to make light of the situation. "In the chest, not the legs."

Just as I was about to try to push to my feet, the nurse came in and clucked her tongue at me.

"The man doesn't listen," Frank commented and waved at Daniel, basically tossing him and me under the bus. "When can he get moving?"

"Let get his vitals," She shooed them out of the way and took her time going over everything.

"Well?" Frank asked as he looked at his watch. I felt just as impatient. I didn't do well sitting still. None of us did.

"I wouldn't say this to some patients, but I know what you tough guys are like. If you're careful, you can leave today, but you need to follow instructions and take it easy—"

Frank cut her off and dropped my boots by the bed. "You have my word he will."

Daniel shook his head and took the nurse by the arm and walked out with her in quiet conversation.

"If anyone asks, I don't necessarily agree with this. It's too soon. But we need you moving, soldier."

I wasn't about to argue. "Yes, sir. Copy that." He tossed my clothes on the bed, and I began to struggle into them.

Cole suddenly appeared in the doorway. "They're letting you out? I didn't even know you were awake." I struggled to lace up my boots. I didn't want to wait around for the nurse to return with a change of mind. Frank headed for the door with a quick look at Cole.

Cole stepped forward to help me, but I held up a hand. "Thanks, but I've been dead before and made it. Believe me, this is better than that." He stepped back without a word. I wobbled slightly and my head felt a little off now that I was upright, but I'd been through worse. "I got the all clear."

"Oh, yeah?" Cole chuckled, knowing damn well he would have done the same. "Anyway, just so it's said, the house knows we're coming home with your son."

"Good. What do the kids know about him?" I sat on a chair and leaned down to flip one lace of my boot over the other and attempted to make a bow so I wouldn't trip. Got it on the first try.

Cole eased his shoulder into the wall after the doctor had tracked me down, thanks to Daniel's concern. "They think it's like any other guest arriving at the house. They know he's a baby without a family and that he'll be staying with us until we get orders from Frank, and we'll go from there."

I eyed him briefly. "And what about your PI of a daughter?"

He smirked, knowing that nothing got by Olivia. "I explained this was a sensitive matter and that she wasn't allowed to dig into it. If I say no, she respects that. Just like she and Brandon would never breathe a word about who you were when you were under cover."

"Good." I couldn't risk anything at this point, not when it came to my son.

"This is a need-to-know case. Which means only the teams, Savannah, Mia, Doc Ivy, and the elders know the truth about who Chase is. I hate to leave the other wives out of it, but that's your call." I nodded, relieved he was being as careful as he was. With Nicole coming back to Shadows, I couldn't risk her finding out he was mine. It was bad enough that most of the people at the house knew I was Eric Noah. I shuddered at the thought of her finding that out. She made it very clear that she was happy he was dead.

"Remember, brother, this is what we do," Cole went on. "We protect the ones who need protecting, and right now, that's Chase, you, and Nicole. Focus on healing so we can get that exceptional brain of yours back behind the drone. I've gotten used to having our eye in the sky."

"Copy that." I tested out my legs as I stood when something nagged at me again. "Cole?" He looked up from his phone. "How could Bruno possibly have known Nicole and Chase would be at that border crossing?"

"That's a million-dollar question." He rubbed the space between his eyes like it had been weighing on him too.

"Makes you think—"

He shook his head. "Don't even go there. If we have another mole in our house, Frank might shut down the entire operation himself." His arms dropped heavily. "Look, my guess is that, yeah, he has someone feeding him information. It's the only explanation unless our phones have been hacked."

"Impossible."

"Right," he agreed. We had the best phone technology on the market. "But the other thing is, Bruno was there, yes, but so were all the other Cartel families. Maybe Bruno's got a mole too. Let me handle that, and you get a handle on all of that." He waved a finger at my chest.

"All right."

"Good. Now, I know you had some fancy surgery done on that chest of yours and they said it should heal faster. But stab wounds are still stab wounds in my book, so I'm leaving before Frank sees you standing." He chuckled as he left the room.

When the door closed behind him, I sat back down and used the edge of my hoodie to wipe the sweat from my forehead. The simple act of getting my shoes tied actually made me want to lie down.

I'd been fortunate to get one of the best doctors Texas had to offer on the base, and he told me I was extremely lucky about exactly where I'd been stabbed.

I knew if I had seen a doctor in Mexico, I would be way worse off. He explained the surgery to me, but he lost me after the first few words. I just remembered the part where he told me I had to rest for a week. That wasn't an option. I'd come back from the dead once before, and I could deal with a few holes in my chest. It was just mind over matter.

I shifted myself to a positive headspace and grabbed my zippered hoodie. I took a breath and forced myself back to my feet. I paused for a moment at the wave of pain then pushed it aside and headed out the door. I didn't have time to baby myself. I needed to see where the others were and get an update.

Frank, of course, was waiting in the hallway for me. "Good. You're up and moving."

"I am."

"Scale of pain?"

"Seven," I lied.

"I need you back on solid feet, Paul, so if you need a few days, take them."

"Don't need 'em." I didn't miss a beat.

"Good." He eyed me hard through his glasses. "I have something in the works that I'm going to run by you when I have all the details. Copy?"

"Copy." I couldn't remember when Frank took any time off for himself or his family. He was a work-horse who never slept. There was a time I admired that, but over the years, I started to see the toll it took on him and wondered if it was worth sacrificing everything for the greater good. I knew he was about to be forced into retirement, and he had nothing to look forward to. I sure regretted having no real family of my own. I hated that I'd lost the years with my Blackstone family and all that I'd missed while I was in Mexico. The kids being born and all that. It left a hole, but I was happy to have them now.

"Stay sharp."

"Yes, sir." I watched as he disappeared around the corner.

The hallway was quiet, which made it easier to follow voices, and soon I heard John and moved in his direction.

"Don't let Frank see you in here." John sounded concerned as he looked up from his laptop. I looked around the small, airless room we were in on the base, then looked back to where John sat. I carefully lowered myself into a chair next to him.

The pain in my chest burned, but I breathed through it before I answered. "I passed him in the hallway. He's okay with it."

"He shouldn't be. You look like shit."

I could hear the rasp in my voice as I tried to clear my throat and felt the sweat that broke out over my forehead. I felt the toll the surgery had taken on me, but my head finally felt close to normal now that the drugs they'd shoved in my veins had cleared somewhat. God, I hated all things medical.

"Truth, how are you feeling?"

"I feel like I've been at a rave for a week straight

and then was stabbed as I left." I lifted a hand in lieu of a shrug.

He sputtered a laugh. "Good lord, man. You've had a cocktail of drugs, surgery to close two stab wounds in a chest that was shot to hell a decade ago. You're lucky you can stand at all."

"When do they get here?" I pressed the heels of my hands against my eyes and wished to hell I felt better. My mind was a mess with the fact that my son was moments from arriving with a woman I couldn't get out of my head. Anger at her made my stomach hurt. I couldn't believe she'd used my child for a goddamn news story.

"Anytime now," he assured me. "Dark Water checked in and said the Canoses were heavily protecting the southern borders on an anonymous tip that Nicole and Chase were heading that way." He smirked at the lie Ty had spread. "But they were also spotted leaving the El Paso border ten minutes after Chili grabbed them."

"That's odd. Makes you wonder if the Canoses have some mutual friends."

"Anyone come to—" His attention was pulled by his phone as it vibrated on the table.

"Is that?"

"Yup, they're here. Give me a minute to talk to her first." He reached out a hand and put it on my arm then hopped to his feet. Without a thought, I did the same and gasped as pain flooded through me. He turned and eyed me hard then hurried out the door with me not far behind him. He was almost to the airplane hangar when Cole met up with him. I heard the engine from the big rig rev down then stop. Cole and John glanced back at me then hurried ahead through the big doors.

I managed to make it to the door before it closed and jammed my foot in it so it didn't latch. I awkwardly pulled it open so I could walk through. I stopped dead in my tracks when I looked past them and saw my son. He was still in the makeshift pouch against Nicole's chest. Her arms were around him.

He's here.

I forced my emotions back as a commotion behind me made me turn. The medical team, a doctor and a nurse who Cole had arranged for, came rushing in with Mike and Mark.

"Everything's checked and the jet's ready to go," Mike called as they came up behind me. Keith had been in conversation with Frank on the far side of the hangar, but when they saw me, they walked over. Keith coughed like he was unsure of where my head was. I didn't know either.

I looked toward Nicole and saw Cole nod at her as her mouth moved, and I quickly stepped close enough to hear what she was saying. I saw her gaze on my face as she continued, but I couldn't muster a smile, and she looked down at my son.

Nicole filled us in on Chase's condition. "He had Tylenol a couple of hours ago, but he's still hot, and I've been worried about his breathing. He'll drink a little but not enough. He'll hardly eat at all." The doctor reached for him, but when Nicole began to move him, he whimpered, and she paused. "He, ah, he doesn't like to be moved too much." The doctor basically had to peel Chase off Nicole.

"Mama." His little hand reached toward her, and her face fell as he was taken.

"It's okay, buddy. I promise I'm here. You just need to get looked at." Nicole glanced at me with a worried expression. "Hey." She tried to focus on me, but Chase's cries clearly affected her.

"He needs an IV. He's dehydrated," the doctor said to the nurse, "and his lungs are full." He held the stethoscope to the little guy's chest, and my own contracted as I watched. I squinted to listen over his sobs. "My guess would be he has pneumonia, and God knows what else he may have been exposed to. Logan," he called over his shoulder, "we should go soon. I need to do some bloodwork and get an x-ray."

"Copy that, Doc." Cole turned to me. "He needs care, and you need to sit down." Before I could answer him, he said to Nicole, "You and Chili need to get scanned for trackers. Frank will take you. Go with him and get it done."

"But if I am chipped, what am I doing here?" Nicole's eyes were wide, and she looked nervously toward Chase.

"Everyone else, get on board." Cole nodded at our private jet. "The entire base has scramblers, Nicole, but we can't take any chances." Frank waved at them to follow, but Nicole glanced at me then back toward the doctor and nurse who were already headed to the jet with Chase.

"He's in good hands, and it won't take long," Frank promised Nicole, who still looked at me. I gave a slight nod so she'd leave.

Keith still stood beside me as the place emptied out. "You're quiet."

"Says the man who barely speaks more than three words at once," I shot back but then felt bad. He was only checking in.

"Right, because being quiet is my thing, and you can't have that. Just like neither of us can be the hungry, loud, flamboyant one. That's reserved for Mark." He lightly hit my arm. "C'mon, you're hurtin', and I know you want to be with your son."

He was right; I didn't want to let my son out of my sight, so I walked with him.

"My head just isn't sitting right at the moment," I confessed. "And yeah, my body aches, I'm a stranger to my son, and the woman I…" I stopped myself and let out a careful sigh, unsure what the hell Nicole really was to me. She was more than a woman I simply kissed; I knew it was more than that. Wasn't it? Betrayal pushed to the surface, and I relished it for a moment. I physically felt shitty, and my head wanted to join it. "I just need to get back on our mountain so I can breathe."

We crossed the tarmac and waited for Chase, who was now hooked up to an IV and on a stretcher. They began to load him onto the plane. The jet engine was loud, but Chase's cries were louder, and it did something to my gut.

Keith ran a hand through his hair as we stood at the bottom of the steps. "He'll be okay. He's tough. Take it minute by minute and go easy on Nicole. She went through a lot to get him here. That counts for something. You may not like the way she did it, and I have to admit it might have been morally gray in some areas, but we've all been there before." I knew he didn't mean it as a dig about my other life, but the comment still hit hard.

"Yeah." I headed up the stairs and joined the others on the plane.

The Gulfstream G550 was a sleek private jet the military had bought a few years back. It was a thing of beauty with its black leather seats and rich mahogany wood finish. It seated nineteen people, so there was plenty of room for the team, as well as the medical duo, Frank, Nicole, and Chase. The pilot was a good friend of Frank's, and the staff were friendly and discreet.

Chase was in full panic mode, and I quickly moved to his side, at a loss as to what to do. His eyes were tightly shut, but tears leaked out from them as he flailed about. I took his waving hand and held it. "Remember me." I tried to speak to him the way Nicole had shown me. "Friend, remember." He rolled his red face and opened his eyes to see me, then he squeezed them shut again and sobbed even more. *Christ, I suck at this.*

"Frank, I've been cleared, and I'm fine. Please, I just need to make sure he's okay." I heard the stress in Nicole's voice, and it made me step back from Chase. I noticed that her cheek had a fresh bruise, and she had a cut in her hairline that looked pretty nasty. So, she wasn't totally all right.

"Nurse, please hold him." The doctor leaned down and juggled a needle with his free hand while he tried to hold Chase still. Chase screamed harder, and I stepped forward again to block Nicole as she reached for him.

"Hang on." My tone wasn't friendly, and her confused, hurt look almost made me drop my guard, but then the image of her on camera as she held up my son fueled my anger again. "Let them give him the medication."

"Of course. I just need him to know I'm here." Her eyes became glossy, but she stepped back and folded her arms. "Are you okay?"

"A solid ten." I looked back at Chase, who had just spotted Nicole.

"Mama!" He reached for her, and I swallowed hard at her words and thought about how much this entire thing would have hurt Talya. She was his mother.

"Maybe let her by," Cole muttered next to me. "He's been through so much, and he trusts her." My fingers curled into fists. "I don't know what's going through your head right now, Paul, but do this for your…" He didn't need to say it; I heard him.

I rubbed my chest, which ached with a deep burn, and moved so she could sit on the edge of the gurney.

"Hey, sweetheart." Nicole instantly went into mother mode as she gathered his hands and smiled down at him. "I know this is scary, but I'm here." She leaned down and kissed his head, then placed a hand on his chest as it heaved. His sobs eased off a bit.

"Mama," he cried, and I heard her sniff as well.

"Nicole," she corrected him gently. "Mama is with the angels, way up there." She pointed to the roof. "Maybe when we're up in the clouds, you can feel her." She patted his heart, and he put his arms up to her and tried to sit up.

Everything inside me coiled into a new pain, or maybe it was an old pain I had suppressed. I didn't realize how hard I rubbed my thighs, but it was enough to have Keith look over.

"Deep breaths, friend." Chili was suddenly beside me. "Lose it when we're alone. Hold it together for now."

His familiar tone instantly calmed me. We'd been through a lot together over the years, and it wasn't the first time he'd given me the same warning. He'd been right back then, and I knew he was right this time. I needed to chill out and get myself together for my son's sake, if not for my own.

"Can I?" Nicole looked at the doctor, who seemed

pleased she had been able to stop his high-pitched cries. He nodded, and she carefully scooped him up and pressed him against her chest. He instantly tucked his head under her chin. His bottom lip was stuck way out, his eyes were wide, and his hiccups made him jump every few seconds, but the entire plane seemed relieved that he'd finally begun to calm down. He looked so small and broken that it crushed my heart all over again.

"He's young. These memories won't stay with him." Chili kept his head down as he scrolled through his phone. "She's great with him." I sat and tried for long, even breaths.

The pilot finally let us know we were about to taxi for takeoff, and everyone took a seat and buckled up. It wasn't lost on me that Nicole chose a spot a few rows back from where I was. The doc arranged the little guy's IV as she settled back with Chase in her arms. Mark handed her a blanket, and Frank slipped into the seat next to her with his tablet. I knew he'd need to spend some time debriefing her, but he could have waited a beat.

Once in the air, I concentrated on my breathing to ease the pain. *In through the nose, out through the mouth.* Then I remembered my meds and swallowed a couple with a swig of water. I moved my head and shoulders around a little, then closed my eyes and let my head go back home to Shadows as I permitted myself to drift off to a drugged sleep.

* * *

My brain fired back up instantly when I felt the plane touch down. Everything hit me at once, and I whipped around to look back at my son. He wasn't in Nicole's arms.

"Easy, brother." John, who had taken Chili's seat at some point, kicked his feet out with a yawn. "The meds the doctor gave him kicked in, and he's out cold. He's with the nurse in the back. The doc needed to check out Nicole."

"Nicole?"

"Yeah, she's got a nasty cut on her head, and her cheek started to swell, probably from the altitude and such." I glanced back at her again. I saw she fought sleep as her head bounced up and down. She had a bandage high on her forehead, and her face looked red and sore. "Mark had her studying our family photos," John went on. "Wants to help her feel more comfortable when she gets to the house." Mark was good at making people feel at ease, it was something I admired about him. "She's exhausted," John's lips pressed together, "but worried Chase might wake up before she does. They seem to have grown close."

"Yes, I bet they have." I heard how I sounded but didn't care. The last few days had been a nightmare. I leaned back and closed my eyes as I remembered the video she had broadcast to the world about how my son was a pawn in a game of power with the Cartel. That was forever out there, he'd never escape his past because of her. How could she be so reckless and all for a fucking story.

"Hey," John hit my arm, "come on. We've landed at the hospital, and they're already getting off."

I shook the cobwebs away and looked out the window. Chase's stretcher was being wheeled toward an ambulance that would take him to the North Dakota hospital.

"Mia is waiting at emergency with Savi and Dad," Cole said over his shoulder as we climbed down the steps. "They'll take the boy to x-ray first, then he'll get bloodwork. Meanwhile, the rest of us get checked over one last time before we head to Shadows."

"I'm fine," I grunted as a knee-jerk reaction.

Cole turned and threw a look at me. "Well, it's not your call or mine, so suck it up, princess," he growled.

I knew I needed to get back in line. "Copy that." I headed for the SUV and caught Nicole's zombie-like expression as I took the seat in front of her. Even looking like death, she was friggin' beautiful, and I hated it.

It was a short drive from the tarmac to the hospital, not far enough. I hated that place and shuddered at the memories. I'd gone from living my best life to being *dead* in that hospital. Then I had to leave my family behind and live a whole different life in Mexico, which had only brought me pain and heartbreak. Now, a decade later, I was right back in the thick of that shit again.

As always, we used our private entrance to the hospital, which was reserved for our special ops teams, thanks to Frank and Daniel. Those two made sure everything worked like a well-oiled machine. Mia waited by the door and threw herself into Mark's arms as he hurried to see her. He lifted her and kissed her hard, then put her back down.

"I'll let you know what's happening as soon as I can." She was instantly all business. Mia didn't work at the hospital anymore, but Daniel made sure that whenever anyone from our teams arrived with an injury, Mia was in charge. The perks of the military and lots of gracious funding.

"Mia," I called as she headed down the hall. She turned and nodded to show she knew how important it was that Chase wasn't to be left alone.

"Copy that," she confirmed, then looked over my shoulder at Nicole and gave her a warm smile before she hurried away.

Savannah hugged Cole and whispered something in his ear, I caught part of it. She asked if Nicole knew that Chase was my son; he said no. Everyone knew not to say a word. That was what was great about our house; secrets were never spilled. Ever. At least until they weren't a secret, and this time it would be for me to tell.

"You must be Nicole." Savannah smiled and slipped right into hostess mode. "I'm Savannah, Cole's wife. It's lovely to meet you."

"Nice to meet you." Nicole shook her hand, then

looked embarrassed as she brushed at a stain on her shoulder that was probably left there from Chase. "Sorry we're meeting under such circumstances."

"You look a hell of a lot better than I did when I first met them all." She chuckled. Savi was always great at putting people at ease, just like Mark. "Would you like to grab something to eat while the guys get checked out?"

"I'd love to, but first I need to find out what the hell is wrong with this guy before I can think about eating." She head-pointed at me.

Savi grinned, and I could tell she was in love with Nicole already. "Now you're speaking my language. I'll be over there when you're ready."

John tried to hide his laugh as the guys scattered to leave me alone. *Assholes.* Daniel began to walk toward us, but Cole turned him away mid-stride.

"Thanks, Savi." Nicole turned and crossed her arms as she looked up at me. "So, you're pissed at me?"

"Pissed doesn't begin to describe it."

Her brows pinched as confusion raced across her face. "All right, why?"

"Seriously?" How could she not know?

"Seriously," she shot back.

I rubbed my face and leaned against the wall behind me. "You used us."

"I'm sorry, what?"

"Was everything that happened just a part of your plan?"

She shook her head. "Paul, you need to let me in on the conversation inside your head. You're only giving me bits and pieces."

I pushed off the wall and towered over her. "You used that kid for a fucking story!" I boomed and saw Frank look over.

Her chin pulled in, and her eyes widened. "What?"

"Don't act dumb, Nicole. It's an ugly look on you." So much of the frustration I had held down tight to that point raced to the surface. I let loose like an angry bull finally getting a chance to take a run at its rider. "All the signs were there. You always had your camera, filming everything!" I flicked my hand at her. "The first chance you got, you stuck the kid in front of a camera and told the world what happened. I'm sure a raise is coming your way, and I hope it was worth it."

Whack! She slapped me hard across the face as tears spilled down her cheeks.

"How could you say such a thing?" she hissed. "I was surrounded by Cartel, with no way out, and you," she jabbed a finger right into my sore shoulder, but the pain didn't register because of how amped up I was, "told me to use whatever means necessary." She swiped at her eyes with her sleeve as more tears fell. "I was following *your* orders. I did *my* job. I brought that sweet boy back to safety. You have no idea what I went through to do that."

"Okay, you two," Frank stepped up with his hands raised, "let's take a beat."

"So, you had no other choice but to turn on the camera?" I ignored Frank. "I find that very hard to believe, considering the connections you have. Maybe you should have called your mystery guy. You know, the one who calls out of the blue."

"What is your problem, Paul?" She ignored my dig. "Why are you so upset? The boy is safe."

I wanted to scream *because he's my son*, but I couldn't. "It was my extraction! I had orders to get the boy back home."

"Mission accomplished! He's here, so what the hell?" Her cheeks flamed with anger.

I went to open my mouth, but Frank held up a hand.

"Enough, Paul," he warned, "before you say something you can't take back."

"Oh, trust me," Nicole laughed as she angrily brushed her tears away, "he's way past that."

"Am I? Or does the truth hurt?" I knew I was a being the biggest asshole in the world, but my world felt like it was slipping out from beneath me, and she just aired it all on the news.

"Take a walk, Paul," Frank ordered, and I stepped back, but I wasn't leaving. "Nicole—"

"You know what, Frank?" she said. "I appreciate the ride from Chili, but I'm done. They're not my unit, and this isn't my home. I need to get back to Mexico so I can do my job."

She was crazy.

"I can't let you do that."

She raised her chin. "Yes, you can."

"You have orders to come to Shadows with us."

She let out a dark laugh. "I never got that order."

Frank held up his phone and showed her something, and her face fell. "You didn't, but I did."

Nicole tipped her head back and took a deep breath. "I need some air." She headed toward the door, but not before she shot me a nasty glare.

"Hey," Frank pulled my attention back to him, "not the time, nor the place, to be having this conversation."

He was right. It wasn't, but I didn't care. "What did you show her?"

Frank looked at the ground and shook his head. "Paul, there's a lot more going on here. Right now, we just need to get back to Shadows before anyone gets word we're here with the child. Copy?"

I locked my jaw, pissed he wouldn't share. "Copy."

"Frank," Mia was behind him, and my stomach twisted, "the little guy is ready to be loaded on the chopper the—"

"What's wrong with him?" I interrupted, growing more impatient with every second.

Frank placed a hand on his daughter's shoulder. "Has the doctor said anything?"

"Yes," she looked back at me like the professional she was, "he has bacterial pneumonia. I won't lie, it's a pretty bad case, and given the little we know about his life, he might not have gotten all his vaccines." She paused when she saw my face. "It's okay. The doctor thinks we got to him in time."

"Thank God," I huffed with relief.

"We gave him a good shot of medication, and he'll be on it for the next few weeks. Once we get back to Shadows, I'll check in on him frequently and monitor him from there. He needs lots of rest and fluids, but most importantly, he needs to be in a stable environment. The less stressed he is, the better." She eyed me when she said it and stepped forward. I knew I was about to get a tongue-lashing from her. "That means whatever the hell you have going on with Nicole better get wrapped up soon because that little boy needs *her* to get through this, and after that he's going to need *you*. So, hash your shit out and move on. You copy me?"

Frank smirked while I fought not to roll my eyes. I knew better than to push Mia. She always gave it to me straight, no matter what. All the wives were the same. "Copy."

She looked at her dad. "I'll spread the word we got the green light to ship out."

"Good." He glanced at me, but I didn't wait to hear what he had to say. I headed for the SUV. I needed to get home.

PRESS

FOUR

NICOLE

One would think I would be delighted to finally get to see the famous Shadows safehouse. Most of the population would never see the place or ever hear of it. Its reputation within the military and other private circles went back as far as I could remember. It had been such a success that they built two more. Dusk was the second to have been built and was supposedly in North Carolina somewhere. The third, only recently finished, was whispered to be in Washington. That particular one I knew had been created for Frank's team, Eagle Eye. I'd heard rumors of a fourth, but I couldn't find anything concrete on it. Safehouses like those had saved countless lives and had given us a leg up on the Cartels.

So, why did I struggle to look over the contract

Cole handed me while we were still in the air once we took off for Montana? Perhaps it was because I'd been accused of using an innocent child just to get a story by the man I had begun to have feelings for. I should have known better. History had proven time and time again I wasn't meant to find happiness with another person. Especially with a friggin' soldier.

The chopper shook as we flew over high mountaintops, and I gripped the sides of the seat, hating that my stomach wanted to leap right out of the beast. Of course, Mark grinned at me while I rode out the turbulence. The others seemed completely unfazed as well. Even Mia and Savannah didn't seem to notice that we were being swung around like a child with a yoyo. I much preferred to have my feet on the ground looking up rather than looking down.

I went back to reading and tried to look relaxed even as my stomach swore at me for putting her through such an ordeal. My fingers turned white as I held on with one hand. That was when I read the part about what happened if you were to reveal the location of the safehouse or say anything about what went on there or who might be there. I swallowed past the lump in my throat when I saw the words *shall be punished with up to life imprisonment without the chance of parole, and a two-million-dollar fine.* I didn't need to read the rest, I knew I never had it in me to tell such secrets anyway. My focus was pulled when a flash of movement caught my eye.

Paul used his hands to sign something to John,

who nodded, then signed back. I wondered what they said.

"Any questions?" Cole's voice crackled over the headset and pulled my attention back to the task at hand.

"No, sorry." I swiped the pen across the page to sign and date the contract. I handed it to him when he reached out his big, strong hand.

"Welcome to Shadows, Nicole." He pointed out the door. "Look for a chimney in the direction of that huge oak." If you didn't know where to look you wouldn't be able to spot it. I could see why they'd built it there; it had a bird's eye view of its surroundings while still being heavily protected by the rough terrain all around it. The roof was camouflaged so well that I had to look twice to really see how massive it was.

"Now that I've signed, can I ask a few questions?"

He nodded. "You can."

"Can't anyone fly over and discover the house?"

"The story my father had come up with years ago was that the property is owned by a multi-generational family into green energy. We even have people in place to step in and set the record straight if needed. Anyway," he waved off that direction of the story, "because it's green energy, we have a no-fly zone for miles. Of course, commercial airlines can fly over, but they're so high up and Shadows is camouflaged enough that we don't run the risk of being seen by them."

"What about drones?"

"It's a restricted area. If our radar detects a drone, it's shot down before it gets anywhere near our property line."

"What about those people?" I pointed to what looked like a small town.

"The town of Redstone. They know that the military has a contract to train on some of the green energy property, but that's where the story ends. It's a tourist town, so many people are in and out, and the locals are just pleased we help patrol the area along with the local PD. Honestly, less is more when it comes to it, and people only see what they want to anyway. Besides, we have a few tricks up our sleeves about the location if we ever need them."

"Tricks?"

He simply tapped his head and winked. "We do a lot for the town, and it keeps the focus over there while we are over there." He pointed to Shadows again.

"Smart."

"It's worked so far." He smiled and looked over at his father, Daniel, who I'd had the pleasure of meeting at the hospital when I needed to cool off from Paul.

To my utter delight, we landed just ten minutes later. I released my death grip on the seat and undid my belt, then watched as the second chopper's door opened. Chase, who looked to be out cold, was carried toward the house.

"Be ready." Mark smiled again as he helped me down from the chopper. "You're about to be greeted by a whole lot of people. Hope you studied the digital flip book I made you." We began to walk toward the house.

"I did." I chuckled, but it was short-lived when I saw the group of kids that rushed toward us. I stepped back and watched them jump into the arms of their fathers, then moments later, there were hugs happening everywhere with happy smiles and laughter. There were dogs and even a white furball of a cat that had raced out from somewhere. Total pandemonium but an amazing sight. I almost wanted to reach for my camera. The love, laughter, and relief from the men, women, and children was very moving.

An emptiness spread through me as, for the first time in my life, I realized I really wanted something like that for myself. How amazing it must be to be greeted by people who truly loved you, who waited for you to come home and cared if you didn't. These men put everything on the line and still were able to have it all.

I felt out of place and took a step back, only to bump into someone. I turned and found Paul's cold eyes on me. I swallowed and began to walk again.

"Are you being nice?" Savannah was by my side and she looked over her shoulder. "That doesn't look like a nice face, Paul." She threaded her arm through mine and urged me to walk with her. "Come on, Nicole. I can only imagine what you've been through, let alone the last five days with Chili and the trip here. I bet you could use a hot shower and some clean clothes."

"I could, thanks." I didn't glance back at Paul and followed her up the stairs of the sprawling porch and into what looked like something from a movie. "Wow."

"This is home." She beamed. "Look, we can do the tour later, but before the rugrats bombard you, let's get you settled."

She read my mind. We took more stairs to the second floor and down a long hallway to the fourth door on the left.

"This is your room."

"And the others?"

"Most of team Dark Water are up here, and they're home tonight. Paul is over there, with some of his teammates—"

Wait. "His teammates?" Mark didn't mention a third team.

"There's a lot to learn, but we'll take it day by day," she assured me. She was right; there certainly were a lot of people to meet and straighten out how they all fit. "You'll be happy to know that right next door is your cameraman, Ben."

"Ben's still here?" That made me perk up. "Can I see him?"

"Once he's back from physio, of course." She smiled warmly as she opened the door. "This is your room."

I stepped inside to find what could only be described as a small cabin all its own. A huge sleigh bed was surrounded by windows that looked over the property, and I could see what looked like a lake. There was a stone fireplace already lit, and it gave off some delicious, much-needed heat for my bones. I'd forgotten how cold Montana could be at that time of year. A dresser and a long mirror sat on the opposite side of the room next to a couch and TV.

"Your bathroom." She opened another door, and my jaw nearly hit the ground. Again, another large room with a stone tub, vanity, and a shower fit for three. "This is where it might get a little strange," she opened a glass door into a closet, "this part was hard for me at first, but trust me, you'll adapt." She chuckled and stepped back so I could see the row of clothes hung by color. "They're your size." I looked at her oddly. "I know, strange, but look, most of our guests don't have much after they're extracted, and they can't exactly go in town to shop, so part of my job is to do my research on who is coming and build them a small wardrobe so they can feel a sense of normalcy again. Whatever you see here is yours."

I stepped around her and ran my hands over the soft fabrics and thought how expensive it must be to do. "Savannah, this isn't a small wardrobe. It's more than I have back home."

"So, maybe I went a little overboard, but fashion is my thing, and, well, you deserve it."

"That's up for debate," I muttered then closed my

eyes as I realized how that must have come off. Frigging Paul, he had my anger at a ten. I stepped out and tried to smile. "Sorry. That was rude."

"No, it wasn't. I get it." She pulled out some fluffy white towels and set them on the counter. "Look, Nicole, when people come to Shadows, it's usually under very difficult circumstances. Some are guests— that's what we call the victims who have been rescued —and some come because they're in danger here in the US. Sometimes they end up staying at the house because they've fallen in love with someone here, or they turn out to be a huge asset to the house and are asked to stay."

I leaned against the counter. "What am I?"

"You're a hero," she grinned, "and... the rest, only time will tell."

I huffed at her comment. I felt nothing like a hero. "Can you tell that to Paul?" I didn't mean for it to come out as a snicker, but it did.

She turned on the shower and pulled me farther into the bathroom. She said quietly, "I'm going to give you a little info on Paul so you can understand him better, because Lord knows he won't share shit with you."

I liked this woman. "I'm listening."

"He had someone he really loved once. That's," she hesitated, "gone now, and he hasn't dated since. He's pretty closed off and can be a bit cold."

"You can say that again." I rolled my eyes.

"But he's like a brother to me, and the fact that he

blew up like that back at the hospital tells me that he *can* with you."

"Lucky me." I dripped with sarcasm, and she chuckled.

"My point to that comment is Paul doesn't let his emotions get the best of him until he feels strongly about something or someone." She gave me a pointed look. "I've seen women hit on him, and he shuts them down fast. He doesn't allow himself to feel anything, but with you he must have. Did anything happen between you guys?" I looked away, and I could feel excitement radiating off her. I hated that I let a tiny smile slip, but I pulled it back as the memory of his hurtful words pushed my walls back up.

"I knew it." She did a little wiggle through her shoulders. "God, I knew I caught wind of something."

I laughed. "Don't get ahead of yourself." I closed my eyes and blew out a breath. So much had happened, and there was still a lot that needed to be worked out in my head. The Cartels weren't going anywhere, and I needed to think about me and what would come next.

"Hey, Nicole." She patted my arm, and I looked into her kind eyes. "I know this is a lot, but sometimes having a normal moment is just what you need to help you get your head back on straight."

She'd read my mind. "And Paul is a normal moment for me?" I couldn't help but feel what she was saying. There was a lightness to my chest I hadn't felt in, what, years? She grinned when she knew she had me. I waved her off. "What do you think you caught?"

"When Frank separated you after your spat, Paul watched you all the way down the hallway until you were out of view."

"He could have been making sure I left."

"Nope," her eyes lit up, "not with these guys. They're all the same. They're wonderfully protective. Shit, Cole knows I'm up here with you right now. He knows where I am pretty much all the time. Some might think its controlling, but it's not. It's their love language." She started to fan herself. "Girl, don't even get me started on their alpha qualities." She chef-kissed into the air and growled. "Once he realizes you weren't just trying to get a story off his mission, you'll get the Paul back who made that smile push through your hurt."

I rubbed my sore arm from where Bruno had grabbed me. "Maybe, but I'm only here until I get cleared to go back. So, he can take all the time he wants, but I won't ever be questioned on my motives again."

Her expression turned serious. "Please give Paul a chance. Trust me when I say he's been through more than you can imagine, and he really is a great guy."

"I'm sure he is." I tried to play nice.

"Okay," she stepped back, "we can girl talk later,

but right now have a shower. We'll have dinner in the dining room in an hour."

"Where is the dining room?"

"Main floor, just follow Mark's voice. He'll be the one gushing over how great the food is." She chuckled and stepped out and closed the door.

I turned to look at myself in the mirror. The bags under my eyes were dark, I looked like I hadn't had a good meal in days, and the bruises on my body were embarrassing. "Holy shit, you look like death, Nicole," I cringed out loud.

"Left side of the closet," Savannah called as she closed the bedroom door behind her.

Left side?

***

Apparently, the left side of the closet meant fancy. As much as a tank and shorts and the plush mattress called my name, I wouldn't be so rude as to not attend dinner. Besides, I was hungry, and the soft gray dress with long sleeves and square neckline looked good. It seemed to draw away from my cuts and bruises. Plus, the fact that the dress stopped mid-thigh made me feel like I had long legs, even though I didn't think I did. There were only a few times a year that I felt this way, so it was nice to have the added boost to my self-esteem. I slipped on a pair of heels, amazed that they fit, and pulled my hair into a low ponytail. A few pieces fell out, but they framed my face, so I was all right with it.

I fiddled with the thin bracelet I'd chosen from the things on the dresser as I headed down the stairs. With a job like mine, I was used to quietly finding my way in these situations. I always tried hard not to look out of place, and I got my game face on. Though I much preferred being in the field, I could enjoy myself anywhere, and I liked these people.

"Wow," Mia blurted when I found my way to the kitchen. "Sorry." She shook her head. "No, actually, I'm not. Wow, you look fantastic!"

I stopped at the island where she sat and laid a hand on the smooth stone counter. "Thanks, Mia. The hot shower and clean clothes certainly helped me feel more alive. Now I just need to eat and sleep for about six days, and I'll finally be myself."

"That, we can do." She smiled and looked over her shoulder.

"How's Chase doing?" I knew my voice told them how I missed the little guy. We'd been inseparable for what seemed like weeks, and it felt strange not to even know where he was.

"He's asleep, poor kid. He'll probably be out of it for the next few days. He is one sick little boy. Once the medication kicks in, we'll get a better idea. He's so lucky you got to him when you guys did, or I'm not sure what state he'd be in." I felt my chest tighten at the thought.

"The whole thing is terrible. I hate that he had to go through any of it." I cleared my throat of emotion and looked around the kitchen, as I needed to change the subject. I admired the stunning kitchen. It had everything you could imagine to cook and bake. The huge stoves and ovens, the walk-in pantry, the massive island to prep food, and a sparkling stainless commercial fridge that would make any chef giddy over such luxury. "This place is something else."

"Sure is." Mia beamed, and I was thankful she let the topic of Chase go. "When you get the chance, you can fill your boots. If you like to be in the kitchen."

"I very much do. I'm a bit rusty, but I could get lost in here." I grinned as I admired the red KitchenAid on the counter.

She laughed. "Don't tell Savi that. She'll have you in an apron so quick."

"I would be fine with that."

"Then I'll pass along the idea." I heard her tap her finger on the countertop. "Look, there's a lot of people to meet, but something tells me you're pretty good in a crowd."

"I've had a little experience." I smiled when I heard laughter from the next room. "However, Mark did send me a digital flipbook from his phone, so I have some idea of who is who."

She laughed and grabbed two huge bowls filled with corn and bean salad. "That's my husband. He's always looking out for people. In that walk-in pantry right there," she used the bowl to point, "are some extra napkins. Could you bring those for me?"

"Of course." I watched her disappear into the

dining room as I made my way across the kitchen to the frosted door. It felt strange to dig around someone's kitchen, but I figured that was what this place was here for. "If I were napkins, where would I be?" Then I spotted a stack of napkins with bears printed on them in a cute basket. "There you are." I took a bunch, and as I stepped out of the little room, I ran straight into someone's big chest. "Oh!" A set of broad hands clamped down on my arms to steady me. My eyes followed them up to a handsome face. *Paul.*

His eyes raked down my front as he held me. I could feel the heat from where his gaze left a scorched path. The memory of his lips on mine while my legs were wrapped around his lean waist in the water back in Mexico surged through me, and my heart went wild in my chest.

The sound of footsteps had Paul drop his hands away, then he took a step back.

A sweet voice came from behind him. "You must be Nicole. I'm Abigail." A warm smile instantly smoothed out the lines on her chin. "It's lovely to meet you."

"You too." I forced a grin, but it was tricky, as Paul's intense eyes pierced me from where he stood. "You have a sister named June, right?"

"I do." She seemed pleased I knew that. "She's in the other room. Why don't you come and join us?"

"I'd love to. Thank you." I held up the napkins. "Mia asked me to bring these." I glanced at Paul but had no clue what his thoughts might be. He stayed quiet.

Abigail was just as lovely as everyone told me she was. She wore beige slacks and a yellow cardigan. A set of pearls dusted her collarbone with matching pearl studs. Her snow-white hair curled softly around her face. I loved how put-together she was, and something told me it was effortless for her. I followed her into the dining room, where a massive wooden table stood. It was surrounded by many different faces, and I swallowed hard as my brain tried to recall the pictures from Mark's flipbook. *Just breathe.* Three cast-iron chandeliers cast a warm glow throughout the room. I half expected to see the children, but as none were present, I wondered if they had eaten somewhere else.

"Well, shit, you're alive." Ben stood up and wrapped an arm around my shoulders. I was thrilled to see a familiar face as I hugged him back. I stepped away and looked him over. "I'm okay," he assured me. "Just got a little banged up, but this place," he waved an arm around, "well, let's just say it would heal most anything."

"I'm glad." I gave him a pat and a warm smile. Ben was my oldest friend in the industry, and I was beyond happy that he was all right.

"Come on, sit down. The food here is unreal." He grinned as he pulled out a chair for me next to Mike, who smiled as I sat down. Ben took his seat again across the table from me. It was obvious that he was very comfortable there. I glanced around at everyone as I settled in. All the guys wore black t-shirts and camo pants, but the women wore a variety of styles and colors. I silently thanked Savannah again for the outfit I wore.

I mentally flipped through Mark's photos in my head then looked over at the man who sat next to Ben.

"I'm Nicole. You're West, right?"

"I am." He smiled and shot a quick look at Paul in the kitchen. I followed his glance and saw Paul nod slightly. *What's that about?*

"Which team are you with?"

"Stonewall." He sipped his water. I tried to remember if that was the other team Savannah had mentioned.

"Hey, Nicole," Mark waved a fork with a potato speared on the end of it, "I'm going to put you on the spot here."

"Of course you are." I chuckled with the rest of the table.

"Let's see how great your memory is. Start with Ben and give everyone's names."

"Mark," Mia shook her head at him, "give a girl a break." But I didn't mind.

"I got this." I sat straighter as everyone looked at me. I cleared my head and mentally pictured the flip-book. I looked at Ben, then started, "Keith, John, Sloane," I gave a wave, "nice to meet you." She waved back. "Mia and Mark. Savannah, Cole, Abigail, and her sister June." Again, I gave a wave. I waited for a beat, then went on. "Ivy and Ty," I nodded at them, "Moore, Lee, and Perez." My body threatened to break out in a cold sweat with the mention of Perez, but I had to remember it was as common as Smith in America. Then I looked around as I realized something. "Isn't Gear missing?"

"Yeah, he just left to join Frank's team," Ty answered. "He needed to be closer to his family."

"I'm sorry I didn't get a chance to meet him." I looked to my side. "West and Rush."

"Impressive!" Mark beamed with pride. "I taught her all that."

"And I appreciate the help, so thank you." I smiled at him. Then I looked at the man next to Rush. "And you must be Summit?"

"That's right, ma'am." Summit rubbed the scar that ran down the side of his chin under his bottom lip. He gave me a wave. "Us three," he pointed to Rush and West, "are on team Stonewall." Paul finally joined us, but I didn't look at him as he sat down. "And that's our team leader." Summit nodded at Paul as he took his seat.

"Oh." I glanced at him then. He seemed a little uneasy. "So, do you guys get to jump onto different teams for certain missions?" I wondered why Paul had been with Team Blackstone to rescue Chase if he was Stonewall's team leader.

"That one was a little different than the norm." West stepped in before Summit could reply. "We all have our place in the working wheel of Shadows. Blackstone and Dark Water are the teams in the field, while Stonewall works from downstairs. We fly the drones and give a bird's eye view for the teams in real time. Give them a heads up, if you will, of any potential danger lurking ahead." He nodded at Paul. "It was Paul who discovered what the Cartel was up to when the teams rescued your buddy, Ben."

"And for that, I'm forever grateful." Ben looked at Paul and placed a hand on his chest. "That was ugly, and a time I don't ever want to relive. I'm so glad you were able to go on the mission to rescue that poor child. Not to mention my gorgeous friend over there, and she's still in one piece." He pointed at me and grinned.

"Barely in one piece, but I'm here." I pretended to wipe sweat from my forehead.

Mike held up a glass of beer. "To coming home in one piece." The table raised their glasses, and new conversations took off among them.

Dinner was fantastic, and afterward, we moved into the living room to have drinks and mingle. It was a casual gathering, and I was sure it was meant for me to relax and get to know the housemates.

This place was spectacular. The cast iron chandeliers matched the iron railing that went up the grand staircase. The stone fireplace made a gorgeous focal point in the living room and gave off a delicious warmth that relaxed your body as well as your mind. I could imagine myself just sitting in this room for a whole day doing nothing. My eyes went to the stone archway that led into the dining room. The huge table looked like it was made from the same wood as the mantel above the fireplace.

I gave a sigh as I moved to the large windows that gave a stunning view of the mountains and the lake behind the house – no, mansion. Whoever their decorator was needed a serious raise because w-o-w.

"Overwhelmed yet?" Savannah appeared by my side and replaced my empty wine glass with another. "I was when I first came here."

"No, not overwhelmed, just taking it all in." I glanced around the room and loved how happy everyone seemed. "Is it always like this when they come back from a mission?"

She swallowed. "They have a dangerous job, and every time they come back, it's celebrated with hugs, a family dinner, and normally a trip to Zack's restaurant and bar in Redstone. Which, by the way, we plan on doing, but we wanted you to have a chance to get your head on straight first."

"That's kind of you." I glanced around. "Where are the children?"

"Olivia, that's our oldest," she nodded, "has the kids under wraps. Believe me, they can be quite a handful. We don't want our guests overwhelmed right at the beginning." She laughed. "You'll meet them all soon enough."

I nodded then studied the row of photos on the wall above the bar top. They were all in black and white, and it took me a second to recognize a young Daniel staring back at me.

Savannah's eyes followed mine. "That's Cole's grandfather, Edison. He created Shadows after his son got back from Vietnam. Daniel was struggling, and Edison knew he desperately needed something, so he created this masterpiece." She pointed to a photo. "That's Cole's mother, Sue. She'll be back tomorrow, so you'll meet her then." She glanced around the room. "Frank was a huge part of all this right from the beginning, and he still is."

"Frank and Mia are family?" I tried to piece everyone together.

"Yes, Mia is Frank's daughter."

I made a surprised face. "Wow. Did Mark know she was the general's daughter when he asked her to marry him?" I sensed a story there but pushed it down. It wasn't the time to let my reporter imagination go to work.

"No, not at all. But he loves that woman, and Frank knows it. So, that's all that matters."

"Agreed."

"Excuse me, but Savi can I speak to Nicole alone?" Mike joined us and looked a bit uncertain.

"Of course." She looked at me to make sure I was fine with it. I deeply appreciated that she felt the need to check with me. I forgot what it was like to have a real girlfriend. I nodded at her, and she left us.

"Hey, what's going on?" I studied his face.

"You tell me." He folded his arms over his massive

chest, and I suddenly felt very small. "You said you knew about my wife because you did a story on Catalina and her family. I dug a bit, because that's what I do, and I didn't find any story, article, or even a photo attached to your name. So, how do you know so much about my wife?"

Shit.

I opened my mouth but decided not to fib. Lord knew these guys could sniff a lie out of thin air.

"Actually, what I said to you was I had been asked to do a story on her and her family, but I didn't end up doing it."

"Why?"

I hated my work being questioned. "Because he found all the answers he needed."

"Who?"

"Look, Mike, you don't know me, so this is a lot to ask, but please trust me when I say I can't tell you."

He narrowed his eyes at me and slowly shook his head. It caught Cole's attention, and he headed toward us. Or maybe Savannah, who hadn't moved very far, had motioned him to rescue me. "Why?" Mike hadn't given up.

"Because I can't." I wasn't going to back down and knew my body language would be like a beacon to the others. I tried to relax.

Mike didn't like my answer, and I understood why, but I couldn't say another word. I would never write an article on someone or give out information about someone until I knew it was okay to do so. We were in a standoff.

"Secrets aren't something we do here at Shadows, Nicole." He rubbed his head. "We're talking about my wife here, and I don't like secrets when it comes to my family. Secrets lead to problems." I glanced at Cole, who now stood silently next to Mike.

"It's not what you think." I huffed out a breath, and I felt my heartbeat speed up as the room went silent at my raised voice.

"What should I think?" It was clear Mike wasn't going to let it go.

"Despite whatever some of you might think," I glanced at Paul, "I'm a good person. I don't use people. I just try to help them. I can't help it if there's things I'm not able to tell you, just like you guys can't." I desperately looked at Cole. "You and Frank wanted me to come here, so that's got to count for something."

"It does," Cole assured me, "but the women here all have something in their past that has scarred them. We're very protective, so when you tell us a story and we find out it's not true, you can see how one would get nervous."

"Understood, but I never lied." I looked at Mike. "I didn't. You just misunderstood what I said at the time. I never asked to come here," I said again. "I have orders to follow, too."

Cole let out a long breath as he mulled over my words. "Of course, Nicole. Mike, stand down." He put a hand on Mike's arm briefly. "Sorry if we're all on edge here."

"I'm good." I eyed Paul again, then glanced around the room and spotted the exit. I headed for it. "Excuse me."

I moved around Mark as he entered and slipped out the door. I heard him say "Was it something I said?" as I hurried off. I found the big door to the front porch and stepped outside. The chilly air raised goosebumps across my skin as tears slid down my cheeks.

"Nicole, are you okay?" Savannah had come to check on me.

I nodded and folded my arms around me as the cold seeped through the fabric of the dress. "I am." I wasn't, but I wasn't about to show it.

"Just so it's said, years ago, there was a teammate who almost took down Shadows. He worked with the Cartel. It was a scary time. It really made the team sit back and reset how they do things. Since then, the guys find it hard to trust. I'm sorry about how they questioned you, but you have to understand where they're coming from. I know you've had a rough go of it, and if it wasn't for you, that child wouldn't have made it. Please know I'll always be here if you want to talk."

"Thanks, Savannah. You have no idea how much your friendship means to me." Even if it had only been for such a short while.

"I'm happy to hear that. Please take all the time

you need." Her smile faded as she turned to go back inside.

I leaned my shoulder against the porch pillar and gazed out at the night sky. It looked like a black star-spattered canvas, the mountains carefully placed just so to catch the light of the bright yellow moon. The beauty of Shadows did not disappoint.

I took a deep breath as I tried to clear my head. So many things hit me at once. I had no idea when I could return to Mexico. I wanted to visit Chase, but I knew he needed to rest. Then there was Paul. I couldn't believe he thought I'd use Chase just for a story, and now he and Mike questioned my integrity and my job. I tried to push back the tears, but it was no use. They burned down my cheeks.

I heard the door open, but I didn't turn. I was exhausted. "Savannah, I promise I'm fine."

"You don't look fine." Paul's voice made me spin around.

I raised a hand. "No, please, I can't handle any more judgment."

He crossed his arms against his chest, and I glanced down at his tattooed sleeve. "You and I need to figure this shit out."

The nerve of him.

"Seems to me you're the one with the problem. Apparently, I can't be trusted." I used the back of my hand to swipe my cheeks. "I'm super glad I put every-thing on the line, only to have everyone question my intentions." I knew I sounded bitter. I eyed the door and wished I'd never come down at all. I should have stayed in my room. "Have a good night, Paul." I stepped around him, but his hand slapped around my wrist.

"We gotta figure this shit out, Nicole." I glanced down at his hand, and he flexed it but didn't let go, only softened his grip a little.

"Why?" I couldn't figure him out.

"Because," he pressed his rock-solid body against mine, "you're screwing with my head."

I stepped back and shrugged. "That's a *you* problem." I whisked around him and headed back inside. I slipped through the entryway and up the stairs to my room. When I shut the door, I took a deep breath and got ready for bed. I pulled back the covers and slipped between the sheets. I was more than exhausted and allowed sleep to take over.

FIVE

BRUNO

"Impossible." I couldn't believe who I was seeing. Nando didn't comment as he showed me the footage from the border. "Rewind that." I watched the video again and saw Nicole interact with Chili, one of Eric Noah's old friends. They talked briefly then disappeared out of view of the camera. "How on earth did those two hook up?"

"Maybe he saw her on TV," Nando suggested. "Maybe he made a play to get the kid for himself."

"It doesn't matter now, though, does it?" My cane clicked against the floor as I moved closer to him. "You lost her, and you lost the child." I pulled out my gun and shot him in the head. It was time he was gone from my sight. "Armondo?"

He struggled to wipe the fear from his face. "Yes, sir."

"Find me someone capable of doing his job."

"Of course."

He quickly dragged the body from the room as I waved at another of my men to clean up the mess then sent everyone away, as I needed time to think. It had been over a week since I saw Nicole and she drilled that bullet into my foot. I was lucky there wasn't as much damage as there could have been. She'd pay for it. She'd pay every single day once I had her back. She'd be mine forever without a chance of leaving. I shivered with delight at the thought of how I'd break her and make her mine.

I heard the click of heels as I made a drink and reached for another glass.

"There you are." Maya, my old friend, had come downstairs. She had taken care of my sexual needs earlier, and I felt much more relaxed. She stood and looked down at the nasty spot where Nando's life had just ended. She merely shrugged and reached for her drink.

"I was thinking we should go for a drive to the ocean. I'm bored of the city."

I hobbled over to a chair and took a sip from my glass. "I've got to work, but if you want a car to take you there, I can provide that."

"I want you to come with me." She pouted, and her red mouth looked inviting.

I leaned back and studied her. I liked Maya. She had wonderful attributes, mostly in the bedroom, a lovely body, and above all, I knew I could trust her.

I'd tested her more than once, and she never disappointed me. The issue was she demanded a lot of my time when she was around, and I was much too busy with the task at hand to give her the attention she wanted.

"Bruno," Rio, Mama's right-hand man, appeared in the doorway of my office, "you should see this." He glanced at Maya, and I knew whatever it was, it wasn't meant for her eyes.

"Go use the pool out back." I motioned for her to get moving.

"The pool?" Her nose scrunched, but she lifted her hands in defeat as Armondo came rushing in. He must have heard that Rio had arrived. Maya looked at Armondo, then Rio. She made a show for them as she crossed the room to kiss me and let out a loud sigh. "I guess I'll go entertain myself." She turned dramatically and left the room.

I admired her tight ass as she walked, then a thought hit me as she disappeared through the door. She was pretty and had her attributes, but she wasn't the one I really wanted. I heated as I pictured Nicole again. In time, I *will* break her, and she'll be mine until I get my fill.

I caught Rio watching me, so I sat straighter. "I don't want to have to remind you that this is my house and coming over unannounced is breaking rule number one."

"I'm under orders from your mother to show you this and ask if you know anything about it." He raised an eyebrow, and I wanted to slap it right off his cocky face. Instead, I extended my hand for him to give me the tablet. "It was uploaded from a new account this morning on YouTube. It seems *Señorita* Winter isn't the only one making waves in the media."

My curiosity piqued, I hit play on the video. The pain in my foot soon subsided as I watched with great delight.

"One down, ten to go." I grinned, but then something hit me. I backed up the video and paused it on his face. "Armondo, why do I feel I met him before? It's something in the eyes."

Armondo followed my train of thought. "He does look familiar."

"Let's do a little recap, shall we?" Rio made himself comfortable on the chair across from me. I thought of all the ways I'd kill the son of bitch when my mother was finished with him. "The American reporter brings a date to Sully's party, a party where he's entertaining an unlikely guest, Rafael Cruz. The very man who is selling the child and the only one who knew where the child was being held."

He fixed his tie with a sigh and continued. "No one can find information on this Dan from LA other than the past few years. You get confirmation from Nicole herself that she's working with Blackstone to get the baby across the border, and then suddenly the Ruiz cousins kill one of the Blackstone soldiers? Tell me you can see this for what it is, Bruno." I imagined ramming my cane through his pretentious face. "Your girlfriend failed to mention the truth to you too. That she brought in a member of Blackstone right under your nose and played you for a fool."

"Get the fuck out!" I screamed. He shrugged and slowly rose from his seat with a head shake and left.

I tossed the tablet on the table and let it all sink in.

"Armondo, get the car." I pushed to my feet and grabbed my cane. "We're heading to the United States."

SIX

PAUL

Nicole stayed in her room for most of the next day, only coming out to see if Chase was up, which he wasn't, and to have a quick bite. I missed her because I was in a meeting with Blackstone.

The following day, Savi said she needed more sleep. I couldn't help but wonder if she was avoiding the house. We needed to do damage control, as much as I wanted to believe Nicole didn't try to sell my son's story to advance her career, the fact that she was holding on to secrets bothered all of us. We were a house built on trust and love. It seemed we had another version of what I assumed Lexi was like here, and it didn't sit well with anyone.

I rubbed my bottom lip as I stood on the porch and watched the dogs chase each around the property.

A big stick hung from Wellington's mouth. The pup was our newest addition, a huge golden retriever Mark had fallen in love with after Butters passed. I thought of that old dog and had to shake my head and smile. How he'd lived for as long as he had was amazing.

Wellington's antics made me laugh out loud as he dropped his stick and barked at Captain. He'd been found on the side of a road somewhere and had been taken to the local shelter by a tourist. No one ever came for him, and when Mark got wind of it, the rest was history.

I missed Tripper the most. He was such a sweet boy. I only had the pleasure of knowing him for two months before he got sick and passed. John was heartbroken, but I thought Sloane took it the hardest. She was near tears half the time. One day I heard a border collie had a litter in town, and I took a chance and brought one home for her. Captain was nothing like old Tripper, but he was a sweet little guy with crazy energy, and Sloane loved him immediately. He and Wellington were best friends in no time.

Chase's scream snapped me out of my thoughts, and I rushed for the door and up the stairs.

"Sorry, Paul," Savannah's face was sweaty as she knelt by Chase's bed, "he woke up, and still has a fever. I gave him his medicine. It wasn't easy, and now I can't get him to stop crying."

"It's okay. It's just that he's seen so many strange people lately." I gathered him in my arms and felt how small he was. He took one look at me and screamed louder. Savannah reached up and rubbed his back as I pressed him against my chest. "I can get Mia to come and help. I just need a minute."

"It's fine, I've got him. I didn't even know he was awake." I hadn't seen him since we got back, and I missed the little crier.

She gave me a sympathetic look. "Poor guy. He'll come around. He just needs time and patience."

"I know." I smiled at her. "Thanks Savi. I know it's an adjustment for all of us."

"A great adjustment," she nodded, "especially for you. He'll soon learn to trust us."

After she left, I tried to bounce him in my arms as I walked around the room. "It's okay, big guy. Look at the puppy dogs, *el perrito*. Can you see?" I said the word in Spanish and English as I held him so he could see out the window, but his bottom lip poked out and he hiccupped as he caught a breath.

"Mama," he said in the most heartbreaking voice. It nearly brought me to my knees. Christ, I fought back the tears that threatened to show just how much that one word could break me. I knew he loved his mother, Talya, but I also knew he was referring to Nicole.

"Fuck," I muttered and walked to Nicole's door. I'd do anything for my son, and if that meant taking him to her, I'd do it.

I knocked, and Chase, who was still very upset, copied me and did the same action with his fist. I smiled at him and knocked again, and this time he tried with me.

"Look at you." I beamed with pride and patted his shoulder gently.

"Mama," he whimpered again, and I saw more tears start to form. *Screw it.* I opened the door and poked my head in. Nicole looked to be asleep in bed, so I stepped inside and closed the door behind us. When Chase caught sight of her, he wiggled like a wet noodle, and I quickly put him down on the bed next to her in fear I might drop him.

"Mama!" he cried, and her eyes popped open. She reached out and pulled him into her arms with a deep intake of breath and kissed his head.

"Hey, buddy, I've missed you." She smiled down at him. "Oh, my, are you upset?" The little guy let out a loud sob, and she pressed him to her. She glanced up at me standing there and then pulled the blanket up over her thin top. We both knew I could see she was braless under it. It was hard not to see how pretty she was with her messy hair and sleepy eyes.

"He was crying and wanted you. It's the first time I've seen him up." I cleared my throat and felt uncomfortable. "Sorry to wake you."

She hooked the blanket and moved up to sit against the headboard with Chase in her arms. "He's still very warm. Did he get his antibiotics?" Chase pressed his head under her chin and settled in, so she tucked the blanket over him as well.

"Savannah was with him when I went in. She

managed to get it in him, but then he wouldn't settle."

"It's fine." She looked at the clock on the nightstand. "I don't remember the last time I slept in like this, let alone two days in a row."

"It's good that you did." I tried to sound friendly, but I knew we were far from all right. "I think he missed you."

"At least someone does," she blurted, then her eyes went wide when she heard herself. I shifted my weight and the floorboards outed me. "Is Frank here?" She changed the topic, but before I could answer, Chase's hand moved to her plump breast, and I sucked in a gulp of air. Her face went pink as she eased his hand away.

"Ah, Frank, yes, he is, and, ah, he said he wanted to meet you tomorrow afternoon." I hated that my words were jumbled. "I think he wanted to give you some time to rest."

"That was nice, but I need to figure out when I can get back into the field."

Internally, I rolled my eyes and wondered when she'd figure out that wasn't going to happen. Not unless she planned on returning to Mexico with a body bag in hand.

"Don't hold your breath." I shrugged, and the lines deepened around her mouth as she pressed her lips tightly together.

"Paul, despite how much you hate me, I've been working on something for the past five years. It's an important story, and all the Perez and the Canos shit that's been happening tells me it probably runs deep into the Ruiz family. I'm going to be the one who tells the story, and I hope it will take down several tiers of the Cartel."

"Well, we all know what you'll do for a story." I glared at her. "What will this one cost? Your life?"

"Maybe." She glared back at me while I stared at her like she had three heads. "Our jobs aren't that different, you know," she went on. "I may not carry a gun or rescue kidnapped victims, but I'm there to help the people too. I do whatever I can in my own way, and this story will give them hope to maybe be able to live without the threat of violence."

I folded my arms and watched as Chase moved restlessly for a moment then reached up to hold a piece of her hair. He coughed but seemed content, and it screwed with my head even more. "And if you ever do get to tell your story, what exactly do you think is going to happen then?"

She looked away. "I'll cross that bridge when I get there."

"Because it seems to me you'll be hunted down like a dog." I made a face. "Oh, wait, much like you are now."

"Paul, don't exaggerate."

"I'm not, Nicole. The only difference is Bruno wants you for himself, at least at this point. What happens when he learns you were working with us to get the boy over the border?"

"He already knows." She didn't miss a beat, and my face fell. "Oh, yeah, right before I shot him in the foot, I told him I was working with Blackstone."

I covered my face with my hands and let out a long breath. "Nicole," I couldn't believe what I was hearing, "now you really can't go back."

"That's up for debate." She kissed Chase on the head again when he stirred and gave a little cry. "I don't know why you care so much. You've made it abundantly clear that whatever happened between us is over. So, no loss for you if I go back."

I opened my mouth but clamped it shut. *Am I done with her?*

Chase reached for her breast and took a nosedive toward it. Quickly, she pulled him back. "Oh, no, those girls are out of commission for you, sir." She giggled. "But you know what that tells me? Your tummy is finally hungry, and that's a good sign." She swung her legs over the bed and got up with him in her arms then moved toward me in her shirt and panties. "You go with Paul." She held him out, but Chase scowled at me. I got it. I didn't have breasts or smell like she did. I took him from her, and he let out a loud cry of protest.

"Just let me get dressed. I'll be right back." She grabbed some clothes and headed into the bathroom. He wiggled to get down, and I scanned the room for anything he could get into, then set him on the floor. He, of course, bolted for the bathroom door. I scooped him up and tossed him over my shoulder. To my utter surprise, he giggled.

"You like that?" I carefully turned him around in my arms then threw him over my other shoulder. His feet kicked out as he let out the best belly laugh I'd ever heard. "I knew you were one of us." I did it again, and pure joy erupted from him. Then a small cough started, and I stopped, not wanting to set off his lungs. I lowered him down my front and admired his happy smile. "You're so cute."

"So, you're a softy under all that brooding." Nicole ran her hands through her hair as she crossed the room and picked up her phone. "Did I finally get a peek at what the real Paul is like?"

That comment hit hard, but I tucked the Eric Noah part of me back in its box. Only problem was Chase looked like me—well, at least I thought so—so I couldn't escape my past completely.

"Knock-knock." Olivia popped her head inside. "Hey, Uncle Paul, I was hoping to meet the baby and —" Her eyes widened when she saw Nicole. "Oh, my God, you're even prettier in person."

Of course, Olivia would know who Nicole was. She seemed to know everything. The girl never missed anything that happened around Shadows.

"Olivia, this is—"

"*Washington Post's* war correspondent, Nicole Winter," Olivia gushed. "When Mom told me you were coming, I watched all your videos. My favorite was where you chased one of the Ruiz cousins to El

Salvadore and right into the hands of Jim Canos. He never saw it coming."

"I won't lie, that one was really fun." Nicole put on an earring, and it sparkled when she let it go. *Why do I notice these things?*

"Fun is an understatement." Oliva laughed and sounded about twenty years old. She came close to see Chase and tickled him under his chin. "Hi, little fella. I'm Olivia. You're pretty cute. Ms. Winter, do you think maybe we could talk more about what you do sometime? I have a few ideas for the house, and I'd love to run them by you."

"I'd love that too, Olivia. Just let me get settled today, and I need to chat with Frank, then I'm all yours."

I scowled playfully at her as Chase reached out for Nicole and threw his whole weight unexpectedly in her direction. I managed to hold on to him. "What about me?"

"I love ya, Uncle Paul," she raised her chin the way she often did when she wanted me to take her seriously, "but I've dug into your head about my ideas and got all I needed. And, well, she's fresh meat." She grinned when Nicole laughed. "Ms. Winter would have a whole different perspective to offer, plus she's a woman, so that just adds the cherry on top."

"Hell, yeah, it does." Nicole high-fived her. "You can call me Nicole."

Chase threw himself toward Nicole again. I put him down, and he made a beeline for her. His crawl was comical with his big diaper making a swooshing noise as he went. Without a second thought, she gathered him up in her arms and placed him on her hip. Instantly, he settled. *How does she do that?*

"First, and most importantly, I need to get this little guy some food," Nicole smiled.

"I can help with that." They both left for the kitchen, and I followed. I was totally in awe of Nicole. The woman probably didn't even realize what a natural she was with my boy.

Chase got tired after he ate a bit of food, and they managed to get him to drink some juice. He began to yawn and got quiet again. The girls took him off for a nap.

I headed to meet up with my team to fix a small problem on the drone. It had been transported from Texas.

I hit the top of the stairs when Dr. Bash caught me mid step. "Hey, Paul, I know this mission was a hard one on you. Would you like to set up a session?"

"Nope."

He licked his lips. I knew it was hard coming into a house like ours, but Bash wasn't Doc Roberts, and my assigned doctor was Ivy. I didn't have to take suggestions from him, even though Doc Roberts encouraged us to.

"I'm really not the enemy here. I'm only trying to offer help."

I rolled my wrist and checked the time. I was sure I acted like a jerk, but I had so many things on my mind, and letting Dr. Bash inside my head wasn't going to help. "I appreciate it, but now isn't the time."

"Tomorrow, then?" he pushed.

"No."

"The next day?"

I shook my head. "With all due respect, there's a way to approach us, and this isn't the way." I continued down the stairs, leaving him to figure it out.

"You know, I'd actually consider working here." Chili looked around our tech shop, admiring all the new technology the safehouse has to offer. "Now that you're gone, the job doesn't seem to run as smoothly as it once did. I wish you were back."

I glanced at West, who had his headphones on and his nose deep into some blueprints. My team knew about my past, but it wasn't something I talked about freely. They knew I'd been undercover in Mexico for ten years and that I'd done so for the sake of the house. My alias was never shared, nor would it be. I had hoped the name Eric Noah would die when I left Mexico, but truth be told, he's still very much alive inside me, and that proved to be a whole other problem I had to deal with. Bottom line was the team didn't dig, and I didn't offer any more than I had to.

"That was another life," I grunted and went back to soldering two tiny pieces of metal.

"Yeah, I see that you've tucked that life away behind a sleeve of ink." He pointed to my tattooed arm where it had been necessary to cover up the past.

"It's a work in progress."

Chili pulled out a chair and rolled it over to be closer. "Do you miss it?" I didn't answer. "Come on, Paul, it's me. I won't tell a soul."

I finished and turned off the gun then removed my gloves and glasses. "Some of it, I do." I held the drone. "It fits perfectly."

"Like?" he dug, and I couldn't help but wonder if Doc Roberts asked him to try to pry some of my feelings from me.

I pressed my hands against the table and opened that part of my head I normally kept tightly shut.

"I miss doing my job without all the boundaries. If someone fucked up, I dealt with them. No questions asked." I ran my fingers through my short hair. "You know, Chili, parts of me kinda miss the uncertainty Castillo brought to every day. Sure, there was a lot more action there than being stuck here." I shook my head as I realized my words came out wrong, but I knew Chili understood what I meant. "I'm glad he's gone, but life's sure thrown a lot at me since."

"You got a son out of it."

"I did but lost his mother along the way," I sighed deeply and instantly felt that horrible tug and pull that came with thoughts of Talya. I cleaned my hands with a rag. "I don't know, things are different. Then there's –" I shot him a look when someone knocked on the frosted glass door.

I glanced at Chili and thought it was strange. The

wives all knew that if the light wasn't on outside, they could come in without knocking.

"Come in," I called then studied the drone a little closer.

The door slid open, and my vision shifted off the drone and on to the visitor in the doorway.

Nicole looked around, and her eyes widened at all the things around my shop. "Ah, sorry. I was looking for Cole."

She had changed since I'd seen her last, and I noticed her silk blouse tucked loosely into her jeans showed a slightly thinner figure than before. She'd lost a little weight since we'd been in Mexico. I found my voice. "Next room over."

Her head dropped forward in defeat. "I already checked."

"Everything okay?" Chili asked.

"Yeah," she held up a black cell phone, "I just needed to give him this."

Suddenly, my training kicked in. "Is that an outside phone?"

She looked at it. "Yes."

"The fuck." I hopped to my feet, and she took a step back as I got closer. "You brought an outside phone to Shadows? What were you thinking? You signed a contract explaining all this shit."

Chili came to her rescue. "Let's take a breath there, buddy."

"You mean the three-hundred-and-five-page brick he sat on my lap five thousand miles up in the air?" she snapped back at me. Her eyes flashed in anger. "Sorry, I must have missed that part!" Her face twisted, and she pulled her chin in like I was nuts. "And second, despite your opinion of me and my job, I wasn't born yesterday. It's off, and the SIM card has been removed and put in a Faraday cage. So, take your condescending complex down to a three because it's friggin insulting."

Chili let out an unexpected laugh, and I turned to glare at him. I shook my head and returned my attention to the spitfire in front of me.

"Who does the phone belong to, and how did you obtain it?"

"Obtain it?" She let out a laugh. "Okay, well, it's Bruno's, and I obtained it after I shot the shit in the foot."

"What the hell?" My face must have said it all because she just shook her head.

"Right, while you digest that, I'm going to go hand this over to Cole if I can ever find him."

I reached out and grabbed her arm and swung her around to look at me. "Does he know you have it?"

She stared at my hand on her arm, and something passed through us. Something deeper than frustration. It was like she ignited a flame inside me. One I constantly fought to keep to a spark.

"No," she said quietly, and her face told me she felt it too. "The man was in too much pain to notice."

"Whatever you do, don't activate the SIM card. Chances are he's closed the account, but that SIM card will hold a lot of information for us. Not like he can wipe it clean."

"I know." She nodded at my hand. "Can I go find Cole now?"

Slowly, I let go, and she glanced up at me with a look I couldn't read. "Good thinking." I tried to play nice. I wished I could erase the vision of her and Chase on the news from my head.

"Thanks." I watched her disappear down the hallway.

I turned to find Chili texting someone. "Not a word."

"Sorry, man, but John needs to hear about this one."

I rolled my eyes and knew I'd be the one to hear plenty about it.

At dinner, Nicole kept to her side of the table. Ty and Moore had plenty to catch up on now that they were back from Rosarito, and they picked her brain on the Canos family. I hated to admit it, but the woman had a wealth of knowledge on the Cartels. She knew the history of the Canos family inside out. I noticed she did sidestep on some of the questions that had to do with Bruno and their past together and a few on Sully. They didn't push, and I just watched and listened.

Later that evening, I saw her sneak upstairs. I guessed she went to check on Chase, and I took that time to speak with Cole.

"Hey," I joined him at his favorite spot by the fireplace, "did Nicole give you Bruno's phone?"

"Yeah, that was a surprise."

"Think you can get any information off it?"

"We're going to dive into it tomorrow," he said quickly, his eyes on Olivia. She was making a beeline for her dad. She threw her arms around him and hugged him.

"Copy that." I grabbed Liv once she let go of her dad and pulled her in for a hug too.

"So, Nicole seems nice." She gave me a mini shit-eating smile that matched her dad's, and I knew her mother was probably somewhere watching us. "She just went upstairs."

"And on that note…" I shoved her back to her father and made a point of heading downstairs to my office. I closed the door and went to work on the drone.

I slept in my office as I often did when I needed my head to settle, only this time it didn't. I just stared at the wall with my mind in an endless loop of how Talya must have felt having Chase all on her own. The fact that my choices in life meant that I not only missed knowing she was pregnant, I missed my son's birth, and I wasn't there to protect his mother from being killed. That would forever weigh on me.

I stayed downstairs the next morning, after getting word from Abby that Chase was eating now but sleeping a lot because of the medication. I slipped upstairs a couple times to check on him. She was right; he was out cold. I knew he needed it, but I missed the guy.

My body was healing well, and I was antsy with not being able to train with the guys. I tried to disobey Cole's orders and get in a little exercise, but he'd already caught me in the gym once, no thanks to Frank, who seemed to be keeping watch.

Lost in thought, I didn't hear the door slide open.

"Why are you avoiding everyone?" Dr. Ivy stood there with her arms crossed over her chest. I caught a lightness in her eyes, so I knew she wasn't really pissed.

I gave her a small smile. "Just got a lot on my mind."

She nodded and stepped inside the office, closing the door halfway behind her. "Lucky for you, there are people here willing to listen."

"Are there, now?" I teased. I knew I needed to try to release some of the tension that was building inside, but I had to get a handle on it myself first.

"Mhm, look, Paul, Dr. Bash is ready and willing to listen."

"Pass," I shot back.

"Why?" When I didn't answer, she let out a long sigh. "You boys really hate change." I shrugged and fiddled with a new lens for the drone. "You know Doc Roberts is retiring, and I can't take on Dark Water, given the team leader is my husband. So that leaves me with Blackstone and the kids. But I could have one spot open for Stonewall."

"Good, me, then." I flashed her a grin.

"It would be better if team Stonewall all stayed with one therapist. You know Doc Roberts would only bring in the best of the best. He sees something in Bash. He'd be good for you and the team."

"What do you see?" I challenged.

She shook her head. "This isn't about me."

"If you want me to jump to Dr. Bash, sell him to me." I popped the lens inside then lowered it to give her my attention.

"Paul?" Cole popped out of thin air and gave Ivy a nod as he said, "Please join us next door."

"Copy that." I set the drone down and looked at Ivy. "You think on that answer and get back to me, yeah?"

"All right, Paul." She shot me an unimpressed look. "Meet with me later today for a session, and we'll talk it through." She stared hard at me. "And don't think I don't know about you and Frank and your evening sessions." Christ, she saw a lot. "Yeah, that's what I thought." She smacked my arm as she stepped out of the office.

Frank, Cole, Daniel, and Nicole all sat around the conference table.

Daniel rubbed his hip like it hurt him to sit. For a man in his eighties, he was still pretty spry, but the years had taken a toll on his body. "How's our tiniest houseguest?" he asked Nicole.

"Sleeping now. Abigail's keeping an eye on him. He's got a way to go before he'll be the active little boy I'm sure he'll be one day." I noticed that the guys avoided any eye contact with me.

"What's going to happen to him?" Nicole looked at Daniel. "I mean, do you have a family lined up for him?"

Daniel cleared his throat. "For now, he'll stay here. He's too valuable to the Cartel to put him with anyone else, at least for the foreseeable future."

"All right," Frank thankfully started. "First off, General Bruce wasn't able to make his flight, so he won't be here. Apparently, something happened with an Eagle Eye member." That caught my attention.

"Who?" Cole and I said at the same time.

Frank paused for a second and glanced briefly at Nicole. He pursed his lips but seemed to get past that she was in the room and continued. "Mills. Someone took a run at his truck about ten minutes after he got through the last security checkpoint at the safehouse. It's mostly likely nothing, but the kid he was training with got a busted-up shoulder. The truck was hit on that side, and Mills got a bit banged up, nothing serious. Driver of the other vehicle didn't stick around, and there weren't any witnesses. Things like that do happen, but they're looking into it."

"Shit," Cole shook his head, "I'll give him a call later today to check in."

"Okay." Frank pushed his wire-framed glasses up his nose. "So, that means we'll have to wait until tomorrow to have our official meeting on what's next for you, Nicole." I shifted uneasily on my chair and wondered where she'd end up. "Also, our meeting will be in Washington rather than here."

"Washington?" I said out loud. I didn't like the idea she'd be going anywhere on a plane. "Why Washington?"

"General Bruce has someone he wants us to meet."

"Wait," Nicole also looked worried, "I can't leave. What about Chase?" Warmth settled in my chest for a hair of a second, then I pushed it away.

Cole jumped in. "Abby and my mother will look after him. You can check in with them or Savannah whenever you need to." He smiled, and I appreciated his effort to put her at ease about Chase. I also could see by his glance at Daniel that he didn't like the idea of the meeting being held off site.

"All right," she rubbed her chest, "but for one night max."

"Understood." Frank glanced at me. "As for now, sit tight, and I think you should go to Zack's tonight with the others. A little normalcy will do you good."

"I'm fine," she shot back, but her gaze dropped to the table. "Perhaps you're right. Savannah mentioned it as well. I think I would like to join them." She tried to smile.

"Good." Frank looked at me. "Paul, since you know Nicole already, I'm assigning you to her detail."

Her mouth dropped open, and I knew we were in for an argument. A part of me already looked forward to it. "I don't need a bodyguard."

"It's not up for debate." I egged her on.

She shot me a cold look. "You think he's going to protect me?" She laughed darkly. "He's admitted he doesn't trust me and accused me of using the child for my own purposes. Which, for the record, I would never do. My luck, he'll leave me in the middle of the town to find my way back here."

"Don't tempt me." I gave Cole a smirk.

Nicole raised her arms. "You've got to be kidding me."

"I'm seriously too old for this job," Frank muttered under his breath and ran a hand over his silver crew cut. "I have no doubt that you can defend yourself, Nicole, but there are a lot of things that can happen in town, and we never let any of our guests or family members go there without someone to watch their six."

"And not to mention, one Cartel family that's looking for you because you told them you were working for us." I wanted that out on the table so Frank was aware of how much damage she'd done to herself.

"You did what?" Frank's head snapped up.

"First, I never said *for,* I said *with.*" She scowled. "And second, they'd know anyway. Bruno has eyes and ears everywhere. Christ, he knew Eric Noah was the father of that child before I even got my hands on the birth certificate."

"What?" That shook me. "When did you find this out, and why didn't you tell me?"

"Why the hell would I think to tell you that?" She looked at me like I was crazy. "Before or after you tore a strip off of me for following your orders?"

"Christ," Mark who I'd seen slip into the room to sit quietly by the door, piped up. "I feel like I'm watching Ross and Rachel. We're on a break!" He chuckled but stopped when Cole looked at him, confused. "Sorry, Mia makes me watch it."

"Yeah, Mia does." Cole rolled his eyes. "Anyway, Nicole, are you sure Bruno would've known that? Because if you ask me, he'd kill if he knew that."

"Yeah," her anger tamed some, "he tried to kill me, but I shot him in the foot so he couldn't." She shrugged like shooting a gun didn't freak her out. "He told me when I was at the border. Along with a threat that he was going to find me, the baby, and the safehouse. And that Ben was only the start."

"That might be something to have told us right when you arrived here," I growled.

Frank held up a hand to stop the next fight steamrolling my way. "Nicole, you report anything out of the ordinary to Paul. If you remember anything else, you also report it to Paul." He pushed his thumbs into his eyes. "Paul, you and Cole will come with us to Washington."

I could see Nicole didn't like that. I was pleased until I began to digest the thought of leaving my son behind. I also hated to admit that Chase seemed to be drawn to her. He needed her almost more than me. That thought pissed me off.

"I'd rather be back in Mexico than have to spend any more time with someone that questions my loyalty." Nicole snickered at Frank.

"Look," Frank leaned forward with his hands pressed into the table, "I don't really like this any more than you do." He stood and huffed out a breath. It was clear whatever General Bruce was up to weighed heavily on his mind. "Miss Winter, I've got about four months left with my teams before Bruce takes over. I'm way past retirement, but I've stayed on because…" He glanced at me, and I thought I knew what he would have said the reason was. He wanted to see me home and settled before he left. That was what he'd told me. Lately, though, I sensed that things were different with Frank. He'd changed. His only focus now seemed to be bringing down Perez and his Cartel. "I need to know that this house will be all right once I step away," Frank continued.

"I didn't mean I don't appreciate all you've done." Nicole's face was open and honest. "It's just that—"

"Nicole, Paul has his reasons for behaving like he does." He glanced at me. "But with that, Paul," he lowered his chin and squinted at me, "I need you to set aside your concerns and do what is expected of you. Protect her."

"Of course," I assured him.

"I just need Nicole to hear that."

Nicole raised a brow. "Time will tell."

Frank shook his head and huffed a laugh. "What is it with this place and feisty women?"

"I think it's required for being here." Mark laughed.

"Sorry, Frank." She cleared her throat. "I hear you, and I'm not here to make your life any harder than it might be." She smiled. "I'll go out to Zack's tonight, I'll report to Paul if I need to, and I'll be ready for Washington tomorrow. All I ask is that it only be for one day."

"I'll mention it to General Bruce."

"Thank you." Her shoulders relaxed. "Wait, do you know who is joining us for the meeting?"

"No idea." I could tell by the way Frank's jaw flexed he wasn't happy with not being in the loop anymore. "Now," Frank looked at his phone then back to her, "is there anything else I should know before I go?"

"No, nothing that *you* need to know." She tapped her fingers on the table. I glanced toward Cole at her strange wording.

Cole's mouth twisted. "What about something *any* of us should know?"

"Nope." She shrugged, and it left a bad taste in my mouth.

Mark quickly signed that we should get a few drinks in her and ask again. I knew he was joking, but I loved that idea.

"She's been cleared, guys," Frank reminded us. "Back off a little."

Back off? I tried to figure out what Frank knew. "What? C'mon, Frank, you know something." When he didn't answer, I grew more frustrated. "She gets calls at all hours of the night. She knows things she shouldn't." I looked at her, but her face was expressionless. "She's hiding something."

"I don't actually know anything. It was Bruce who cleared her," Frank admitted.

Cole looked at him hard. "That's not how things are done."

The sadness that flashed over Frank's face bothered me to my core. "Send your complaint to General Bruce. I'm being stripped of my role."

Nicole pushed to her feet. "For men who keep your whole lives a secret," she waved around the room as if to say Shadows, "you sure don't mind trying to force me to crack."

I folded my arms. "So, there *is* something."

"I'm saying you're hypocritical." She looked at Cole. "Can I go?"

He nodded. "Yeah." I waited for her to leave and shot Cole an uneasy look. He nodded because he felt it too. "All right, boys, let's get back to work," Cole ordered, and we quickly dispersed.

* * *

Later that night, we piled into the SUVs and headed for Zack's. When we arrived at the front door, I felt a sense of calmness settle over me. These were the times when we felt normal; we were just in town like regular folks for some fun. A group of friends who wanted to shed the stress of our work lives.

Our SUV pulled up behind the girls'. We got out first then watched as they exited their car. Nicole's white cowgirl boots hit the pavement first. She wore jeans and a pink halter top and looked damned attractive. I knew she used very little makeup, only what she needed to cover up her various cuts and bruises. Savannah and the other girls were dressed the same, some in skirts, but mostly pants as the weather was cooling off fast. The guys, like me, all had on jeans and button-ups or t-shirts. I stuck to a black t-shirt. I wasn't one for wearing color, like Keith or Mike. Either way, we easily blended in with the locals, and that was all that mattered.

As much as I gave Nicole shit earlier, I wasn't overly happy to be the one to keep an eye on her, and I planned to keep my distance as much as possible.

"You remember your cover story?" I reminded her.

"I do. I'm Hanna from Long Island just in town with my friends for the weekend."

"Good." I gave a curt nod.

"We walk in with the guys," Savannah quietly explained to Nicole as they approached me, "and we leave with them. It sets the precedent that we're all together. Just follow Paul's lead."

"Understood." She nodded in agreement and smiled at Savannah and looked excited.

"Good, we'll meet you in there." Savannah rushed to Cole's side and slipped her hand through his.

Nicole folded her arms and shivered. She didn't have a sweater, and the air was cool. Her shirt barely covered her stomach, and I couldn't help but notice her breasts reacted to the drop in temperature. "So, we just walk in next to each other?"

"Yeah." I motioned for her to walk, but she stopped me.

"Paul." Her eyes softened, and I saw her guard slip. She looked around, and I wondered if she was nervous. When she saw me look down at her, she shook it off. "Never mind."

We stepped inside, and I felt her stop and pull back. Zack's was busy. The restaurant closed earlier in the evening, and the place had more of a western club vibe. Live music blared from the speakers. The dance floor was full of people line dancing. Over the years, the town of Redstone had grown, and there were more tourists than ever before.

I bent and lowered my lips to her ear. "You good?"

"Yeah," she tried to smile, "it's just been a minute since I've gone out at all, and it's such a busy spot."

I felt slightly bad, knowing exactly how she felt. I put my hand on her hip. "It's a lot, but it's safe here." I moved her in front of me.

PRESS

SEVEN

NICOLE

We joined the others in the far corner near the bar. Pool tables and dartboards seemed to have been reserved for us. *That's pretty cool.*

"Hello, all." A friendly looking man set a tray of beer pitchers on the high-top table. "I see we have a newbie." He whipped his hand out and extended it toward me. "I'm Adam, one of the managers here at Zack's and a friend of everyone." His grin went from ear to ear.

"Nicole. Nice to meet you." I shook his hand. "This is a pretty nice place."

He looked around. "I think so, too."

"Hey, Adam," Savannah smiled, "let's see what fancy girlie drinks the ladies want." She pulled him away as Mark held up the pitcher of beer. I shook my head, and he shrugged and poured one for himself.

Savannah called me over to where the girls had gathered around a separate long table. Adam was taking their drink orders as fast as he could.

"What's your poison, Nicole?" Sloane, John's wife, called from the far end. "We always like to try something new. I'm having a Sour Puss, and Savannah's having a Blue Walrus." She laughed and clapped her hands.

"I think I'll stick with a pinot." I grinned. "I might get wild and crazy on those."

"That's the whole idea." Savannah patted the chair next to her, and I sat. "You need to let your hair down a little."

"Yeah, we'd like to see that," Mark called from where he stood with the guys. He held up a beer and wiggled his brows at us.

"I just bet you would." I allowed myself to get into the fun. "Okay, Adam," I glanced quickly down the drink list, "I'll have a Random Ruckus."

"One Random Ruckus for the lady." Adam wrote it down and laughed as he headed for the bar.

"Make them all doubles," Mark called, and all the guys but Paul whistled and clapped.

I saw Paul watching me, but when he caught my glance, he turned to say something to John. I hated that we had something between us. He and John went to the pool table, and the other guys followed.

They began to joke with each other as Ty handed out pool cues.

"He likes you, I can tell." Savannah patted my arm. "You just need to give him time to see that he's wrong about you. He is wrong about you, I know. I've seen you with that child, and it's obvious you care a lot for him. So has Abigail, and she always gets a good read on people."

"She's sweet. Thanks for that. I'd do anything for the little guy. I felt it was the only thing I could do to get him out." I noticed that the other girls were listening.

"Listen, Nicole," Ty's wife Ivy smiled from across the table. "These guys are hardwired not to trust. You can't blame them." I hadn't missed the fact that she glanced at Catalina, who played with her string of small pink pearls. "When Ty and I met, he was dealing with the death of one of his teammates. He'd been killed by a fellow soldier. He shut down on me, and it was very hard on our relationship, but I knew I liked him enough to weather the storm, and I'm glad I did." She smiled and glanced over toward the guys' table.

"Have you even met Cole?" Savannah snorted and leaned in. "He was so used to having things go his way, the man trusted no one." She raised her brows. "Well, maybe a select few." She shrugged. "Until *I* came along." She gave me a wicked grin. "We might love their alpha-asses, but we sure as shit don't back down when we need to. If you feel you have to stand your ground with this whole media thing, Nicole, we have your back." She raised her glass to mine, and the other girls all chimed in their support.

"Thanks, you guys." My heart swelled.

Savannah held up a finger. "That being said, you can stand your ground, yes, but know where he's coming from too. Like Ivy said, they're wired differently than most, so don't walk away from something that could be just because he isn't open to it. He's a great guy, but his shell has hardened over time. He just needs a little love in his life before he'll soften up." She arched a brow at me.

I looked around the table at these strong, gorgeous women who had let me inside their circle and decided to share. "Okay, truth?"

"Please." Sloane nodded, and her serious eyes went to mine.

"I've only known the man for a short time, but we've shared some amazing moments." I felt my cheeks heat and pressed my thighs together when I remembered that kiss at the safehouse. "But maybe they only happened because of the danger we were in."

"Like the whole 'in the moment we could die' kind of thing?" Keith asked as he sat in a chair across from me.

"Oh!" I felt my whole body seize up. Apparently, he'd been listening. I quickly glanced around, but the girls didn't even flinch with Keith's sudden arrival, so I allowed myself to relax. *Okay I guess this is how it is here.*

"Exactly." I smiled at him. "So, how do you really know if that person is for real or only reacting to the situation? Is he worth fighting for? Can I even trust him? Because he doesn't seem to trust me." I took a deep breath.

"Okay," Keith stopped Mia from speaking, "sorry, Mia, but I want to take this question."

"Go ahead." She grinned and leaned back in her seat.

He spun his beer through his fingers as he thought. "Nicole, I had a wife who was tough as nails. We met in high school, and I loved that girl. Then something tragic happened, and everything went to shit. Years later, I found her again and fought for her." He paused then waved a hand as if to dismiss something. "Let's just say after some time and skipping over a number of significant events," he made a wry face, "we found ourselves married with two kids.

"Trouble was, over the years, she began to resent me, and it became too much for her. All the signs were there, but I chose not to see them. Then she was killed because she did something stupid." My mouth sagged open, and my eyes went wide. "You want to know how I got her back? Her body back, I mean. How I got answers about her death and how I got closure to move on?" He pointed at Paul. "Because of that man."

"How?" fell from my lips.

"The how is a whole other story." He pursed his lips. "Just know that despite his cold demeaner, he has one of the biggest and most selfless hearts I've ever met. I think it's fair to say he's done more for our operation, our family, than any of us."

"Agreed," Savannah added. "He's a saint." There were murmurs of agreement from the others.

"So," Keith leaned his elbows on the table, "I'm going to ask you this one time, and whatever your answer is, we'll believe you."

"Okay." I felt my chest tighten.

"Did you use the child for your own personal gain?"

I licked my dry mouth and looked at him straight in the eye. "Keith, I've never really been loved by anyone, so when I say this, know I mean it from the bottom of my heart. I swear on that little boy's life that I didn't use him for a story. I was in a bad situation, surrounded by a magnitude of Cartel, and it was the only way I could think of to get him out. Trust me, I lost a lot more than Paul's trust when I made that call. I had no choice."

He waited a beat and held my gaze intensely. "All right, I believe you."

"No," Ivy shook her head, and my stomach dropped, "we all believe you, Nicole."

I let out my breath and let my shoulders sag with relief. "Thank you." I rubbed my forehead and felt the tightness of a headache. "And for what it's worth,

Keith, I'm really sorry about your wife. I'd like to have met Lexi."

"Thank you. It's worth a lot."

I looked around the table and felt like for once in my life I might be among people I could have a deep friendship with. I glanced at Paul then caught Savannah's smile as she watched me. "You guys really want us to date, don't you?"

"You know what it is, Nicole?" Cat said, and I found her Hispanic accent comforting. She had been the quiet one of the group, and I found myself getting worried Mike had warned her to stay away from me. "The house needs a certain breed of soldier to handle what they do, and it takes a certain kind of woman to live with them." She looked at Keith. "Correct me if I'm wrong, but there's a reason you and Paul took a while to settle down with someone. You needed to see that fire inside."

Keith nodded. "You're right on the money. You know when it's there and when it's not."

"Right, and we women can spot it too. When Savannah and Mia met you, Nicole, they saw it."

"We did." Mia agreed.

"You have that fire that we all have and that they all want. We," she waved around the table, "push because we know it can work with you two. Of course, there's more to it than that, but it's worth giving it a try, though, right? I mean, life is too short not to take a chance."

I looked down at my drink and absorbed what

she said. I had put my life on hold and put myself second for the sake of my job. Maybe it was time to have a little fun and see where life would take me next. The only problem that stood in the way was I loved my profession. I lived for the challenge of digging up clues that helped me piece together a master puzzle. In the perfect world, I could do both, but sadly, that didn't often happen.

Suddenly, the music changed to *Austin* by Dasha, and the place went wild. Mia's face lit up as she grabbed Savannah's arm.

"Do you know the dance, Nicole?" Mia beamed at me. She positively vibrated out of her chair.

I wondered if I should fib, but she looked so excited. "If I say yes, are you going to pull me out there?"

"She does!" she shrieked, and before I could protest, I was dragged onto the dance floor and into the straight line that had quickly formed. It took a few minutes for everyone to find their rhythm in the dance, but we soon had it and fell into sync.

The lights flashed, and the beat pulsed through me as I kicked and swayed and stomped. The laughter from everyone was infectious. I tossed my hands up and tilted my head back, soaking in the normalcy that flooded my chest like a drug. Someone grabbed my arm and pulled me toward them.

"Look at you!" Mark grinned at me. He added an extra step to the dance and raised a brow in a challenge. I seriously loved this guy. He was just so damn fun. I apparently missed having fun.

"Oh, you think you can outdance me?" I added an extra step, and his smile grew wider. Then we were off, both showing off our skill. He tipped the cowboy hat he stole off Mia's head and grabbed my arm and sent me into a double hand twirl. I spun right into someone else's arms. When I stabilized myself, I looked up to see I was in the arms of a stranger.

"Howdy." He slapped his hand around my waist. "Let's see how you do with a real dancer." I glanced at the girls, and Savannah gave me a slight nod to let me know they had my back if needed. I could see Ivy's eyes on me as well.

It felt wonderful to know they were there. I'd seriously underestimated how much I needed people like them in my life. I'd pulled back from the happiness of having friends for so long that I almost forgot what it was like to have that kind of comfort. Someone who genuinely cared about my well-being.

"All right, stranger, let's see what you got." The song morphed into *She's Country* by Jason Aldean. I let him spin me around the floor, and we fell into step when the chorus came. I'd never tell a soul, but Ben and I used to hit up the local bars in Mexico, and that's where we learned these steps. Moments like this made me truly miss that country.

My dance partner slipped an arm around my mid-section when I had my back to him and pulled me closer.

I glanced around the room and saw Paul's pissed off stance. His arms were crossed, his jaw seemed to be locked in place, and his eyes shot to mine like the opposite side of a magnet.

I wanted to look away, but I couldn't seem to do it. That irritated me. I wasn't the type of woman who could be swept off her feet. Over the course of my career, I'd worked with a few men who'd tried, but I'd never felt that spark, not until Paul.

The man's hand on my waist tightened as I missed a step, still lost in thought. I wondered what it was about Paul that made me feel the way I did. We were like Cheerios and milk in a bowl, nice at first, but if left too long, we'd go off.

"You still with me?" The guy turned me again.

"Yeah, sorry." I smiled at him then felt my eyes drawn right back to Paul. He leaned his head to the side and held up three fingers then started to do a— *countdown!* What the hell. When he got to zero, he started toward me.

"He your boyfriend?" My dance partner asked in my ear, and I shook my head no. "Brother?"

"No."

"Husband?"

"No." I kept dancing.

"Bodyguard?"

I rolled my eyes. "Something like that." The song switched to a slow melody. "What's your name?"

"McGray."

I tapped a finger against my chest. "Hanna."

"All right," I heard Paul's voice, "that's enough for tonight."

McGray lifted his chin and stepped toward Paul, but Paul simply leaned down and said something quietly to McGray and his face fell.

"Sorry, man, I didn't know." McGray held up his hands, shifted his gaze to mine, then stepped back and disappeared into the crowd.

What the hell just happened?

"Seriously?" I was livid. Who did he think he was, chasing off that nice man? I caught Cole's huge smile as he watched us. He tried to use his beer to hide his lips from me, but it was too late. He quickly turned away to say something to Keith, who nodded in agreement.

As I stood there beside Paul, various options went through my mind. I could get mad, I could throw a tantrum, but it just wasn't my style. No, I had a better idea. I held up a hand and put the other on his shoulder.

"All right, cowboy, you wanna chase off my fun, then you be my fun."

"I don't dance." He just stood there.

I beamed up at him as *Burning House* by Cam flowed through the speakers. "Somehow, I doubt that." He didn't move, and my fun took a dive. "Fine, never mind." I turned to leave, and he grabbed my arm, spun me around, and hauled me to him. I knew from Savannah that he was close to being healed, but I pulled back a little from his chest and slid my hand over his shoulder.

We began to sway to the music, as I tried to settle my pounding heart. I prayed he wasn't going to say something to ruin the moment. I tilted my head back a moment later when he hadn't said a word to sneak a peek at him. He was watching me. I looked away and swallowed hard to try to ease the stress in my throat. I opened my mouth to say something, but nothing came out. I couldn't think of what to say at that point anyway, and I sure as hell wasn't going to apologize for something I didn't do. It was there between us; I could feel it in his body. The tug and pull of secrets and sins, I thought as I danced with him. I guessed we were all guilty of something.

I found myself getting emotional and I had to blink away pesky tears. *Get a grip, Nicole. You barely know the guy. Why do you care so much?* I dropped my hand away. I needed space before he saw how much his accusation affected me.

His hand flexed on my lower back and drew me closer. His lips skimmed my temple as he breathed in deeply. "Nicole," he said just above a whisper, and his cool breath brushed across my ear, "we need to figure this out." The growl in his voice made my head go light. Maybe it was his strong arms around me, or maybe it was the command in his voice. Regardless, I felt it deeply, and my stomach coiled into a hungry knot.

"So you keep saying," I shot back with a hiss so he wouldn't know how much I hurt.

"You've got a quick tongue."

"And you think you know everything." I held his gaze.

He looked toward the stage, and I followed his gaze. John had gone up to speak to the DJ. He grinned over at Sloane as he mouthed something then walked over to pull her into his arms. The song changed to *Love the Lonely Out of You* by Brothers Osborne, and they moved along the dance floor together.

"If we were alone right now," Paul's voice broke my fairytale moment and made me look up at him, "I'd have you under me, pinned so you couldn't get away. I'd kiss you until you begged me to do more." I blinked at his words and rewound what he just said. A light sweat broke out on the back of my neck at the thought of his hands on me that way. "The pink in your cheeks tells me you'd like that." He wasn't smug, and he wasn't wrong either. I was definitely turned on by the idea.

I waited a beat. "Let's remember I'm not the one with the problem here," I reminded him. I took a breath as the spark that built between us was about to hit full blaze. "I wish you'd take my word on what happened."

I felt his chest rise and fall against mine. "I want to," he admitted.

"Why can't you?"

"It's complicated."

"Says every man." I sighed. "Look, Paul, we barely know one another. We were thrust together because of an extraordinary situation. Maybe what we had in Mexico was caused by an adrenaline rush and nothing more."

His forehead wrinkled. "I don't believe that."

"You don't believe much of what I say," I huffed. As the song ended, I stepped out of his hold. "I just thought maybe…" I stopped my words when I realized he wasn't having it. "Thank you for the dance." I turned and began to walk away, feeling raw and my heart bruised.

"Nicole," he called after me, but I rushed toward the hallway where the bathrooms were located. I just needed two minutes to myself, so I could re-center. It was a lesson I'd had to learn very early in my career in order to cope.

I was almost to the hallway when my phone buzzed in my pocket. I pulled it out as I made my way through the crowd.

Jack: I'm sorry, Nicole.

Huh? Another message popped up.

Jack: I'm sure you've seen it by now but just in case I thought you should know. I know you were working with him. Call me if you need a friend.

The attachment pushed through, and I quickly pressed play. Agustin's face came into view. "We are the family that will end this war." He said in English and held up a finger. "One down, eleven to go." The camera then swiped down to where Paul lay nearly unconscious on the ground. I could hear him moan. I stopped dead in my tracks and pressed myself to the wall.

Agustin's face came into view again then whoever held the camera panned it back down as a needle was pressed into Paul's arm then tossed aside. Agustin then lifted a knife and stabbed it into Paul's chest. I slapped a hand over my mouth and watched in horror as he yanked it out, and as plunged it into his chest a second time. A terrible sound came from Paul, then his body went limp. The camera zoomed back in on Agustin's face. "And hey," he waved at the camera, "media bitch," he licked his lips as the camera zoomed in, "we're coming for you too." He stuck out his sloppy tongue and ran the bloody knife across it, sending crimson drops everywhere. He laughed like a hyena as the screen went dark.

Rage hit hard, but it was quickly replaced by fear and then the realization that Paul was supposed to die that day. Everything hit at once, and I felt my cheeks and forehead start to tingle as my mouth went dry.

"Yikes," Ty suddenly appeared and put his hands on my shoulders, "you look like you might be sick."

"Ty." I couldn't get the words out, I was so traumatized. The image of Paul being stabbed was so horrible I shuddered.

"Paul!" Ty yelled over his shoulder as the shakes began to set in. Mark appeared next to him then stepped back as Paul rushed up to us. His hands replaced Ty's, and he bent down to look into my eyes.

"What's going on?" he asked, and I handed him my phone. I watched as he replayed the video, holding it so the others could see. "Where did you get this?" Paul's voice was all business.

"Jack," I swallowed hard, "my contact at the *Washington Post*. Oh, my God."

"We've seen it." Paul's tone was low and cold. "It was released that day."

I shook my head and tried to push the images away. I had been so out of it lately catching up on sleep, worrying about Chase, my career, that I didn't think to look at the news.

"You should be dead, Paul. That video is horrifying."

"Yeah, it was." He shrugged and leaned against the wall next to me. "You see the kind of people that are after you? It's not just Bruno, it's everyone. You're on their list now."

"I've always been on their list. I just keep myself useful, so they don't rush to take me out."

He chuckled darkly. "Christ, woman, you really have no regard for your safety, do you?"

"Never had a reason to care too much about it." I ran my hands through my hair and took a deep breath. "I'm glad you didn't die."

"Yeah, me too." He looked toward the table where Ty was filling them in. "You looked like you were having fun out there."

"I was," a smile pushed through, "until my bodyguard came and scared off McGray."

"McGray?" He rolled his eyes.

"What's wrong with that name?"

"Nothing."

"Sorry he's not like you with your one-word name like Drake or Madonna," I teased.

"I have a first name. I just don't choose to ever use it."

"Why?"

"Reasons."

"Okay," I figured he wasn't about to share the reason, so I switched the conversation back, "what was your reason for chasing off McGray?"

He stared down at me so hard I felt it in my knees. "Because he was touching the last place I touched you." He looked down at his hand between us then slid his fingers along my exposed skin and stopped where my jeans sat low on my hips. The coil in my stomach tightened so quickly I felt lightheaded.

His fingers hooked in the fabric and jerked me toward him. I used his arms to stabilize myself. He leaned forward, and his breath brushed over my sensitive neck.

"Does this mean you finally believe me?" I needed him to say it to address the elephant in the room.

He vibrated out a sexy growl as he kissed the side of my neck and lingered there like he was deciding on how to answer my question. His hot lips raised my body temperature to a dangerous level. "It means I don't like men touching you where I have."

He hadn't said he believed me, and my *fire,* as the girls called it, came raging back, and I welcomed it as I knew the other women would.

"Well, you know what, Paul? I remember all the places you've been and where you haven't. So, I'll remember that the next time I meet a man."

"What?" His mouth opened in surprise.

I stepped back and watched anger flicker across his handsome face. Call me crazy, but I loved that I affected him the way he did me. I turned away and headed toward the table where everyone was gathering their things.

"Cole says you guys need to ship out in the morning, so we'll head back." Savannah handed me my purse. "I hope you had fun."

"I really did. Thanks for this."

"Any time. We love coming here. It's one of the only places we get to let go and enjoy ourselves." She linked hands with Cole, and we started to walk toward the door.

McGray stopped me in my path, and Cole instantly stepped into security mode.

"Sorry, man," he looked at Cole, "I just wanted to give Hanna my number." I reached out and took his card.

"Thanks." I smiled politely, and he waved and left, but not before he shot a glance at Cole's predatory stance. *Yikes, that was damn intense.*

"Nicole, stay with Paul," Cole ordered, and Savannah gave me a nod.

"One thing you'll learn real quick," Ivy leaned in, "the guys are thick as thieves. They know Paul has feelings for you, so they'll scare off any man who comes your way. Trust me. And don't be fooled by that one," she pointed to Mark, "he's the worst. He gave me so much grief for taking a guy's number one time, and I was only being polite."

"That's all I was being." I shook my head but loved that she made me feel a little better about pissing off Cole.

Paul came up and placed a hand on my lower back and steered me toward the door. Just as we stepped outside, he plucked the card from my hand and tossed it in a trash can.

"Hey!"

"You said you were only being polite."

"Oh, my God." I laughed. What world did I step into with these guys?

I noticed the change in the way the vehicles were loaded. When we came, the girls had all traveled in one van and the guys were in the other. Now we seemed to be doing couples. I looked at Mia for clarity, but it was Paul who said something first.

"We like to keep our girls close on the way back home. Just in case we're being followed." He waved for me to get in, and I took the seat in the very back. Paul swung in beside me and rested a hand along the back of the seat. He was a big guy and needed as much room as he could get. Moments later, the engine started and we were off.

I could practically hear the wheels turning in Paul's brain as we headed back to Shadows. The mood was very different in the SUV from when we arrived earlier all carefree and excited. The girls had been so fun, and Mark was a riot as he drove us. Now I was in the very back with Paul, Cole and Savannah were in the middle seats, and John and Sloane sat in the front. No one said much except the occasional comment by one or another of the guys, but they spoke in French. I saw an occasional nod of agreement.

I glanced down at Paul's arm at the bandage that covered where Agustin had marked him. It made me burn with anger. Damn *savage.*

My phone buzzed in my purse, and I hurried to get it out. I wanted to see if it was Jack with more information on the video. My stomach sank when I read who the text was from.

Unknown: We need to talk. Call me ASAP.

I rolled my eyes. Who did he think he was? I wanted to fire back how in the hell he got this number, but I knew he had his ways.

Nicole: We have nothing left to talk about.

Unknown: I disagree.

Nicole: Your problem, not mine.

I saw the little bubbles pop up, then stop, then start again. I knew Glen; he was trying hard to curb his asshole-ness.

Unknown: Got something new on our target. Trust me, you want to hear this.

Shit. He knew he had me.

Nicole: Can't call now, I will when I can.

I tucked my phone away and turned into Paul who I realized was looking over my shoulder.

He leaned down and brushed his lips against my hair, and it sent my head into a tailspin. Lord, the man smelled so good, and his whole rock-solid body and delicious lips just about tipped me over the edge. I'd had a taste of how the man could kiss, and that alone did things to my body that I couldn't describe. "Who was that?"

"Someone I work with." I didn't lie. I just didn't offer any more.

"Does this person have a name?"

"They do." I looked out the window at the moonlight. The way it shone through the trees made me realize just how deep the forest around us was.

His big hand landed on my thigh and drew my attention back to him. I looked up at his eyes then without thinking they dropped to his lips. His fingers flexed and I knew he felt it too. It was pure lust, and I was more than ready to let it take over. The fact that he obviously felt it too made my heart pound and the spot where his hand sat on my leg heated to the point of pain.

"Answer me this." His warm breath blew over my face. "Is it a man or a woman?"

"Does it make a difference?"

"It does to me."

"Yeah?" I turned to see him better and raised my chin as my feisty side kicked in. "Why?"

He reached up and gently pushed back a piece of my hair then ran his fingers along my collarbone. I shivered.

Cole whispered something, and Paul's hand dropped away. He closed his eyes and answered Cole back so fast I couldn't tell if he said it in English or

French. He did, however, leave his hand on my thigh.

Once we got back to the house, everyone went in their separate directions. I hurried to go check on Chase, and when I got to his room, Abigail was slowly closing the door.

"Hello, dear." She smiled warmly at me and put a finger to her lips. "The little one finally fell back to sleep."

"Oh, that's good." I smiled. "Did he eat anything?" I wanted to see him, but I knew how important sleep was.

"He did, but not much. Maybe tomorrow you can try before you leave."

I nodded. "Of course."

She gave me a gentle squeeze on the arm and left me alone. I glanced at his door then forced myself to turn toward my own.

I pulled out my phone and tapped on Glen's number. Just as he answered, the phone was snatched out of my hand.

"Nicole?" I heard Glen snap, and Paul's eyes narrowed in on me as he hung up my phone.

"What the hell are you doing?"

"Who is he?" he snarled.

"None of your business, that's who." I took my phone from him and pushed open the door to my room. I used my foot to try to slam it shut on him, but he grabbed it and stepped in behind me.

I whirled around, and my gaze flew to his face,

but he didn't say a word; his expression had changed from anger to something more like pain. His eyes shifted like he battled with something internal.

"Is this how it's going to be between us?" I blurted. "Because I don't know about you, Paul, but I'm basically maxed out. I told you the truth, I never used Chase for a story, so until you get past your own mental block and see the situation for what it is, I can't do this anymore." He took a step toward me and closed what little space there was between us. "I wish you'd trust me."

"I want to," he admitted and stared down at me like he was trying to figure something out. "I hate that we kissed before because it's consumed me in ways I can't describe."

I looked away briefly and carefully framed my reply because I knew what his problem was. "When was the last time you had sex?" There it was, point blank. No beating around the bush there.

"Don't insult me, Nicole." His brows pinched together. "A kiss can be even more intimate and impactful than sex." My gaze dropped to the floor, and I felt like a jerk. "I've dated one person in the last decade, and since we split, I haven't slept with anyone else. It's not who I am." His jaw flexed and his breath came out in a short huff.

"Sorry." I cleared my throat. "You just seem angry with me again."

"Mm," he mumbled from somewhere deep in his throat.

"So maybe it's best we cut our ties here before any more feelings get—"

He hooked an arm around my waist and pulled me to him.

"No." He ran his other hand through my hair, along my jawbone, then his thumb tugged at my bottom lip. He let it flick back into place then squinted as if lost in thought. "You remind me I'm not who I was." He moved so fast I barely registered what he had said. *Who he was?* The thought flickered at the back of my brain, but before I could get my mind around it, his lips found mine. His tongue broke the seal of my lips and dove inside, making my entire body tense then slowly relax into warm jelly. His hand on my back flexed as he drew me closer. His solid body felt like steel against mine. I ran my hands over his large shoulders and enjoyed the feel of his muscles as they flexed under my touch.

Paul had a way of demanding my body that even I couldn't control. He kissed like we were saying goodbye.

Hold on!

"Wait," I muttered into his mouth, but he didn't stop. I forced myself to rip away and pressed my fingers to his lips. "Does this mean you believe me about Chase and that I'd never use him?"

Something flashed across his face, and I wished I knew what it was. Then he squeezed his eyes shut for a moment and went still. When he opened them again, his eyes seemed darker – almost like he was channeling someone else.

"I've got a taste for you, and I can't take it anymore."

"You need to answer my question first." I turned my face away to the side when he leaned forward. I needed to know how he felt before I let my guard down again.

He started to drop kisses up my neck to my ear then stopped and took my chin in his hand and forced me to look at him. "Yes, I do believe you, Nicole, and I don't trust easily."

That was what I needed to hear, and I let a smile spread across my face as I looked up at him.

He opened and closed his mouth like he wanted to say more but didn't. I wanted to push, but something told me now wasn't the time. Besides, we had just made progress. I didn't want to run the risk of screwing that up.

"I'm happy to hear that." I kissed the side of his jaw like he did mine. I loved the way his light stubble scratched my lips. Paul was rugged and tough, very different than the men I used to date. I'd always refused to date a soldier in the past, but I'd have to question myself on that later, as Paul made me feel more alive than anyone ever had, and that included Justin.

His hands moved back into my hair and tugged gently at the roots. He leaned his forehead to mine, and his warm breath brushed across my heated cheeks.

"I hope you can handle the kind of man I am." It sounded like a warning.

"So does that mean we're dating?" I hated to sound like a teenager, but I needed to know where we stood. We'd had our fair share of ups and downs to this point.

His gaze dropped and took my stomach along with it. That strange look I'd seen earlier, the one that seemed like he wanted to say more, flickered across his face again. Confusion washed over me.

"Let's take this slow," he whispered. "I've been out of the dating pool for some time, and I have some things to work on before I can fully date someone. Let's say we're talking, just getting to know one another."

I appreciated his honesty and, as his words sank in, I had to agree. Our future was unknown, and if my past had taught me anything, it was that long distant relationships didn't work. I had no idea when I could return to Mexico, but that was where my life was. Where I needed to be. *Right?*

"Slow sounds good." I smiled and used his shoulders to help push myself up to give him a closed lip kiss, careful not to press into his chest. Though I didn't think he could feel much pain with the way he'd squeezed my body to his. He deepened the kiss again. It was raw, passionate, almost animalistic. My legs wobbled when a rush of endorphins burst through me like a firework shooting off in all directions. A strange noise found its way to me, and I felt him stiffen then he pulled back.

"Seriously?" I laughed like I was drunk as he read something off his phone.

"Shit, we have a meeting." His hands slowly lowered, and I noticed he was just as turned on as I was.

I stared up at him with disbelief. "Now?" I swiped my hair back out of my face.

"Yeah," he rubbed his eyes in frustration, "I've never wanted to disobey an order so badly in my life," he groaned.

"It's fine," I lied.

He smiled right up to the corners of his eyes, and I found myself mirroring him. Then he turned away and reached for the door. "Get packed, Nicole. We leave at sun-up."

"Yes, sir," I teased, and he looked back as he opened the door.

"Sir?" He raised a brow. "I like the way that sounds." His gaze dragged over me, then he swiped a hand over his face, muttered something, and left with a growl.

EIGHT

PAUL

My head had been in a fog after the meeting with the teams the night before. The Cartel grew steadily bolder with each passing day, and if we didn't step up our game, we'd soon lose our edge.

After some careful planning, we decided to release a statement to the media that I was alive. If we didn't control the narrative, fear would spread along the border towns, and that might be what they were banking on. Spreading fear was their specialty.

I may have gotten four hours of sleep, and that wouldn't normally faze me, but because I was still healing, it took a toll. I dug my thumbs into my eyes, and an image of Nicole's smile and soft lips suddenly came up behind my closed lids. She had been so soft and warm in my arms that it was nearly impossible to—

I shifted my head when I saw Keith come in from outside.

"Hey, man, you good?" I held up the coffee pot, and he gave me nod.

He took the mug I offered him and settled onto the island stool. "Depends on what you mean by good."

"Is it the kids?" They seemed to finally have accepted their mother's death, at least outwardly. It would be years, if ever, for them to completely heal. I knew behind closed doors it was probably a different story.

"No," he chuckled, "for once, it's not them." He rubbed his forehead. "Liza wants more," he blurted, and I felt my body sag with sadness. Keith, rightfully so, had put his kids first after Lexi's passing, then he finally met someone, but we all knew he wasn't ready. He and Lexi had been together since they were teens. Even when she pushed him away, he refused to accept it and fought for her. A relationship like that didn't just go away. A whole piece of who you were was stripped from you.

"What'd she say?"

"Just that she wanted *more*," he huffed. "She doesn't play mind games, I'll give her that. She just comes out and says what she's feeling." He paused. "God, that's refreshing, but terrifying at the same time."

"Agreed." I sipped my coffee. "What did you say?"

"That we should talk in person. She deserves to hear it face to face." He sighed heavily. "She wants to meet the kids." I frowned. I knew he wasn't ready for that, and I doubted the kids would be either. "I just got Brandon back on track. I mean, you've seen him training with us. Christ, he's a better soldier at his age than I was. Regan is finally participating in school and just joined the soccer team." He squeezed his eyes shut. "I can't risk rocking that boat. I've worked so hard with them."

"Then don't." I leaned toward him. "If Liza likes you as much as it seems, then she'll get it. But she has to remember you had a family way before she ever came into the picture. That your kids will always come first. You say she's a straight shooter, so be one back."

"Yeah," he sipped his coffee, "you're right."

I heard a tiny cough and turned to find Abby with Chase in her arms.

"Look who woke up in time to say goodbye." She brought him over to me, and I smiled at his little army tank jammies.

"Good morning, big guy." I rubbed his back as he coughed again. "How are you feeling?"

"His lungs are still congested, and he needs to eat more, but he's better each day." Abby handed him to me, and Chase looked up at me, wide-eyed. "Have you seen Nicole yet this morning?" She eyed me up.

I waited for Chase's bottom lip to stick out, but

he just stared at me, a bit unsure. That was okay; that was progress.

"I'll leave you to him." Keith ruffled Chase's hair. "Morning, bud. Hey, thanks for the ear." He made an apologetic face.

"Anytime." I smiled at him. Then I addressed Abby's question, as she had put her hands on her hips. "Not yet." I handed Chase a rubber giraffe that I took from the island. Savannah had gotten it for him. He jammed it in his mouth without a thought. "Are you hungry, buddy?" I took the mashed strawberries Abby handed me and sat at the table. I leaned over and plunked Chase in the kiddie seat that I knew had been Olivia's.

"I just wish I knew what he ate before he came to us," Abby huffed. "We'll just have to try different things. We'll start small and work our way up."

I nodded and held a spoonful of the strawberries to his lips, but he just turned his head away. I tried to remember the few babies I'd been around as Eric Noah. I'd missed most of the baby stages at the house.

"Come on, little guy," I moved the spoon around, "here comes the Blackhawk." I made a funny noise like propellers cutting the wind with my mouth, and to my absolute delight he smiled. "Oh, do you like that noise?" I made it again, and he made a little squeak, and I took the opportunity to gently slide the spoon into his mouth. His brows went up as he spat it back out. He let out a cry and rubbed his eyes and nose with both fists, smearing the berries all over his face. "Chase, you have to eat." I switched to Spanish to see if that would work. It didn't.

His gaze moved off me, and he bounced in his chair. I didn't have to turn to know Nicole was coming up behind me. "Mama!" He reached his arms out as she came to sit next to me.

"There's my big boy!" Nicole kissed his head. "Are you eating for Paul?"

He nearly wiggled out of his seat as he lunged toward her. She swooped him up, and he rubbed his head all over her face.

"Eww, someone is affectionate today." She laughed and grabbed a napkin to wipe his face then her own. Abby laughed as she put a plate of avocado toast, sliced bananas, and a hardboiled egg in front of Nicole. "Oh! Thank you, Abigail."

"Of course, dear."

Nicole looked at me as Chase settled on her lap. He really was attached to her. I understood it; she was something special. Just as his mother had been. *Talya.* I flinched at the pain even the thought of her name brought. I hated that Chase would never know who his mother was. With that came the thought that I prayed he'd never know his blood mingled with that of the Cartel. Although the logistics of that were beyond the scope of my imagination. It would be hard to shield him from it as he got older, and now there was a video circulating.

One day at a time.

"You okay? You look sad."

I slammed the lid closed on Talya and forced myself to be in the present. "Yeah, just lots on my mind."

She nodded as she bit into her toast. Chase seemed to find that interesting, and when she set the toast down on her plate to take a drink, he snagged it.

"Hey, you little thief." She laughed as he jammed it into his mouth with a giggle. She broke off a small piece and held it out to him as she pried the bigger piece from his tight little fist. She was a natural mother. Then she started to eat the slices of banana. She didn't use her fork, just picked up the slices and put them in her mouth. Just like before, he watched her then went in for a slice for himself.

"Hey." She pretended to be mad, and he laughed and shoved it in his mouth. I tried not to be grossed out as wet banana and toast showed through his open mouth. I leaned back and watched the two of them interact. He held up a half-eaten piece for her to try, and she leaned down and snagged it out of his fingers which he found to be the funniest thing. His head tilted back, and a full-blown belly laugh erupted from him. I had to turn away for a moment to keep my face from showing how much it affected me. I pulled out my phone, as I needed a distraction to let the emotion fizzle out.

"Gah! Gah!" He pulled my attention back to him, and I saw he was offering me a piece. I grinned, made the Blackhawk sound as I bent down, and did the same thing Nicole did. His laugh was so infectious that I joined in.

Daniel and Doc Roberts moved into the kitchen and watched from a distance. We played the game a few more times until he had eaten most of Nicole's breakfast himself.

"You've gained his trust." Doc Roberts grinned as he slowly approached us. "That's huge."

"He's always trusted Nicole." I nodded. "Today was a first for me."

"Children typically feel a bond with a female in the beginning, and given that this little guy was raised by his mother alone, it doesn't surprise me that he would gravitate toward you." He smiled at Nicole. "It also helps that you have a natural maternal instinct, and children at this age pick up on that. I'm pleased you're here for him and, well, for all of us."

"Thank you." She glanced at me.

"Keep playing with him, Paul." Doc inched his glasses up his nose. "It won't take long. He can already tell you're a good person too."

"How long do we have?" Nicole asked.

I glanced at my watch. "We leave in ten."

"No, I mean how long will Chase be here? I know I've asked that before, but to be honest, I'm letting him in, and I'm unsure if I should be. Saying goodbye is something I'm going to need to prepare for."

Doc Roberts eased into the chair across from me. "The child is still being hunted, so it will be a while. Best for him to stay at Shadows until we know the coast is clear and we have a plan for his safety." He glanced at me. "After that, we'll see. To be honest, there's enough love here for this little guy. Who knows," he smiled, "maybe there's a way for him to stay."

"Can you do that?" She shifted as Chase lay his head on her chest and reached for her hair. *His favorite spot.* "I mean, it would be awful for him to fall into the system. Lord knows, that's a total crap-shoot." She looked hopefully at Doc. "Do you actually think keeping him might be something you'd all do?"

"Yeah," I blurted without thinking. "He has no one, and Cartel life isn't something any kid would want to be born into." I'm sure Nicole thought it wasn't my choice to make, but in fact, it was. "There's plenty of space here and plenty of people who would give him love."

"I guess there is. I hope you all can make that happen. Wouldn't that be wonderful?" She rubbed his back tenderly as she thought. "You're a lucky little guy. I hope you know that," she whispered, and I could almost feel her own heart squeeze. I know mine did, for her.

"Hey," I leaned forward, "sorry, but we really need to go."

She wrapped her arms around Chase and hugged him tight, then took a deep breath. "I promise I won't be gone for long, okay, little guy?" When she looked over at me, I could see how much it hurt her to leave him behind. "What if—"

I cut her off from going dark. "He's safe here, and it's only for two days and one night." I acted like leaving wasn't bothering me, but inside, my chest hurt in a whole new way. "Come on."

I stood when she did and tickled Chase under his chin. "See ya soon, little fella." She took an extra minute to kiss him then handed him to me. I hesitated then kissed him on the top of his head before handing him to Daniel. He whisked him away, saying something to Chase about finding Cole's old flipbook.

As we walked toward the entryway, Nicole checked the time. "Can you give me a minute? I just need to speak to Ben before we leave. I know he's nervous they're going to pull him from his next assignment. I'll be quick."

"I'll meet you in the driveway."

"Copy that." She smiled then quickly made her way up the stairs. I couldn't help but watch her hips sway as she climbed the steps.

I grabbed my duffle bag from the bottom of the stairs and felt someone come up behind me.

"You know, she's good for you." Mark bit into an apple and chewed with a smirk. He always appeared out of nowhere. "Pretty too."

"Why is it the first time a woman shows interest in one of us you think it's a match made in heaven?"

"History has proven to me I have a special gift." He tapped his head then leaned against the banister. "Let's be honest. We need a certain kind of woman. Example," he twirled a finger at me, "those girls at the bar, you chased away without a thought, but Nicole," he made a face, "you can't take your eyes off her. It's obvious she can handle the shit we deal with. She's tough, and it shows. She's like our women, strong and fierce. They keep us in check." He smiled wide. "And we love them for it."

"You done?" I headed for the door, but of course he followed.

"Maybe take this trip to get to know her better. I've got a feeling she'll be around for a bit."

I turned to speak over my shoulder. "Just because two people are single and I might be attracted to her, it doesn't automatically make her the right one." I knew a lot more than Mark did, and I knew I had to be careful with her. She didn't know I was Eric Noah, and it was no secret she hated who that man was. It ate at me, but I couldn't see a way out.

"Why are you so hardheaded? I don't ever remember you being this way." Mark's voice pulled me back from my internal struggle.

"And I don't remember you being like one of the wives," I shot back, then softened my comment with a grin. Mark had always been a Savannah, even before she came into the picture. He was always stirring up trouble and poking his nose in places he shouldn't be. But we loved him for it, and his heart was always in the right place. No matter how frustrating he could be at times.

He made an exaggerated gasp. "You know you wouldn't want me any other way."

John opened the truck as I got closer, and I tossed my bag in the back. I turned to face Mark, as I knew he wasn't finished, and he pressed a finger against my lips. I batted it away in disgust.

"Fine, keep her at arm's length, but tell me one thing." He tilted his head.

Oh, my God. "What?"

He pointed at Nicole and Dr. Bash as they walked toward us. They laughed together at something. "She's most likely staying awhile, and you're not the only single guy here." He pointed his chin at them.

My stomach twisted, and I looked away. "You're an ass," I breathed.

"Don't know about you, John," he called, ignoring my comment, "but I haven't seen Dr. Bash laugh once since he's been here. Do you see what I'm seeing?"

John looked at them then caught my eye. "Man has a point." He grinned and hopped into the truck

Jesus.

"Oh, yeah," Mark put up a finger, "Frank told me to tell you before, guess I forgot. Dr. Bash is joining you guys in Washington." He turned and chucked his apple core in the woods. "Have a good trip." He waved and patted Nicole's arm as she came up to put her suitcase inside the truck. I grabbed the handle and slid it in next to mine, feeling all kinds of mixed emotions.

"I see you met Dr. Bash." I tried to curb my discomfort about him joining us.

"I did." She smiled right up to her eyes, making them light up. "He was just telling me a funny story about Chase trying peas for the first time."

Dr. Bash laughed. Who was this man? Normally, he was as quiet as a cat in the corner of the room, always watching from a safe distance. When the guy did make an attempt to approach, he was like a meek little rabbit, and that turned me off. I squinted one eye and wished I could read his mind. I also hated that Doc Roberts was talking of moving out of the house with Abigail. They wanted to be closer to Daniel and Sue in town. I knew they were way past retirement, but no one was happy about the idea of them leaving.

"Well, peas are gross, so I get his reaction." I sounded off, and she caught it. "Ready?" I opened the door for her, and she gave me a strange look before she got in. "Bash, why don't you take the front?"

"Oh, no, I'm more of a passenger." He opened the door across from Nicole. "I'll take the back."

I took a deep breath as I got in the front. I closed the door a bit harder than necessary, and John couldn't hide his smirk. I glared at him to get moving.

Once we got through the checkpoints and out onto the main road, John and I immediately started to look for anything out of place or different. It was engrained in us to scan everything around us. Our eyes never stopped as we monitored the terrain to make sure no one was around. John's eyes constantly checked the mirrors.

"He's got some meetings in Washington, and Frank thought it would be wise for him to travel with you," John said in French. We both knew Bash and Nicole only understood English and Spanish.

"I didn't ask." I switched to Dari just in case. Nicole was smart enough to quickly use a voice app to figure out what we were saying, and I wasn't taking any chances. I remembered the time Doc Roberts did it when trying to catch Keith after he skipped a session. We never forgot it.

John side-eyed me and went back to French, knowing what I was doing. "Maybe you didn't ask, but I can hear the wheels turning in your head."

"I just don't trust him yet."

He rubbed his head and let out a small sigh. "Me either," he confessed, and I glanced at him.

We spent the rest of the drive in silence and made it to the airport in good time. We boarded and sat in first class. Dr. Bash took the window, Nicole sat in the center, and I took the aisle. I hated the window. It was too constricting, and I couldn't do my job from there. Plus, I was big and needed the aisle to stretch out my legs. We took off, and once in the air, Bash put on earphones and closed his eyes and Nicole pulled out her laptop. I did the same and sorted through the emails from my team. Rush had made some improvements to the second drone we were creating, and I needed to go over them.

Nicole leaned into me. "Don't you like Dr. Bash?" She kept her voice low.

My brows pinched together. "Why do you ask?"

"You're cold toward him."

"How so?" Lord, she caught a lot.

"As someone who's been on the receiving end of your coldness, I recognize it." She gave me a knowing look. "He's quite nice, you know. Funny too. You might want to let him in a little."

"I will when and if I can." I didn't sugarcoat my answer. She studied my face for a moment then nodded slowly. "What?"

"Most soldiers hold people back at about an arm's length, but you keep them miles away."

"I have my reasons."

"What are your reasons with me?" She lifted a brow, and I felt my heart pick up speed.

"I let you in last night," I reminded her.

She nodded as she typed away. "And I'm waiting for the door to slam shut at any moment."

Flashes of me as Eric rushed to the surface, then Talya's beautiful face, and then Chase.

When I didn't answer, she sighed and went back to typing.

We didn't speak the rest of the flight. She worked, and I sat there and fought the battle inside.

Bash woke just as we landed and jumped right

back into conversation with Nicole. I couldn't get off the flight quickly enough.

We were greeted by a young soldier who was to drive us to our Washington headquarters. I didn't retain his name, as my head was elsewhere. Again, I took the front and scanned the hundreds of cars that flooded around us.

"We're about ten minutes out," I commented as I glanced at the time. Nicole's pen wildly rattled against her notepad as she looked out the window.

"You good?" Bash whispered, but she didn't seem to hear him. I turned in time to see him slip a hand over her wrist to quiet her fidgeting. "Nicole?"

Her head whipped around, and so much was written in her wild eyes. She looked at me then Bash, then down to his hand on her which he slowly moved away. "Yeah?"

"What's wrong?"

She blinked at him. "Wrong?"

"You're suddenly very tense."

She let out a short huff. "I'm fine, thanks." She went back to looking out the window, and I turned around in my seat.

I caught Bash in the side mirror studying her, and that horrible knot formed in my stomach. I hated the feeling of jealousy, especially when I had no right to be. I had it for years with Talya and Grim, even though I knew she didn't love him. She loved me. The fact that I had been keeping a secret about who I was then, and now I was doing it again, made my insides twist.

We parked and thanked the young driver. He would look after getting our belongings to the hotel.

"It's understandable to feel nervous, Nicole," Bash said gently as we were about to enter the building. "Anxiety can come out of nowhere. Remember you're a badass." He winked, she smiled, and I fought not to roll my eyes then felt like an asshole. I wasn't good verbally, so I showed my support physically. Again, another roadblock, thanks to my past.

"Thanks, Bash. Good luck with your meetings." He waved and smiled at us as we walked away.

"Paul?" Nicole pulled me from my frustration, and I looked up and saw she was waiting for me. "You coming?"

I nodded once, and we walked inside together. Once we stepped from the elevator and headed down the hall, Cole suddenly popped out of a doorway.

"Logan!" I coughed. "Logan." I was happy to see one of my bothers and felt instant relief. The stress of the situation and the fact that our Washington head-quarters had never been my favorite place had made me overreact at the sight of him. I saw him raise a brow. "I thought you were in New York," I covered in a normal tone.

"I was, but I had a hunch I'd be needed here more." His lips pressed into a firm line, and I knew he was just as uncomfortable with General Bruce as I was. "Let's see what shitstorm comes our way this time," he added quietly.

"Cole," Nicole stepped forward, "if I am being stripped of my position, does that mean I need to show—"

General Bruce stepped out of his office, and Nicole's words faded away. "Please, come in. Ms. Winter, it's nice to see you again."

"You too, sir," she said quickly then stepped up to do as he'd asked. "Let's get this over with."

I wanted to pull her aside and hear the rest of her question, but it wasn't the time. Cole and I exchanged a worried look as we followed them inside.

General Bruce kept his office freezing, which I welcomed because I always ran hot. I figured he did that to keep people from staying too long. *Smart tactic.*

"Please take a seat." Bruce stood at the head of the table and then to my utter discomfort and annoyance the door opened, and Dr. Bash suddenly appeared with an apologetic smile at Nicole. *What the hell?* He took a seat at the back. I glanced at Frank, who entered next. I shifted my gaze to Bash then back at him, but he just lowered his head and dropped the files he carried on the table. "Doc Roberts thought it would be best for Dr. Bash to join us," General Bruce offered as an explanation.

What was I missing here? I glanced at Dr. Bash, who kept his facial expression neutral.

"Nicole, I'm going to just jump right into this."

General Bruce pointed the remote at the TV and brought up a photo of Bruno. "First, I want to let the record show that your assistance in helping Blackstone retrieve the young boy has not gone unnoticed. I know what you sacrificed to do so." He cleared his throat. "I also know exactly what else it cost you." Nicole tilted her chin like she was about to brace for impact. "Normally, I wouldn't disclose such a secret—"

"Secret?" fell from my mouth.

"Yes, secret." I could tell he didn't like my interruption. "Ms. Winter, maybe it's best for you to introduce our guest?" The door opened, and before I saw who it was, I had my gaze trained on Nicole, who had paled to the point of looking translucent.

"I wish I could say it was nice to meet you all, but frankly, I'm pissed to even be here." The man dressed in jeans and a polo entered the room with his eyes shooting a death glare at Nicole. He waited for her to speak, and when she didn't, he rolled his eyes. "I'm Glen Digby, and I work for the DEA, and Ms. Winter," he pointed to Nicole, "is my CI."

"What?" Cole and I said at the same time. I did not see that coming. I whirled around to look at Frank. He was the one man who knew all our secrets, and I knew he'd take them to the grave no matter how much they cost us.

He raised his hands, and his face mirrored our shock. "I had no clue." I believed him.

"No one did." Nicole's voice cut the silence. "I

was approached years ago by the DEA and knew I had an opportunity to make a dent in the drug world. I was assigned to Agent Digby." She looked at me, and I immediately made the connection to the person who kept calling her. "I'd been working with him on the side." She addressed the room with confidence. I was impressed in spite of my instant annoyance that she'd told us nothing of this. "At that time, not even General Bruce knew. That came later."

"Later, as in the past forty-eight hours," General Bruce added rather bitterly.

Cole tapped his fingers on the table. "How long were you working as a CI?"

"I signed on my second year in Mexico."

"Jesus." Frank adjusted his glasses as he digested that.

"Was Digby the only agent you worked with?" Cole continued.

"Yes," Glen answered for her, and Nicole sent him a nasty glare. Something told me he was difficult to work with.

"He's a dick," Cole barked boldly to me in Dari from across the table. "I'm surprised she lasted that long with him. You ever worry about a man in her life, it sure as hell wouldn't be that one."

"English, please." Frank cleared his throat as everyone stared at us.

Cole looked at Glen. "I've heard of you, Agent Digby, and you've got a reputation for pushing limits and getting your way."

"He does and tried." Nicole's voice held a sharp tone as she looked at the belligerent man. "But my moral compass can't be broken. When Glen told me to ditch that poor child at the border so as not to compromise my position," she glanced quickly at me, "I couldn't believe it. And, of course, I ignored him."

"Amateur," Glen snapped at her. "A professional would have known better. We all have to make sacrifices if we ever want to win the war against the Cartels."

Nicole raised her hand. "I'd never sacrifice a child. I told you no and kept my word to you, Paul." She gave me a hard look. "Chase is just a baby. He never asked to be in that position. He can't help that he was born into a world with Cartel blood in his veins and a monster for a father." I felt the pain in my gut like a knife.

"And look where it got you." His voice dripped with contempt, and I could barely hold myself back. I wanted my hands around that bastard's throat. The guy had a death wish, and I hoped to make it come true.

"I know there was some question about you using the child for professional gain." Frank glanced at me, ignoring Glen. Nicole suddenly stood, and all eyes went to her. She made a show of pulling out her GoPro.

"Yes, there was," her tone was angry, "and as I said before, I would never do that but in case there are any lingering concerns, I can prove that my only motive was to get the child to safety." She removed the cord from the laptop at the center of the table and stuck it in the side of the device. A moment later, her footage popped up on the TV. We all watched in horror as my son's red face came into focus. He clung to Nicole's shirt, his mouth open as he screamed in fear.

My fingers dug into my thighs as we continued to watch her footage, and when Bruno put his hands on her and Chase, we could see she fought him with everything she had. The look of pure shock on Bruno's face when she shot him made my entire year. We all listened to her conversation with Glen telling her she should ditch the child and get back to work.

"The fuck," I growled and glared at Glen with pure hatred. He simply shook his head.

"Easy," Cole softly warned.

I tried to breathe as I tuned in to the conversation with her *Washington Post* friend, Jack. Then I heard her desperate public plea to find help to get Chase across the border. Nicole's face was filled with pure terror and desperation. As I watched the entire situation unfold, it made me see it was the only move she had left. Not once did she show his face on camera when she was on air with the viewers. She never divulged anything about him, not his sex or name.

"Holy shit," I whispered at how wrong I had been. Then I spotted Chili in the background in one shot. I appreciated that he had my back enough to risk being seen at all. I breathed a sigh of relief as if I was there in that moment when she weighed her options and decided to step into the back of his truck. I felt myself relax a little as Chili closed the door on them.

"That clears things up," Frank said, very matter of fact, as if the footage had no effect on him. It bothered me that Frank, in his older age, was becoming almost robotic. He seemed to care more about the job and less about the people. Had he always been that way?

"You guys got your mark, but I potentially lost my eyes and ears out there. A lot of work and time goes into these things. You must know that," Glen said. The guy had no idea how close he was to having his throat ripped out. The fact that he even had the balls to try to explain himself astounded me. Nicole looked at my expression then at Cole's, then turned to Glen.

"Glen, if you want to live to see another day, I'd suggest you shut the fuck up." His eyes bugged out at her words, but he did close his mouth.

I saw Cole shoot Frank a look. Then he turned to Nicole. "Smart of you to wear your camera." I could see the wheels turned in his head, and my own were at full speed. "Glen, where does this leave you? How do you see your and Nicole's working relationship from this point?"

I was stunned. What kind of a question was that?

"I thought for sure I was fired," Nicole held his gaze, "but then—"

"I think we can do damage control," Glen cut her

off, "get Nicole back in the field. There's a direction we can go where I think we can expose something within the next six months."

"What the hell?" My blood boiled; he was crazy! "There's no fixing this. Plus, Bruno knows she was working for us. If Nicole goes back, she'll be as good as dead."

"Given the level of intel, it outweighs the risks." *The bastard.* I jumped to my feet, unsure I could control my actions at that point. Cole stood and kept himself between us. Glen looked at Nicole. "She thinks there's a chance. You didn't say no. Did you?"

"What? How could you ever consider this?" She really was reckless and crazy and…

"Because Glen knows what I know." Nicole bit her lip as the tension in the room grew.

"All right, all right." General Bruce banged on the table then held up his hand. "We can play 'who knows what and who goes where' later. But I will not have a brawl in my office this morning. So, with all that's come out, Ms. Winter, it goes without saying that you've been compromised. You'll certainly not be returning to Mexico as a US war correspondent. What you do with the DEA is up to you."

"I understand, sir, but I think that might be a mistake." Nicole set her bag on the table. "I have some serious intel that—"

"Do you have more intel than what you gave me?" Glen dared to speak again.

"Glen," she sighed heavily, "I have more information than you can even imagine."

He stepped toward her then, and I made my move, but this time Frank grabbed my shoulder.

"Enough!" General Bruce's phone rang, and he ripped it from his pocket and murmured into it. "Shit," he growled. He shot Nicole an unimpressed look. "All right, everyone out but Ms. Winter and Agent Glen."

"Nicole." I stood and made a move toward her, but Frank stepped in my way.

"Paul," he held up a file, "we need to talk, now."

I watched as she tucked her GoPro camera away in her bag, avoiding eye contact with the rest of us. "Can it wait?"

"No, Paul, it can't."

NINE

BRUNO

"You have time to look over the menu, sugar?" The waitress stood there in her stained uniform with a finger pressed into a pancake she was about to serve and grinned down at me. Her voice had a thick southern accent.

"Coffee. Black."

"Sure thing, just let me drop this off and I'll grab that for you."

I pretended to glance at the menu as I sat in a booth well back from the entrance. My eyes were on the door, and I wondered when she'd show. She was supposed to meet her father here, like she always did the last Monday of every month. Sadly for her, he wouldn't be making an appearance. I knew he would be dealing with a flat tire and a dead engine.

"Your coffee, honey." The woman plopped

down the thick brew in an old white mug that looked to have been around since the early 1950s. "Cream?"

"No."

"Sugar?"

"No."

"Anything else?"

"No."

Her smile wavered. "Well, just holler if you need anything."

"I'd rather rip your apron string from around your neck and choke myself with it."

She blinked a few times, studied my face, then gave a weak smile. "You're funny." She slid some napkins next to my hand. "I'll check on ya in a bit."

Fuck.

As I reached for my phone, I heard the bell over the door then the click of her shoes as she walked toward the booths. Her steps slowed as she looked around the room, then she tossed her coat and purse in a booth and slid in next to them.

I watched her for a moment, then stood and made my way slowly toward her. She held her phone and tapped away on it, probably texting her father. I waited until she picked up the menu then slipped in next to her.

"Oh!" She jumped. "Ah, hi."

"Hello J. I'll give you a moment to make the connection as to who I am." I looked into her wide eyes and waited. "So, do you know who I am, J?" I repeated. She opened her mouth then shut it as she connected the dots. "Good. Now we need to speak."

"My father –"

"Your father has been detained." At her worried look, I held up a hand. "He's fine. Just a little car trouble. Let's keep it that way, shall we?"

She cleared her throat and sat a little straighter. Smart girl.

"All right. Let's go through a little history to set the scene. A few years ago, you had nothing, and your father's pathetic little business was sinking, I helped you get into the Army and arranged to have you stationed at Camp Green. Correct?"

"Yes."

"You were instructed to lay low and find out the details on the whereabouts of a certain American special team until instructed otherwise. Correct?"

"Yes. Blackstone."

I nodded, very pleased with her short answers. "I pulled the rip cord, so to speak, to activate my sleepers. You are one of those sleepers, J, and you know what you were to do. What was that, exactly?"

"Follow the first rule." I saw her throat constrict.

"Did you do that?"

She shifted and her hands shook as she took a tissue from her purse. "No."

"Why?"

I held up a hand to the waitress as she approached the table and waved her off. She wisely retreated. I waited for "J" to speak.

"I-I don't know. I guess I panicked."

I shook my head slowly to show I was highly disappointed but didn't get angry. I needed her to stay focused, as she had what I needed. Information. "Why did you panic?"

Tears filled her eyes, and I knew she was scared. Good. She should be. I could end her life right here in this disgusting vinyl booth before she could even whisper.

"B-because they-they," she stumbled and broke eye contact with me. I knew she was about to lie. "I haven't had the time to get what you need."

I gave her a long, hard, solid minute stare before I tugged back my jacket to allow my gun to show against my dress shirt. "Try again." I held up a finger. "Remember who I am and how easy it was for me to find you and your father. My people are everywhere, J."

Her mouth dropped open, but she quickly recovered. "All right." She nodded, and a tear ran down her cheek, and she dashed it away. "I had to lay low. One of the girls I work with sticks to me all the time. I have a hard time avoiding her, and she almost caught me when I was digging through the files after hours. She keeps wanting me to join her and the others after we get off. Camp Green employees like to socialize." She made a helpless motion with her hands. "She wants to be friends."

"And what did you find in those files?" I ignored her excuses.

Her eyes briefly met mine. "That's the problem, I found nothing to lead to where that Blackstone safehouse is. Honestly, no one will talk about it. I can't even get a general idea as to the location. It's some weird kind of pact or something. Or else everyone there has undergone some kind of brainwashing where they'd take it to the grave no matter what." She rubbed her forehead. "If I even bring it up, people clam up. I did figure out one guy is a doctor and supposedly works with them. I tried to follow him once, but I lost him."

"Which one? The name."

"Ah, Dr. Bash."

"And did you ask about him?"

"Yeah, but as I said, people on the base just don't talk about Blackstone. I get nothing." She pressed her lips together. "But I do have this." She reached in her pocket and dropped a little white box into my hand. I examined it with a tilt of my head. "That's a starting point, at least." Her voice was hopeful.

"This," I held it up, "just saved your life, but I'll need a lot more." I gently tucked it in my breast pocket and took a deep, controlled breath. "I'll leave you with these words, J. I am bringing a war your way, and when we invade, you're either with us, or with them." I leaned in and lowered my voice. "And I have no plans on losing."

PRESS

TEN

"Nicole." Cole was on my heels as I pushed through the sea of military men making their way down to the mess hall. My head was reeling as I wondered if I'd made the right choice. I'd never withheld anything from my bosses before, but General Bruce didn't want to hear what I had to offer. Every time I tried to speak, he'd cut me off and tell me how hard it was going to be to find a replacement. I explained that if he teamed up the person with Ben Bale, they'd be fine, but again, he didn't seem to want to hear me.

Then there was Glen, who was right there at every breath trying to get any information he could. I thought General Bruce was going to toss him out of his office, and I hoped he would, but he didn't.

I had no idea where Paul and Frank had gone, so

once General Bruce dismissed me, I rushed off and made my way to the elevator.

"Nicole!"

I needed to get out of the building. With both hands, I pushed through the big doors and took a deep breath of city air. *Eww*. But any air was better than what was back in that room.

Ten years I'd given myself to the job, and for what? To not even be able to plead my case?

I saw a black SUV and recognized the young soldier who had brought us here. He leaned against the vehicle, then when he spotted me, he quickly stood and moved to the passenger door. He opened it, and I slid in without missing a beat. As he went to close the door a hand reached out to block it. I looked up into a set of steely eyes.

"You may not realize it, but my wife is just as fast as you when she's pissed." Cole leaned down and huffed out a breath. "Nicole, we should talk, but not here. I can see you have a lot more to say."

"Honestly, Cole, I just need to get out of here. I want a shower, a stiff drink, and something hard to hit." I looked down at my knees. I felt wrung out and frustrated but somewhat impressed that he could see I was pissed.

"Understandable, and I respect what you're saying. Okay, how about this. Shower, eat, sleep, but tomorrow meet me in the hotel lobby at zero-eight-hundred."

I closed my eyes and remembered who I was

speaking to. Not just a senior military officer but a friend too. I looked him in the eyes again and nodded. "Of course. I'll be there."

"Thank you." He closed the door and tapped the window. I stared out the window with my mind in turmoil until we reached the hotel.

After a shower and a change of clothes, I felt a lot better, but my anger still seethed just below the surface. I decided a trip down to the lobby bar might be a good idea. Maybe a stiff drink would be just what I needed.

I looked critically at my reflection in the mirror behind the bar. I wasn't a soft featured woman. My nose was a little narrow and my face a bit angular, and I was okay with that. I wasn't the tallest or the physically strongest of women out there, but I had passion for my work. I wanted to be taken seriously; I was no pushover. My job should be proof of that. I had never been a girly girl, though I had moments where I enjoyed being one, but I had strong opinions and needed to be heard. I just had to figure out what I needed to do.

The bar was empty, and I eyed a stool off to the side where I could be alone to think in case the place got busy. I eased onto the cool leather seat and briefly contemplated if sleep might not be a better option. *Nope.*

"What can I get you?" The bartender smiled at me, then her face twisted as she read my mood. "You look like you could use something strong."

"You got it." I grinned. "I don't care what it is, just make it a double."

Her eyes shifted up to the left as she thought. "Do you like single malts?"

"I'll take it."

"I like you." She matched my grin. "Be right back."

I rubbed my tired head then closed my eyes and took a moment to center myself. I lost my job—well, jobs. I was jobless. I could resell my soul to Glen and take his mental abuse for a few more years, but what would that say about me? He'd wanted me to hand Chase over to those monsters! I knew how important it was to discover where the drugs were headed and from where in the States, but there would always be another CI to fill the role I'd had and probably do a better job. I was sure Glen could find some other person's soul to take and leave mine alone.

"Cheers." The bartender slid the triple drink my way.

I took a sip and loved how strong it was. "Perfect. Thanks."

"Happy to be of service."

The glass was half empty by the time I noticed I wasn't alone in the bar anymore. My mind was so busy rehashing the last few hours that I hadn't heard anyone come in. A group of women who looked to be airline attendants took up a large table and seemed to be laughing about something entertaining. I loved people watching, especially if it was people having a good time. I shifted my gaze to movement in a booth and spotted Paul as he nursed a beer. He appeared to be deep in thought. He had his elbows on the table and his chin in his hands.

I slipped off the stool, picked up my drink, and made way over to him.

"Hey," I kept my voice low so as to not startle him, "care for some company?" He kept his gaze locked on the table in front of him. "Everything okay?" I touched his shoulder, and he jumped and grabbed my arm, about to twist it. "Oh!" I yelped, and he let go.

"Shit, Nicole," he gasped, "I'm sorry."

"It's okay." I rubbed the tender spot. "I should know better than to sneak up on a soldier." He nodded and rubbed the back of his head; clearly something weighed on him. With Paul, I knew I couldn't push, or he'd shoot his walls up. That wouldn't do either of us any good. "Well, I guess you need some space, so I'll head up to my room. See you in the morning." He didn't respond, so I walked to the elevator. I sipped my drink as I watched the floors slip by and wondered what had happened with him after he and Frank were kicked out of the meeting.

Once in my room, I reached for the remote on the TV and switched to a music channel. I needed something in the background, or I'd go crazy from the silence.

I flopped on the bed and let my body sink into the mattress. The ceiling fan spun above me, and soon my vision blurred and my eyes grew heavy. I jerked awake at an urgent knock on the door, and I scrambled to open it without a thought.

Paul stood there. He looked at me with so much pain in his expression it took my breath away.

"Hi." His shoulders were tense, the muscles in his arms twitched, and his fists pumped at his sides. It felt like he was screaming at me in silence. You could practically see the war in his eyes. Music flowed around us as we stood there. "You want to talk about it?" He shook his head slowly. "Okay," I said softly and tried to gauge how I could help. "Want to come in?" He seemed to think about it, then he took a step toward me.

His hands snagged my face as he leaned close and drew in a deep breath through his nose. It was as though he wanted to inhale my scent. His eyes flickered to the TV when *The Moment of Truth* by Red Clay Strays started to fill the room.

"Paul?"

"I hate him," he whispered, but before I could ask who, he kissed me so hard I stumbled backward. One of his arms snaked behind my back and pulled me to him, then he pressed me against the wall. I could tell he needed a release, and I wanted to be that for him. He slowed the kiss, and I was sure he was being careful not to force himself on me. I respected him for that, but I wanted it too, so I reached down and caught the hem of my shirt and pulled it up over my head. His pupils dilated as he reached out and slid his thumb along the ridge of my collarbone. Suddenly, he yanked his t-shirt up over his head and tossed it to the side. I sucked in a breath when I saw the two puncture wounds on his chest.

I forced myself not to focus on that as the heat built inside me. I reached for the button on my jeans, but he stopped my hand and placed it in the center of his stomach. He leaned one hand on the wall above my head and used the other to stroke down my side. I roamed his stomach with my fingers and enjoyed the feeling of his steel-like body. It seemed to relax him as I took the liberty to explore every curve of his muscled torso. My fingers traveled over the scars, discolorations, and dips in his muscles from years of abuse. I knew it was a hazard of his job, and each one carried its own story, ones that were kept deep within that haunted brain of his.

His head dipped, and he panted in my ear like he was losing his self-control. I tilted my head to the side, and my eyes closed as his lips found the side of my neck, dropping hungry kisses as he went. His hand flexed low on my bare hip, and I slid my hand down and did a swipe of his erection. He was like stone, ready for me.

I knew from Savannah that it been a while since Paul had been with someone, and it was the same for me. I think we both fought to play it carefully and stay respectful with one another because of the situation we were in. Deep down, we both knew we'd end up here; it was inevitable.

He let out a painful groan when I pushed my hips into his. My body hummed with need. Within seconds, he had my jeans and panties at my ankles for me to step out of, and then he kicked off his own. I unhooked my bra and dropped it, and before it hit the floor, his hands were all over me. He hooked my leg over his hip and pressed his erection at my slick opening.

My head spun with all kinds of madness. It was the perfect kind of chaos I needed. It settled all the crap inside and heightened everything else.

"Please don't hate me," he whispered as he lifted me into the air and slid inside me at the same time.

"Don't hate you?" I railed off, and all I could think of was *oh, my God, he's so large*. I gasped as he filled me then wrapped my legs around him and held on for dear life as he slowed and pushed in further. Everything went silent in my head as we locked eyes and he stilled for a split second, then he kept going. My skin heated as my body worked hard to adjust to the delicious intrusion. My heart pounded so hard I imagined he could feel it against his chest. "Too much?"

I broke out in a delirious smile and shook my head. "No, not too much," I gasped.

"Good." He pulled out slightly and slid back in, and my head dropped back to the wall with a happy laugh. He pumped slow and deep, and with each thrust I felt as though he was feeding me a drug. Everything felt amazing, and for the first time in forever, I let my guard slip away. I was truly living in the moment. It had been years since I let myself come first.

I leaned back to look at him, and he smiled, then he hooked my lips and deepened a hard, passionate kiss. Our bodies were slick as he rubbed against me. He never slowed or showed any signs of getting tired, then he suddenly swung me around and laid me on the bed. We never lost our connection, and he picked right back up again devouring my mouth and grinding his hips into mine. I was out of my mind with lust and needed more. With all my strength, I pushed his shoulder so he'd roll over, but instead he hooked my arms and lifted me so I sat on his lap and started to thrust from the bottom.

The new angle sparked a whole different feeling, and I screamed in pure pleasure. "Oh, my God, Paul," I cried as my body built into a tight coil. My nails clawed at his back.

"Say that again," he ordered, but I was nowhere near listening, so he grabbed my chin. "Say that again." His look was so serious that my attention locked in on what he asked.

In a low moan I repeated the words. "Oh, my God, Paul."

His eyes creased as a smile crossed his lips, and I wished I could have read his mind, but in that same moment he leaned in and nipped my neck and it sent me off into a rainbow of colors as one hell of an orgasm took me over. I screamed, bucked, and shook my way through it. I didn't care if the people in the rooms next to us thought I was dying and called the police because in that moment I shed a part of myself and let this man inside my own walls.

I vaguely remembered as Paul tucked me into his side and pulled the blanket over us. What I did remember was his arms stayed tight around me and the kiss he slowly dropped on the top of my head seemed sad somehow. I didn't dare ruin the moment by asking him what was wrong. He needed this, and apparently, I did too. Instead, I relished the feel of my tingling body as I fell into one of the best sleeps of my life.

***

My eyes fluttered open to the sun that shone down between the two buildings next door. Instantly, the night before rushed back to me, and I turned to look at Paul. Only the bed was empty. There was a note written on a napkin propped on the nightstand. It told me to look at my phone.

I quickly read the text message that had come in two hours before.

> Paul: Sorry to leave but Cole called a meeting. Chili arrived this morning. When you're up, let me know. We need to talk.

My stomach dropped for a second; did he regret our night together? Happiness immediately replaced the feeling when I read the message right after it.

Paul: I realized how that sounded. I meant the four of us need to talk.

I sent a message back.

Nicole: I'm up, give me twenty.

Paul: Second floor, conference room 3B

I wasted no time and was showered, packed, and out the door under the twenty-minute mark. I found the conference room and was pleased to be greeted by Paul outside the door with a cup of coffee and a pastry.

"Hey," I stopped myself from leaning in for a kiss, even though my libido didn't take the cue, "thank you." I parked my suitcase next to the door and happily took what he handed me.

"I feel like an ass for leaving, but it was an order."

"I understand. Are you feeling better?"

He broke eye contact with me as he cleared his throat. "Listen, you don't have to agree to what Cole is going to offer you. For the record, I'm not on board, but I'm being overruled here, so…" He shook his head.

"Um, all right." Now, that piqued my interest. "Can I go in now?"

He hesitated then nodded.

Cole and Chili smiled at me as I entered the room, and Cole pointed to a chair across the table from him. "Good morning, Nicole. How did you sleep?"

I didn't risk a glance at Paul. From what I knew about Cole, he'd immediately figure out what we were up to last night. "Fine, thank you."

"Good. I'm going to jump right into this." I gave a nod. "First, I want to know, if you had video evidence that could have cleared you from what you were being accused of with Chase, why didn't you just show it to us right off?"

I spun the coffee cup around between my fingers. "Your word, your reputation, and your trust, mean everything to you, correct?"

"Yes."

"It does for me too. I told you I would never use a child for a story. I needed you to take my word on that. It took time, but I think you eventually believed me." I waited for him to answer my suspicions.

"Correct."

"I need you, all of you," I looked around at them, "to trust that when I speak, I speak the truth. That's important in my world as much as it is in yours. I had every intention of showing you the video, just like how I had every intention of giving you Bruno's phone when we got to a safe place." I gave a light shrug.

"I respect the hell out of that." Cole glanced at Paul, who kept his gaze on me.

Paul clicked his pen. "I have a question."

"Sure," I addressed him.

He leaned back in his seat. "Mike said you were doing a story on his wife Cat, but then you said that the story was pulled because *he* got what he needed. Was that DEA Agent Glen?"

"Yes." It was strange for me to speak freely about someone I'd kept secret for years, but now I was legally allowed to. "He thought Catalina still had ties to her father's drug business and wanted any information I could find on her. It only took me a couple of days of digging to realize that she wanted nothing to do with him or the family money. As soon as I gave him that information, the DEA moved on to one of the cousins."

"Right, but you said story, not drug information. So, you were working a story angle on her as well?"

"That's correct. It was basically turned into a double assignment. The *Washington Post* got word I was digging into Catalina and wanted to know if the rumors were real. That a Cartel daughter fell in love with a US soldier. It seemed a little too convenient." His brows pinched as if he didn't like that comment. "However, once I started to dig, I saw it for what it was. She was a woman who fell for someone she loved, nothing more. Then once I found out that the man she fell in love with was a Blackstone member, I shut it down quickly. I didn't want public attention put on Blackstone. Besides, Catalina deserved to be left alone. She had been through enough."

"We appreciate that, thank you." Cole shot Paul a look. "All right, now that we got that cleared up—"

"Actually," I stopped him, "I have a question."

"Of course." Cole waved for me to go on.

I twisted my chair to face Chili, who took a second to look up from behind his laptop. "Chili, you mentioned that you were good friends with Eric Noah."

I caught Cole give him a quick look, but Chili kept his eyes on me. *What was that? Did Cole not know that? No way, Cole knows everything.* "I am."

"'I am' would imply present tense, as in he's still alive." I raised a brow at him.

"I, ah, *was* friends with him," he reworded.

"What was that?" I kept my eyes glued to his. "You hesitated before you answered."

"It hasn't been that long since Eric was killed. Sometimes, I slip."

I chuckled softly. "You guys don't slip."

"Did you have another question, Nicole?" Chili's voice was cool. I could tell he wanted to slam the door closed on the topic. I had a pretty good idea that Eric Noah was alive, and for whatever reason, they didn't want it out there. I wondered if they were biding their time to take him out. As a reporter—well, ex-reporter—I understood the 'need to know' principle. On the other hand, I was curious.

I squinted at him. "I find it strange that someone like you would be friends with someone as evil as Eric Noah."

"Is that your question?" I could tell he wasn't happy with me grilling him.

"No." I changed directions slightly. "Were the girls I met in the truck taken through the Tunnel of Hell?"

"Yes."

"So that tunnel is still a working operation?"

"Yes, but you know how it works. They're returned to the US." He licked his lips, and I nodded. "Is there anything else?"

I decided to let him loose and backed off. "No, I think I got all I needed for now."

"Great." He forced a smile and went back to the safety of his computer.

Cole tapped his pen on the table. I knew he'd watched our conversation closely. Very closely. I wondered what was going on in his head. "All right, we don't have much time. I have something I want to ask."

"I'm listening."

"You said you had a lead on a big story, something to do with Bruno and his mother?"

"Yes."

"Would you be willing to share the details? Give us a nutshell version?"

I shifted in my seat while I thought about everything I'd put together over the years. "Yes, okay, I can do that. It's a lot, but I'll try to give you my best elevator pitch." I closed my eyes briefly.

"Whatever you can do." Cole smiled.

"About two years into my job, I met Sully Sanchez. I went about gaining his trust, and he eventually introduced me to Bruno Perez. A reporter's dream, to get a source like that, right?" I tried to smile and failed. "Trouble was, Bruno decided he wanted me for himself." I licked my lips and took a breath. "He's a scary man, but I played the game." I paused to take another breath. "He likes to show off and flex his power, but when I didn't react the way he wanted, he changed his tactics and let me see the ugly side of what he's capable of." I moved my hands to my lap and pressed them hard together. "Because I didn't run, he got comfortable with me being around and relaxed a bit, and that was when I started to see things most wouldn't."

"Like, what kind of things?" Paul's voice was tightly controlled, and I refused to glance at him.

"Like how he has American contacts. I got a glimpse over his shoulder once when he got a call, and I saw it was just a letter. When he answered, he stepped away so I couldn't hear, but when he finished his conversation, I distinctly heard him say 'stupid American.' One night he had too much to drink and left his phone on the counter. I tried to figure it out, but with only their initial, it was impossible to know who they were."

"Our numbers are programmed the same way in yours," Cole challenged.

"Right, but I could see the area codes, and one of numbers was in Washington and the other in North Carolina."

Cole's brows went up, and all three men turned to

stone. The tension in the room spread like the tentacles of a squid had slowly latched on to them and squeezed. "What else?"

"I heard Esmeralda on the phone with an American lawyer speaking about the soil being dry."

"Meaning?" Chili finally joined the conversation.

"Well, maybe nothing, but add that to the blueprints I found, and a real estate pamphlet I saw in her office another time, let's say it raised my suspicions to a whole other level."

Paul leaned over the table as things grew even more intense. "Do you have a copy of those blueprints?"

"No. Before I could snap a photo, she came in the room. I pretended I got lost in the house, but I don't think she believed me."

Is there any way you could give us a sketch of what you can remember about those blueprints?"

"I already did that." I reached into my bag and pulled out the laptop Mark had given me. I tapped on a folder and brought up a photo I took of my drawing from that night. I turned the computer around to face Cole. "This is everything I could remember."

"Jesus, Nicole, I'm impressed." Paul smiled at Cole. "Anything else?"

"I have a lot more I could share. It's just pieces of a much larger puzzle, but it's starting to take form. I know if I had another month or two, I could figure it out."

Cole nodded. "Nicole, I can't stress just how serious this could be. We don't have another month. How about a week?"

A week? I ran that around in my head. "I'd have to have an in. I can't work from the outside looking in. If it's seven days, I'll have to jump in headfirst." I looked around the table as excitement grew in my stomach. "I can do this. I'll just need some resources."

"We have endless resources." Cole glanced at Chili then at Paul. "Let's hear what else you have, but we'll have to move fast."

A slow smile stretched across my lips. "Copy that."

ELEVEN

PAUL

We spent the rest of the morning going over everything Nicole had. On the plane, we sifted through all her notes, photos, and possible leads. To say we were impressed would be an understatement. Nicole brought answers to questions we'd been trying to figure out for years. She had a timeline of specific events we'd been involved in and the aftermath of our extractions. Critical information came out that would help us improve our missions moving forward. It was like we got a sneak peek into their world looking at us instead of the other way around.

"Change of plans." I grabbed Nicole's suitcase when we landed in North Dakota.

Mike caught up and fell in step with me. "They're here. First class lounge back in the private room."

"Copy that."

Nicole fought to keep up as her legs were shorter than ours, and I wished I could slow down a little, but we had to hurry. "What's up? Where are we going?" She looked from me to Mike and back.

"We need to check in with some people, and time's not on our side." I spotted the sign for the first-class lounge. We stepped inside and handed our luggage to a man at the desk.

"Where did the others go?" Nicole gasped for air.

"We'll be fast." I addressed the guy and handed him a twenty.

"Of course, Mr. Paul."

Nicole looked confused, but I didn't have time to explain. We quickly moved through the room where men and women who were lucky enough to sip their drinks away from the madness of the airport enjoyed their time between flights. I made my way through to another room where only a select few could go. I waved a card at a rather round man, and he reached down to press a button without comment, and the door opened.

It was dark and cool inside, and the décor was elegant and low-lit. I looked around then turned to Nicole and put my hands on her shoulders.

"Hey," she looked up at me, "I want you to meet some people. They're friends of mine, okay?" I kept a hand on her shoulder but stepped to her side so she could see who I referred to.

I felt her tense under my hold and wished I'd taken a moment to give her a heads up, but there really hadn't been time. "Oh, fuck," she breathed.

"Just follow my lead." I didn't wait for her to answer and steered her in their direction.

"Ms. Winter." Grim Gates stood and loomed over her as he buttoned his suit jacket. I knew that jacket probably cost more than our chopper. "Nice to meet you again. I'm glad it's in a much calmer setting." His eyes seemed to glow under the lights.

"Mr. Gates, I hardly recognized you without blood dripping from your hands," she replied smoothly, and I squeezed her shoulder as a warning to be nice.

"Job hazard." He grinned.

I moved on. "Nicole, this is—"

"No introductions needed." She sat in the chair I pulled out for her. "Trigger, it's been a while." I glanced at Trigger; he never mentioned they'd met.

"It has." His voice carried its usual rasp. He tilted his head and cracked his neck as he studied her. "Nice to see you made it over the border alive."

"Only time will tell." She gave a wry smile then looked around while I tried to process the fact that she knew the two of them as well as she seemed to.

I cleared my throat. "I wasn't aware you knew each other."

"Job hazard." She shrugged a shoulder. "So,

gentlemen," she jumped back in, "where's the third horseman?" Fuck, she had balls sometimes.

"Mr. Capri isn't on this particular trip," Grim seemed amused rather than annoyed, "though I will send him your regards."

"Oh, yes, please do." I really couldn't tell if she was being sarcastic or serious but either way, she was impressing the hell out of me.

"All right," I knew we didn't have much time, "so, I'm going to jump right into this. Nicole, Grim and Trigger have offered their help on this mission." She physically flinched. "We're all in this for the same reason, Nicole," I explained as her face paled. "Grim will be visiting Bruno the same day you arrive. He'll get what you need past security and hand them off to you to plant later. If you have any problem, your code word is to ask him about his wife." I expected push-back, but instead, she looked at Grim and nodded.

"Understood." She raised a hand. "As long as it's us three and not the other."

Trigger's jaw ticked. "You have a problem with Elio Capri?"

"No," she shook her head, "but I do with that FBI agent Colin who tried to take Chase from me. I don't know who sent him, but I sure as hell wasn't giving a child to that slimy—"

"Paul?" Trigger interrupted her and looked at me straight on.

I closed my eyes and steadied myself. "Chili mentioned something about them being intercepted on their way back to us, but we got interrupted, and I told him to take it to Frank. Clearly not a good choice." I sucked in my cheeks. "If I'd known Colin would get involved, I'd have said something."

"Okay, so," Nicole looked around, "who is this guy? And who sent him to take Chase from me?"

I hesitated to reply. I'd always felt there was something off with Agent Colin, but I could never pinpoint it. He had helped us out more than once, but I didn't like that he always made it a point to mention how he liked people owing him favors. Trigger saved me answering as he turned to Grim.

"Maybe it's time to make our move." I saw them exchange a glance. "Nicole, do you remember exactly what Colin said to you?"

"I do, and better. I have the entire thing on camera."

I swung my gaze over to her. "That's news to me."

"And all *this* is news to me." She waved at us. "I'll hand it over if you fill me in. I'm getting a major vibe here. Maybe whatever you've got going on, I can help with. FBI or not, whoever he is, I want in."

Trigger eyed me as he rubbed his chin. I knew he was intrigued by Nicole being so gutsy. It made me nervous that she was willing to go down a dangerous path. I glanced over my shoulder at Mike, who shook his head.

"I don't know what Colin's up to, but we'll check it out." He didn't look happy.

"We'll pick this back up later." I knew things

needed to move along. "But no, Nicole, Agent Colin isn't a part of this."

"Good," she shot back.

"Good," I repeated and turned to Trigger and saw him nod at Mike. I knew they went way back. Then he looked at Nicole. His Mohawk covered part of his eye as he sucked back on a joint, and it went through my head that in a room like this, rules didn't apply. "Trigger will be in town with the rest of his biker club. They'll be trying to locate someone. He'll have one of his men stay down the hill from Bruno's place. There's a guest room that looks over the church—"

She cleared her throat. "I know it."

"Click the light three times if you're in trouble."

"Copy that," she looked at Trigger. "Who are you trying to locate?" I cringed when she asked such a direct question.

Trigger's colorful hand stroked his beard as he sat there, and I was surprised he answered. "Milo Garcia, the VP of the *Cazadores de Sangre* gang."

"I heard his cousin, Vincente, works at the Guerra del Diablo pub in La Gloria." Nicole pursed her lips. "I know Milo sometimes goes there. Wave some money and a hot chick in front of Vincente, and he'll roll over on Milo in a heartbeat. They've got bad blood between them."

"Appreciated."

Damn, she's good.

He raised his hand as if to say something else. It was very unlikely Trigger to speak more than he needed. "Impressive you're willing to go back into the lion's den," he stroked his beard, "but, fuck, you shot Bruno, betrayed the guy, and snatched the kid. That was his bargaining chip to take down the fuckin' Canos clan. You think he won't just shoot you in the face?"

"No, because he's in love with her." Grim stared dead-eyed with Nicole. "He's said it to you before, hasn't he?"

That is news to me. After our conversation in Washington, she assured us she could handle Bruno. She never once shared that the guy was in love with her.

"Yes, he has, but it's more like obsession." She didn't break his stare.

"And you plan on using that to your advantage?" He ignored her correction and raised his perfectly arched brow at her.

She nodded. "I do."

Grim flipped his Zippo lighter through his fingers like a drummer with a stick as he thought. "I was there that night, at Sully's, when Bruno flexed his power for you to see." Nicole visibly flinched. "There's no stopping him when he wants to prove a point."

"I can handle him."

Grim moved his gaze over to me. "I hope you know what she's getting into."

"He does." Nicole didn't miss a beat. "I've been on the receiving end of Bruno's wrath before, and I'm still here."

Trigger blew smoke toward the ceiling. "We'll do our part, but fuckin' stay close."

That was the plan. I nodded.

Grim checked his watch, and I knew we needed to leave. I stood and pulled Nicole to her feet.

"Paul," Grim stopped me as Mike took a moment to talk to Trigger, "you find out who killed Talya?"

Everything around me stopped, sweat broke under my collar, and my gaze flickered to Nicole who, thank God, didn't seem to notice my reaction.

"Not yet."

"When you do, let me know. I'm sure we could come up with a rather amusing payback."

"I'd enjoy that very much," I muttered and gave him a tight smile. Nicole shot me a look, and I knew she'd heard that. I silently repeated what I'd just said in my head. *Shit, that sounds personal.*

"See you soon." I hooked Nicole's waist, nodded at Mike, and we hurried off to grab our luggage. Back in the main airport, I set a fast pace.

"Hey," Nicole sounded pissed, "what the hell? I don't appreciate the blindside back there."

"You blindsided me too with that whole Agent Colin, Bruno in love thing. What happened at Sully's party, anyway?"

She ignored me. "You just tossed me in front of a mafia king and a ruthless MC pres!"

"You handled yourself just fine." My head still reeled with the mention of Talya's killer. I still didn't know who'd done it. Whoever it was, they would pay, and I looked forward to it.

"There's that look again." She pointed at my face.

"I don't have a look." I kept up the pace until I spotted Cole. He stood by an exit talking to Mark. He nodded at us as we joined them and signaled we had three minutes before the car arrived to take us to the helicopter pad.

I needed to do damage control.

"Hey," she'd stepped a few feet back to chug down a water, "sorry we didn't have much time to get that meeting in. Face-to-face time is important with those guys, especially when they're offering to help with a mission."

She tossed her bottle in the recycling bin. "How often does that happen?"

"Enough times that I trust them."

"How do you know them?"

I figured she'd let us in on this whole thing, so I needed give a little too. "I met Trigger through Mike. They go away back. Grim I met through—"

"Talya?" She stared at me. "It makes sense now."

"Huh?" I swallowed hard.

"What you said back there about you both wanting to get her killer. So, you and Talya knew each other?"

"Yeah, we did." That wasn't a lie.

"Sorry." The tension lifted from her shoulders. "I never realized. It must have been hard hearing that she died and had a child who needed saving."

I felt my phone vibrate and looked at Cole. He waved for us to leave. "We need to go."

She started to walk but looked back at me. "Thanks for getting me protection over there."

"Of course." I shrugged.

We made it to the chopper, and the sound of the muffled rotors through my earphones relaxed me. I let my head go back over the last few days. I'd almost drifted off myself, when my earphones crackled.

"She's impressive." Cole's voice found me.

"You should have seen her with Trigger." Mike laughed. "She handled herself like Tess would."

"She'd make a huge asset for the teams." Cole smiled. "Just something to think about."

I looked down at Nicole, who had fallen asleep with her head against my shoulder. For a moment, I thought about what it would be like to have a significant other in my life. I was always on the outside looking in at the other men and their lives. I shook that thought away, and instead my mind went to how every wife had a purpose at Shadows. Nicole's skills were impressive; she would certainly bring a lot to the table. I smiled in agreement at Cole but didn't comment.

One thing I loved most after we got back from a mission or a trip, was when my boots hit the ground on the Shadows property. I always took a moment to suck in a big lungful of air and let it out slowly. This place brought me so much peace. I did just that as I stepped out of the chopper behind the others. I needed it to get my head on straight. I smiled as I saw Nicole make a beeline for the house. I had no doubt she was headed directly to Chase. I grabbed my bags and followed Cole and Chili.

"Hey, look who I've got." Nicole brought Chase over and held him out to me and I scooped him up, feeling more confident.

"You look better today." I noticed his color was improving. He seemed to be more aware as well. His eyes were definitely brighter. "I see you got your bunny." Chase gnawed on its ear, and some drool dripped down his neck.

"He's still teething." She used her finger to swipe the spit like it didn't affect her in the slightest. "Bunny may not have an ear by the time all your teeth come in," she cooed at him.

"We'll just have to sew on a new one." I rubbed the bunny's damp fabric cheek. "Bunny is too important to replace." I felt Nicole watching me. "What?"

"You're good with him." She smiled. "You're a natural."

"I wouldn't say that," I ruffled the top of his head, "but this guy is starting to grow on me."

"Good, because he needs all the love he can get." She touched my arm, and suddenly my head switched to a memory of the time when Tayla and I saw each other in the bar and ended up having sex in the back room. That could have been when he was conceived. I still remembered how she felt, how she smelled, and the sadness that ran so deep inside me when we parted that day. I think we both knew, in some way, that we were saying goodbye forever.

Chase wiggled, and I blinked the memory away. Nicole stared at me. "Where do you go when you make that face?"

"What face?"

"The face you just chased away. You looked so sad."

I forced back the lump that threatened to form in my throat. Nicole didn't need to be a witness to my sorrow; she'd been through enough. Besides that, sorrow leads to questions. "There's just a lot going on right now."

"Yeah, there is." She let it go, but I could see her thinking about it. "Oh, by the way. June is taking me into Redstone tomorrow to get some things I need for this trip. I figured Chase could come along now that he's feeling better. It was Dr. Roberts' suggestion, actually. He wanted me to let you know I was going since you're the one who's been assigned to look after me when I leave the grounds."

"Shit, my day's slammed. My team's got a lot to do before we head off on our next mission as well." I ground my teeth and pushed away my nerves of both of them being out in public without me.

"Oh." She looked disappointed. "It would be so great to have you with us."

"Yeah, no, I get it." I looked around. "But you

can't go without someone to watch your back. Ask Cole who might be free. I'm sure Mark has a run to do."

"Okay." She cheered up as she seemed to like that answer. Her smile faded as she studied my face. "And, Paul, I'm always ready to listen, so let me know if you want to talk about what was going through your head the other night."

"Thanks," I answered too fast and handed her Chase. "It was just work shit." I spotted my teammate West heading downstairs with a UPS package. "Gotta go."

"Okay," she sighed and shook her head, and I turned to hurry off before she could say any more.

Then I stopped at the door. "How are you about leaving tomorrow night?"

"Excited, but nervous to some degree, which will work in my favor."

I knew we had very little choice, and this opportunity was one we had to take, but this mission was starting to scare the shit out of me the more I thought about it.

"I'll be fine, Paul, I'm good at what I do."

"I never doubted your abilities. Things are just different now." I squeezed her arm and knew we both thought the same thing.

"Good different, I hope." She gave me a sexy grin. "We gotta go find Cole." She bounced toward the door with Chase in her arms.

"*Very* good different," I muttered out loud. She laughed, and I knew she heard me.

I spent the day working with my team as we tested my newest drone. I couldn't leave anything to chance. Once I was finally satisfied, the sun was low in the sky. The next morning would be her first full test flight, and I was positive she was ready. I took a breath and let the guys clean up for dinner. I stood back and took a moment to study her. The technology of this one far surpassed my first, and the first one kicked ass. I couldn't resist just a few more minutes to tweak one of her propellers.

A half hour later, I headed for the house and got myself washed up. As I steered toward the dining room, I spotted Keith outside on the front porch. He was hunched over the railing, and I wondered why he hadn't joined the others for dinner. I saw Nicole in the hall chatting with Ty, and I gave her a quick wave as I stepped outside to talk to Keith.

"Hey," I tucked my hands in my pockets when the cold breeze hit me, "you good?"

"Yeah." He wore that distant stare he often got when his head was working overtime. "I decided to cut ties with Liza."

"Oh, shit, really?"

"I like her," he shrugged, "a lot, actually, but when I told her I wasn't ready for her to meet my kids, she got upset. Said, we weren't moving forward together, just standing still." He glanced at me. "She's not wrong. I offered to spend more time together, but she said I was missing the point. That it wasn't just about meeting the kids, it was just about me letting her in more."

"It hasn't been that long since Lexi died." I reminded him.

"It hasn't, but we were finished well before she died." He let out a deep breath. "I think I'd like a companion, but not a wife." He let out a laugh. "That sounds selfish, doesn't it?"

"No, man, it makes you sound like you've been through the wringer and just wanna try life a different way."

"Yeah."

"And look, this doesn't have to be the end with Liza. Maybe take some time, settle your head, and see what happens in a month. If you keep thinking about her, tell her that. If you don't miss her, then move on. But you ended it, so at least while you figure it out, you're not stringing her along."

I gave him a few moments to think then popped him one in the shoulder and laughed. "Hey, what could possibly go wrong? You're doing it the right way, regardless." I could see the stress fade as he laughed along with me.

"Thanks, man, I needed that."

"You got this. Things will work out the way they're supposed to. Just takes a few bumps before the road smooths out."

"Look, I don't want to be *that* guy," John made us

whirl around, "but these little bro talks that you two keep having is giving me a fucking complex."

I rolled my eyes as I walked by him. "You've been spending way too much time with Mark," I growled.

"First, fuck you, and second, whose fault is that?" He followed as I headed into the living room to find my son and eat something. "You know you're still in the doghouse."

I laughed. "You gonna wear a fedora next?"

"Words hurt, guys," Mark, who was fucking everywhere yelled.

John rounded in front of me and stuck a finger in my face. "Okay, tell me what went down in Washington."

"What?" I spotted Nicole and Chase in the kitchen. She smiled at me when we locked eyes. God, she was pretty. John put a hand on my arm and raised a brow at me.

"Soooo, anything else you want to share?"

"What? No."

"Uh-huh. Okay, we'll let that go for now. But hey," he smacked my shoulder, "Cole said Frank pulled you aside, and afterward you went all shut down. What happened?" The heavy weight I'd carried since my meeting with Frank doubled and my face fell. "All right, so it's something big."

"John." I couldn't find the right words to even say it. "I—"

Sloane, who could sense her husband's mood, was

suddenly by his side. "Why do you look like this? What's going on?"

"Paul?" Frank suddenly appeared. Fuck, when had he gotten here? "A word."

I wanted to tell my brother everything, but I couldn't.

PRESS

TWELVE

NICOLE

"What is in these things?" The women behind the counter with the push up bra and plastic boobs snarled as she awkwardly lifted one of the boxes onto the scale. "This is going to cost a lot, you know."

"I know." I gave June a sideways glance as she gently bounced a sleepy Chase in the stroller. He was making great progress but was still not a hundred percent. He got tired quickly and mostly wanted to be held by me. I had to work hard not to hold him as much. Ivy warned he was becoming too attached, and when I had to leave, it would be hard on him.

"This one will be ninety-five." The woman raised her drawn-on brow.

June moved to stand next to me. "She's under Cole's account, Christina."

Oh, boy. The woman's face went from pissy to full-on disgust. "Is that so?"

"Yes." June rolled her eyes then did a three-number countdown on her fingers where the woman couldn't see them.

"Let me guess. Since Keith has some bimbo from out of town, you must dating Paul."

I couldn't help but laugh. June was right on the money. She warned me the UPS office in Redstone held a few generations of crazy women, and this one did not disappoint.

"I'm a cousin of John's, actually." As much fun as it was to play, I didn't need any enemies. "My husband and three kids are down the street getting hot cocoa."

Her expression eased, and I could practically hear her claws retract.

"Oh, good." She tapped the computer screen a little kinder. "The total for the three boxes is $32.55." I handed her my credit card, thinking Blackstone had quite the discount. "You have friends in Mexico?"

"No, just preparing for my next adventure." I smiled and held up the receipt as I headed to open the door for June. "Thank you for your help." I knew I was low on supplies and had to make sure my contacts in Mexico would have what I'd need when I got there. I also made sure I sent my friend Mari her favorite perfume as a thank you.

I glanced at June once we were away from the door. "Wow!"

"Let me guess," Mark rolled his eyes as he stepped out of the running vehicle, "you met the famous manhunter Christina?"

"Oh, yes," June sighed, "she was eyeing up Nicole like her next meal."

"Better you than me." He bent and tickled Chase. "All right, ladies, where to next?"

"I think we could use some fresh lemonade and a walk in the park," June suggested.

I unclipped Chase and gave his diaper a quick check. "That sounds perfect."

"Lemonade and a walk it is." Mark flipped the stroller closed with one hand and placed it in the truck. *Talk about a pro.*

Mark shared many Christina stories and had us laughing so hard my sides hurt. Chase joined in a few times, which filled my heart to the brim. I hoped the energy we showed around Chase would help his mental health. I knew he was still young, but some of it had to rub off on him.

"Okay, ladies and gent," Mark added with a quick ruffle of Chase's hair once he got the stroller all set for us, "I'll park over there, and you two can do the circuit." He waved to Zack, who was talking to someone on the street near his restaurant. I followed his gaze.

"Zack's a really nice guy, isn't he?" I took the handle of the stroller.

"Salt of the earth." Mark shooed us off with a hand movement and went to park the truck.

I pushed the stroller and knew June wouldn't be able to walk very far, as she'd purposely left her cane in the car. She said she'd be damned if she was going to look like an old cripple. I had to laugh; she was one feisty lady. Mark was right when he told me it took a certain type of woman to handle their world, and feisty was differently a requirement.

"I just love this time of year." June breathed the cool Montana air with a happy smile on her face. She was old enough to be my grandmother, but in spite of her cane, she was quite spry. She leaned down and tucked the blanket around Chase. Her eyes held so much love and happiness that I found myself mimicking her expression. "Abby and I used to walk this park every fall. She said she loved to watch the trees as they changed color, but I was dedi-cated to the walk because the college football team practiced here." She grinned. "Everyone says Keith's nan is the dirty one, but my God, they had no idea what was going through my mind half the time." She winked.

I laughed. "Is that the trick to staying so young?"

"Yes, ma'am, that and the fact that someone invented tight clothes. I had quite a figure once." I choked on my lemonade and laughed harder. "Well, that and falling in love as many times as you need to."

I wondered what that really felt like and if it was different with each person. "Have you ever been truly in love, June? Like one man for the rest of your life kind of love?"

"No," I thought her smile would fall, but it didn't, "my heart belongs here with my sister. My first love lived in California. He couldn't imagine living away from the ocean, and I couldn't imagine living anywhere but here."

"And the other?"

"There were two more, and they both have my heart equally and are still very much in my life." She stopped to warm her face in the sun. "Marcus and Cole. Those boys won me over years ago, and the thought of being anywhere they weren't just didn't work for me. I tried," she chuckled, "but I always came back, and then I stayed. What's life without the people who fill your heart to the brim?"

I spotted Mark in the parking lot with a book in his hands, but I knew he was watching us.

I looked away and thought back on my own life. It was empty and lonely. I tried for years to convince myself I was making a difference, but lately I'd started to question that.

"You can always look back and do the shoulda-woulda-coulda game, but it's only the future you can change. Only you can make yourself happy." Chase dropped his bunny, and she slowly bent to pick it up. "Don't think you don't deserve love, Nicole, but love doesn't always mean a ma—"

Whack!

Tires screamed against the pavement, and I saw

June's body lift off the ground, flung up like debris in a storm, her body weightless for a heartbeat before it crashed back to earth. The bunny flopped at my feet, leaving me breathless.

I held the handle of the stroller in a death grip, frozen in panic as Chase screamed in fear at the loud sound. I desperately tried to focus on the car as it sped away but only got a glimpse of the back of it.

My vision started to glitch, like I was watching a movie, and everyone was running around me as I stood there stuck in place. People's mouths moved but I couldn't hear them, just the sounds of my own breathing and Chase's cries. Mark was suddenly there. I could hear his voice and see him bent over June, but I couldn't focus.

Then someone touched my arm, and I slow blinked to see Zack, the man I'd met only an hour before. His eyes were wide and glossy, and he was trying to get me away from what just happened.

June!

Like a light switch, everything turned back on, and I shook myself and saw that Chase was all right. He was just upset.

"Get her out of here!" Mark yelled, and I saw blood on his hands.

"Nicole, you need to come with me." Zack tried to pull my hands from the stroller, but I refused to let go.

I did follow his orders, and he rushed us down the street and into his restaurant where lots of people were on their feet staring out the window. Police and ambulance sirens were deafening as they rushed to the scene.

"In here." He directed me into his office and pushed me gently into a chair. I reached for Chase and pulled him from the stroller and held him close. His cries immediately stopped. "Look at me." I struggled to focus. "Nicole," his voice was firm and commanded my attention, "You told me about your job. You're trained for this, right? Just remember your training. Tell me what happened."

Right.

"June bent down to get Chase's bunny. He dropped it." My voice gave my terror away, "A car hit her and took off. It was an old gray Honda, looked to be maybe early 2000." I squeezed my eyes shut and tried to pull the memory forward. "Holy shit, was this because of me and all that's going on with Chase?" A whole new level of panic ripped through me.

"We have no idea of knowing that right now. So, for now, I have more pressing questions to ask. Who was driving?"

"I don't know. I didn't see anything, just the back of it."

"Okay, what else? Did you hear anything before?" I shook my head. "Was there anything on the car that you remember? Something that stood out?"

"No." I looked down. "Wait!" I remembered something. "There was a red sticker on the top of the bumper near the trunk. I think it was in the shape of a tiger or something."

"Zack?" I whispered and looked into his eyes as my legs shook.

"Yeah, sweetheart, she's gone."

I hugged Chase tighter as I lost it.

I barely remembered Paul picking us up and taking us home. Mike checked a few times, but the call went straight to his earpiece. I made out a few words here and there about how they were checking the traffic cameras, nearby businesses, and working with the police. I was sure they were frantically working any angle to get some kind of answer.

Mark stayed behind, as he didn't want to leave June. I did remember Savannah asked Paul how I was. I wasn't ready to talk, not then. The stairs and the long walk down the hallway to my room felt like it took forever. A hot shower did nothing to rid me of the shock and horror of it all, but I managed to get myself ready to go.

The house was silent and still. I wondered if the guys had found out anything. I decided not to ask. I was sure someone would fill me in. I could only imagine the chaos in the offices downstairs and wondered if I should offer to help. But again, I decided against it. I didn't want to get in the way.

I wished I'd had more opportunity to get to know June better, but I was happy to have known her enough to enjoy some time with her. She had so much love to give and so many people who were lucky enough to have had it. She might be gone, but her memory would always be here. My heart broke when I spotted Mark down the driveway later on, talking to Mia. The raw pain I'd seen on the faces of the family brought a huge lump to the throat, but Mark's face had been the worst of all. The heartbreak he felt in losing his beloved June was hard to see. She'd been like another mother to him since he was a boy. I'd heard the story from Savannah, and it made me feel the depth of his pain.

I felt terrible. To leave the very next day after such a tragedy occurred felt insensitive and cold. I wondered…Paul appeared in the doorway of the bedroom, and he stood there quietly as I stared at the floor. I knew he was there to take me to the chopper, but I just wasn't sure about any of it.

Like the rest of Blackstone, Paul held it together and was strong for everyone else. I wondered if when he was alone if he'd let it out, or if he just swallowed it down.

"Are you ready?" His voice was barely over a whisper.

"I don't know if I should go."

He crossed the room and joined me on the couch. He rested his elbows on his thighs and let out a heavy sigh. "I'm so sorry you had to go through that."

"It's not the first time I've seen something shocking, but, Paul, she was such a lovely person. I feel so terrible."

"I know. We all loved her." He rubbed his hands together as if they were cold. "It sure takes a toll."

I nodded in agreement as tears ran down my cheeks. "We had such a nice talk. She told me about how she and Abby walked the park years ago and why she loved it. She made me laugh."

"Yeah? Why?"

"She mostly went along because the football team practiced there." I ran the back of my hand over my cheeks. "She said Keith's nan might have had a dirty mind, but it had nothing on her." That made him chuckle. We sat there for a moment, letting the hurt seep back in. "You were all so lucky to have had her. She loved you all so much." He took my hand in his cold one as he tried to soothe me. "There's so much love here. June, Abby, Sue, all the wives. So much warmth."

"It's because it was built on a good foundation. Daniel's parents and grandparents were the same way, full of love. Generations of good people doing good things."

"I hope to break my family's pattern," I confessed then felt terrible for turning the moment on me. "I just think you're really lucky."

"Nicole, you—"

"Can I ask you something?" I cut him off, and he waited for me to go on. "When we were in Washington, you said you were against my going back. Was that because of what's going on between us, or because you don't agree it's worth going back in?"

He pressed his lips together as he thought. "It's a high-risk trip, and it involves a third party." He squeezed my hand to show he meant me. "We've never willingly planted a mole. Especially one like you, not that you aren't experienced." His voice was unemotional, as if he was explaining something to his team.

"Okay." I wished he'd answered that a little differently and I hated that I felt like I needed some kind of love and comfort. I shook it off, I realized I felt vulnerable after what happened with June. Also, I had to admit I was more scared about this whole trip back to Mexico than I admitted, even to myself.

"I'm not saying you aren't capable of doing this, Nicole," he continued. "If we can take down the Perez family, then June's death wouldn't be for nothing."

I tilted my head as his words sank in. "Do you think there's a connection?"

"I've no idea. I mean, nothing points to that, but there've been a few things lately." He huffed. "If there's even the smallest possibility, I mean, she was—"

I dried my tears and looked over at him. "I'm sorry."

"It wasn't your fault."

"I know it wasn't directly my fault, but I'm worried it was because of my involvement in everything and with getting Chase out. I can't help but wonder if it was me they were after. Or, God help us,

Chase." His expression told me there was something there.

He shook his head. "Look, Nicole, I know I said earlier that I didn't think there was a connection, but the truth is the guys are looking into it. Pooling every resource. I just didn't want you to feel exactly what you're feeling now."

"Oh, no, I feel so, so awful."

"I know you do. Look, the likelihood they'd find us here is slim to none." He gave a me a hug." Maybe he was right, but it still didn't make me feel any better.

"I'm still sorry for everyone's loss. She was pretty amazing."

"She was."

I nodded a few times and screwed my head back on right. "All right, let's do this for June."

"For June." He pulled my hand up and kissed the back of it softly.

***

The Blackstone team, Chili, and I took the chopper from Montana to Wyoming. Dark Water took a commercial flight to Rosarito. Our trip was long and dead quiet. The guys were like zombies, and I knew they grieved for June and wished they could have been there when she was laid to rest. It was only the urgency of the situation that made them leave, and I knew it hurt.

Cole and Mark were inseparable and often exchanged glances when they thought no one was looking. It was bittersweet to witness, but I was so glad they had each other to lean on. The bond all these men had made my heart swell.

The second part of our journey was a flight to New Mexico, then a drive in a convoy to mid-country where a semi-truck waited for Chili and me. The guys were dressed in their camo, helmets, and full tactical gear, ready to slip over the border once it got dark. This was where we would part ways.

As the guys scanned the truck to ensure it was clear then checked with the local police about the route we were about to take, Paul pulled me aside to talk.

"You remember everything?" He towered above me, somehow looking much larger than ever. His gear must add at least seventy pounds, and I wondered how his chest was healing. It was pointless to ask; he'd just brush me off. "Nicole?"

"Mm? Yes." I tried to focus, as the last forty-eight hours had been a lot, and now I was about to walk into another nightmare. I hoped I had it in me.

"Tell me again," he ordered.

I concentrated before I answered him. "Chili is going to offer me to Bruno and explain the baby's gone. Bruno will, of course, scan us for bugs. Chili has one he'll activate after the first scan so you can have eyes and ears on the initial meeting. Grim Gates will arrive shortly afterward and will drop the tiny cameras somewhere for me." I hoped the fake confidence in my voice would satisfy him. "How will I know where he'll put them?"

"He'll let you know," Paul assured me.

"Okay." I needed to sound like I had everything under control. In truth, I was far from prepared to be alone with Bruno again, especially after I shot him. I tried not to think how furious he'd be with me for that. I knew I'd have to do what I could to get Bruno to cool down and see me again. I swallowed hard and knew, more than anything, I had to look like I had things under control long enough for Chili to hand me off. I didn't want the guys to pull me out before we even got started. I thought of Chase and how he deserved to grow up in a world where he wouldn't always have to live terrified of being kidnapped or killed.

"And what else?"

"I look for the maid with the hummingbird tattoo on her forearm. She's working with us. I let her know where the cameras are, and she'll plant them where the cleaners won't find them. If I get into trouble, I flick the lights on in the bedroom that overlooks the church three times to signal Trigger's men to get me out."

"Lastly?"

"Dig when I can, don't trust anyone, and hopefully get an opportunity to head outside. At that point, I make this signal," I reached up and held my hair back from my neck with both hands as if I was really hot, "so you know I have something to share.

Don't risk trying to share anything with you using the planted bugs. It would be too risky and could make them suspect something. It might out their location in the house."

"Right. Good. Remember, the house is riddled with cameras, and he'll probably have someone watching you all the time. But if something really significant comes up and you can't get outside to give the signal, I guess it might be worth a shot." His lips tightened as he thought of that. "What else?"

"If I need to leave in a hurry, try to get to the garage. At the back, there's a classic Mustang stored there, where the maid will hide a phone for me."

"Where?"

"On the right back tire."

"Correct." He nodded. "If anyone stops you, say Armondo told you to go get him something, like a screwdriver. You might have to come up with something plausible. Act annoyed and irritated." He looked over my head then back to me as he flipped up his sunglasses. "I need you to be careful."

I tried to smile. "Copy that. I'm good at coming up with something." I went for a smile.

"This could get ugly, Nicole."

My mood fell. "When Bruno's involved, it's always ugly."

He suddenly grabbed my face with both hands and smashed his lips to mine, then he deepened his kiss and the world melted away for a moment. "Don't leave the property. Ever. Promise me, you won't leave," he said sharply.

I had no intention of getting myself into trouble. This was unlike anything I'd been involved in before, and I didn't feel as casual with my life as I once did. I had a lot more to live for. "I promise." I looked at the ground and figured I'd address the elephant in the room. "Are you guys all right with this? Not being there at the house, I mean."

"Zack, Doc Roberts, and Daniel are handling everything." His mouth pulled into a thin line. "Our job comes first; it has to. We keep an eye on each other, and we'll get through it. Later, we'll have a small service for her and grieve together. It's how we deal."

"Good." I saw Chase's little face and felt the tug inside at having to leave him. "I can't help thinking of Chase."

"You need your head in the game, not thinking of things like that. Distractions will get you killed."

"Is that what *you* do?" I challenged, and he looked away like I hit a nerve.

He licked his lips and pulled me to him, so I could feel his whole solid body. "Don't do anything more than what we discussed. Just stay alive for seven days, and it'll be over."

"Okay." He kissed me once more, then he was gone, and Chili took his spot.

He held up a thin cloth bag. "Ready?"

Panic coursed through me as my body temperature rose. "Yeah, I'm ready." He walked me to the truck. Then everything went black.

BRUNO

"Bruno, he's here." Armondo found me in the west wing of the new house. I had to admit Mama had said the view of the kitchen was going to be fantastic, and it was. I could see for miles, and that also meant it would be easy to spot anyone coming and we could be ready for them.

A small group of local men came into view. They were installing cameras, and I wondered how many of them would regret working for us. I had to smile at the idea of what we were building. These people had no idea how powerful we were about to become.

"I've never seen that many shades of orange in a single sunset before," Mama said from behind me. "It makes me wonder if we should stay here."

"We own six properties, and this one is the one you want to live in?" I leaned my weight against the wall and felt my foot throb inside my shoe. Though I liked the location of this one, it wasn't my favorite. I had a sudden thought. "How long are you staying?"

"A few more weeks." She stepped into view. "I need the men to understand I'm in charge and there will be no room for error."

Mama never let me forget she was the one in charge of our family. It was the reason my father kept his distance. Two type A people needed miles between them to work. He stayed in Mexico City, and she stayed in Rosarito. Where I hoped she'd soon return.

"Did you meet with your sleeper today?"

"I did."

"And?"

I pulled out the little box "J" had given me and handed it to her. "It's a start."

She read the label and flipped it over. "You're not to make a move until I say so," she reminded me, and I turned to look at her like she was mad. "I mean it. Gather all the information first, then we'll hit all three at once. If you show your cards early, we'll lose the element of surprise."

"If I see an opportunity to take out the very men who killed Uncle Martin, I'm pulling the trig—" She grabbed my ear and yanked me down to her level.

"You know the plan, Bruno. Don't forget I'm the one who brought you into this world and I can take you out. This will be done my way." She twisted harder, and my ear burned. "Do I make myself clear?"

"Yes, Mama."

She let go and patted my shoulder. "Sometimes boys forget where they stand in the family," she said. "Don't let it happen again."

"Mr. Perez." Armondo walked up with a man who positively reeked of America. When he smiled, his teeth flashed so white, he reminded me of a toothpaste model. "Meet your new Nando." The man flashed that smile again as he stepped forward.

"Archie Kidd," he offered. "I'm honored to be working with you."

Mama stared at him hard, and his smile instantly faded. Then she raised a brow at me as if to say, "See? He obeys." She turned and left the room. I waited until the sound of her clicking heels faded, then I turned my attention to him.

I'd already checked the young man's past. He had a less than savory military background and had been dishonorably discharged for fighting. Apparently, he had put his bunkmate in a coma. The US Army didn't approve of such things. It was sure to be my gain.

"You will have only one chance with me," I warned. I waved toward the window. "Can you see the property line?" I stepped forward and looked out.

"No, sir."

"Exactly, because we own it all. Your family will never be able to find your body."

He turned to look over at me. "Then I better behave."

"Bruno." Armondo's voice sounded strange, so I

turned my attention immediately to him. He rarely smiled, and the smile he wore in that moment was chilling. "We're needed back home."

PRESS

FOURTEEN

NICOLE

My hands shook, and the thin cloth bag over my head kept being sucked in and out as I breathed. I struggled to calm my nerves. Tears burned down my cheeks and made the bag stick to my neck and sealed in the heat from my panic.

"Sorry you have to keep the bag on, but we can't risk it. Dig your nails into this." Chili stuck a tin of something between my legs, and I stuck my hand inside to feel something scratchy and damp. "It's dirt. You need to look like I've put you through hell. You don't want him to think we've been staying in some grand place with soap and fluffy, high-end towels, right?"

"Yeah, ha-ha." I awkwardly did as he instructed and rubbed some on my legs and arms, then smeared a little around my neck below the hood. "Any sign of them?"

He didn't answer right away, and I thought he ignored me. "Three cars back."

"How much farther?" I just got the last word out when a loud crunch followed by a quick jerk of the wheel sent me flying into the door. I smashed my head into the glass, and the air was knocked out of my lungs. I hardly had time to react when the door was pulled open and something sharp pierced my skin. For the second time that day, everything went black.

***

My teeth chattered so hard my jaw ached, my head throbbed, and my mouth felt like the Sahara Desert. I blinked and saw things were sideways, or was I sideways? The bag that had been over my head lay next to me. I tried to focus on the small pieces of dirt in the grooves of the tile floor. Then a pair of shiny shoes stepped into view, and I was pulled upright so fast my world spun.

Colors and sounds morphed into one for a moment, then my eyes focused on a pair of cold, evil eyes.

"Welcome home, Nicole." Bruno's smile promised I'd never leave again. He held my arms and walked me backward on wobbly legs until I felt something hit the back of my knees. I fell into a chair and took in the familiar surroundings. I knew exactly where I was. Bruno's living room. The TV was still on the far wall, the large sectional couch sat to my left, the entrance to the kitchen was to my right, and the front door faced me. I forced myself to notice these things to get my mind working.

Then a sudden thought. *Chili?*

I quickly looked around and found him. He sat in a chair and had a mean glare focused on me.

If I didn't know the man the way I now did, I would have believed I was in deep shit. Chili had a way of holding himself that made one's skin crawl.

Bruno grabbed my chin and brushed my hair back to get a good look at me. I drew my chin in and bit at his fingers. "She looks to be her normal self."

"She's got fire." Chili spat chew into a tin can. "Sure put up a fight after she realized she was coming back here."

Bruno traced the scar on my forehead while he thought. "She's a little worse for wear."

"Not my doing." Chili shrugged. "I got ambushed by those fuckers in fatigues. I think they thought I had the soldier the Ruiz guys killed."

"Unsuccessfully killed," Armondo added from the corner of the room.

Chili grunted. "They grabbed them both, but I followed them to a nearby house. I waited 'til dark then moved in and managed to grab the girl while they tended to the kid—" He looked up quickly as Armondo suddenly rushed out of the room.

"And that's where you lose me." Bruno glanced at me then back to Chili. "Just how did you manage to slip by five special ops soldiers and walk away unharmed with the girl?"

"Why, because of me." Bruno whirled around, and as he stepped back, I saw Grim Gates dressed to impress in a crisp black suit and deep gray tie. I knew he'd show, but I couldn't help doing a double take inside.

"Mr. Gates, I wasn't expecting you." Bruno moved to the bar and made a quick drink then handed it to Grim like they were old friends. Chili kept his eyes on Grim but did tap his knee twice and pursed his lips to remind me to breathe.

All it would take was for one of those two men to flip and I'd be gone forever.

"Chili never mentioned your involvement."

Grim paused to take a sip. He seemed completely at ease in the company of evil. *It takes one to know one* came to mind. I knew he was no saint. He was supposedly here to help, but I was very much aware of who Grim Gates was. He was the infamous Vegas Reaper and mafia king. Shit, all I needed now was for Eric Noah to show up and we'd have one hell of a sinful party.

"I'm not one for throwing names around," Chili shrugged, "but Grim was in the area and offered to help out. He caused a distraction, and it gave me the opportunity to grab the girl and get out. I waited them out for a few days and returned her."

I felt such deep pleasure when Bruno limped over for his cane. "What's the catch?"

"Catch?" Chili shook his head. "We're all in this for the same reason. We just want to carry on with our business, but those fucking fatigues get in the way. We need them gone." He waved at me. "It's ingrained in them to rescue the weak."

"Fuck you." I kept my temper at the surface. Bruno wouldn't expect anything different from me. I had to bring flair to the situation.

"You're the one who's fucked, my dear," Chili grunted then turned back to Bruno. "The way I see it, she's bait to tie out in the field. Let her be seen walking around so they get a *visual*." He emphasized the word with finger quotes and grinned at the use of a military term. "It's only a matter of time before they go for it and try to get her. And when they do, we'll be ready."

Bruno rubbed his upper lip as he digested Chili's idea. "What are your thoughts on the matter?" He directed the comment to Grim, who had stayed silent. He took a moment.

"They fucked with a drug deal recently. It greatly inconvenienced Morgan and Jesse, who now have to appear in court next week." I knew Jesse was Grim's right hand man and Morgan was Trigger's Sergeant of Arms. "They've also been causing some major issues for Colin." He drained the last of his drink. "I must say, I think it's time to make a move," Grim said with such ease it was chilling.

"Colin is the least of my concerns," Bruno huffed.

"He should be, Bruno," Grim didn't miss a beat as

he strolled over to the bar and fixed himself another, "because he's planning on bringing more agents in at the El Paso border." *Does Grim know more than Blackstone does? Or is he fishing for information? Or is he trying to tell me something he found out?* My reporter's mind was going full tilt.

Grim came over and stood in front of me. He leaned down, so he was eye level, and cupped my chin in his hand. "I bet you have a lot of helpful information inside that pretty little brain of yours." He whispered the word "umbrella stand," indicating where he dropped the bugs I was to plant. "I'd keep this one around, Bruno. She could be of use to me later." He tucked my hair behind my ear. "And you know I'll return the favor."

I jerked my chin away from him and cursed.

"Be careful, my friend. She might bite." Bruno's smile turned wicked as someone behind me put a cloth over my mouth.

Loud bells drew me back to the living. They rang out and hurt my head. I felt worse than before. They had used drugs on me. *Damn.* Then I smelled that horrible, haunting perfume. It was deeply imprinted in my memory. Roses. Forever, that scent would remind me of rotting souls.

I finally managed to sit up, and to my horror, I realized I was back in the room Bruno had kept me in all those years ago. I looked down and touched the dress I wore; it was the white cotton one Bruno loved to see me in. I swallowed back the bile that rose in my throat, and with shaky legs, I slid off the bed and grabbed onto the windowsill. I looked out at the church down the road and wondered if Trigger's men could see me.

With a sob, I managed to get myself into a chair, and with that terrible scent in my nostrils my head slipped back in time.

"Shhh, hide in here." I helped Raúl and Raphael into a crawl space under the stairs. "Don't move until I come and get you."
"Sí." Rafael positioned himself to shield his teenage son from the door.
I moved the wooden paneling back in place and grabbed Mari by the arm and tugged her with me to the front of the house.
"Raúl is a good boy, Nicole. Please, he didn't know the guy was Cartel," Mari pleaded with me. "He was just trying to get his car started. He was only defending himself."
"Of course, I know that. It was one punch. The guy will be fine." Only it wasn't just a punch. It was an assault on a Cartel soldier, and that might as well be a death sentence. I swung her around to face me and handed her some cash.
"Listen to me. When the police come looking for him, say you haven't seen him since you got home from work. Give them the cash and say you're sorry for wasting their time."
"Wait," her eyes widened, "you're not staying?"

"If Bruno knew I was here, he'd know." I pulled her in for a hug. "It'll be okay, just have them lay low and keep out of sight. I'll get in touch with Jack right away." I held up Raphael's cell phone. "I'm going to take this. You take mine." I thrust mine in her hand. "Wait for my call."

"Okay." She hugged me once more. "Thank you, Nicole."

I hurried out the back door and dialed Jack. "Washington Post."

"Jack, it's me. I need to get Mari and her family out of town asap. Raúl got caught up with some of Bruno's soldiers. He swung and hit one of them then ran. They're looking for him."

"He had one more week to stay out of trouble. Shit," he huffed. "Yeah, give me twenty-four hours and I'll send a car. Just don't tell Emily about this. She'll worry, and with my luck try to smuggle the kid over the border herself." Raúl was like a son to Emily.

"She has my phone. I'll use a burner and text you the number. Thanks, Jack." I hung up, tossed the phone onto the bed of a hay truck going by, and ducked down the next street to the hotel where I was staying.

I stared at the cell phone well into the night. My mind spun and begged me to check in with Mari, but I couldn't risk it.

There was a knock at the door, and I raced to

open it. I was greeted by Armondo, who held up a box.

"Ms. Winter, you've been requested to join Mr. Perez at the Sanchez manor tonight." I felt my stomach drop. "I've been sent to get you."

"I told Bruno I wasn't able to attend." I started to close the door when his foot blocked it.

"I must insist." He pushed the box toward me. "I'll wait outside."

Internally, I let out a string of curse words. I should have known Bruno wouldn't take no for an answer.

An hour later, dressed in the gown Bruno, sent I sat unhappily at a table set with crystal and silver. I saw Sully speak to the bartender, then he approached me with a glass of champagne in his hand. He must have seen me arrive.

He sat down and silently handed me the glass. I immediately tipped it to my lips and took a long draw of the cool bubbly. I knew I'd need another, but before I could ask, the lights dimmed, and the music faded away.

"Welcome, welcome." Bruno stepped onto the stage and played the role of host even though it was Sully's party.

"Any idea what's going on?" Sully eyed me. "Because this wasn't part of my night."

"No idea." I shrugged, and suddenly a floodlight nailed me. Like the proverbial deer in the head-lights, I sat there blind and frozen. "There she is,

everyone, my date for the evening. Come on, sweetheart, come up and join me."

"Over my dead body," I whispered.

"Don't make a scene, Nicole. You better get up there," Sully's voice held a warning.

I put the champagne glass down and stood. A hundred pairs of eyes followed my every move as I made my way slowly to the stage. I could hear whispers as I went. People knew I was an American reporter; they wondered what I doing there. I kept a low profile no matter where I was. I didn't want to be noticed; you got a lot more information that way. That especially applied to parties.

"What are you doing?" I snapped at Bruno, who gave me a warning glare to shut up.

"Isn't she stunning, everyone?" I got a round of fake applause as Bruno signaled to someone. "I'm sure you're wondering why I have this beauty up here with me tonight. It's so I can remind her of who I am and what I'm capable of."

My insides clenched, fear twisting through me like a blade as Raúl and Raphael were hauled up on stage chained together like in some horror movie.

"No," I whispered, and Bruno tilted his head at my reaction.

Armondo stepped forward and handed him a scythe. Blood drained to my feet and my head went light. The crowd went silent, locked in fear.

We all knew there was nothing to be done but be
witnesses to Bruno's cruelty.
"This is a reminder of who I am and not to
mistake my love for weakness."
Love? He was mad. I felt a pair of arms wrap
around me and hold me in place.
"You watch and learn. You forget you are a guest
in his world," Armondo hissed in my ear.
Bruno stood over Raúl than turned to look at
me. "You didn't listen, Nicole, and this is what
happens when you don't obey." He swung the
scythe.
"No!"

I jerked awake when I heard footsteps. I quickly
dried the tears, and then Raúl's sweet face faded from
my memory. He was just fifteen when he and his
father were slaughtered in front of me by that
monster.

"You're awake." An American man stood next to
the bed. "You missed dinner, but Bruno would like
you to eat something." He waved for a maid to come
in with a tray of food. Her hands shook as she lifted
the lid from the plate, and I saw she had the tattoo on
her arm. When I looked into her face, however, there
was no nervousness there, only a cunning expression.
She wasn't nervous at all; she faked it for him.

"You're an American." I pulled his attention.
"Who are you?"

"I'm the man who takes great pleasure in drugging you," he snarled. He reached for the maid and pulled her out of the room. "Eat, or don't. I don't give a shit."

The smell of the food on the plate made me want to vomit, and I put the lid back on.

I remembered the maid's confident expression and gave myself a mental kick. "All right, Nicole, you're here, and you can do this. This is for you, Raúl."

––––––––

"Breakfast." The maid with the tattoo found me in the sunroom the next morning. The white-toothed American sat nearby and sipped a coffee as he stared at his phone. He glanced at the maid then went back to scrolling. After a couple of minutes, he got up and left the room. *Wait, what?* For a split second, I was excited, but then immediately realized I hadn't seen Bruno since the day before, and I was sure he watched me on the cameras in his office. It was unlike him to show patience, and he had a nasty temper. He was up to something. I wondered if he wanted to make me sweat and stew over what my punishment would be for betraying him. My stomach turned at the thought, but I'd agreed to this and knew how important it was. We didn't have much more time to take these monsters out.

"*Gracias.*" I reached for the pastry and looked up at her. Her gaze conveyed she wanted me to be careful. I took a bite of the pastry as she walked toward the door then stopped and made a show of shaking out a lap blanket. As I ate, I casually looked around and kept an eye on her.

I moved my foot and reached down to rub the spot where the metal irritated my ankle. I looked down at its blinking red light and wondered what kind of range the thing had. To say I was surprised he'd used an ankle bracelet and not shackles on me would be an understatement. I'd take this hunk of technology over them any day.

As I watched the maid, I had an idea. If Bruno wanted to track my every move, then maybe I'd give him something to track.

"I heard it might rain today." I popped a piece of gooey crabmeat in my mouth. "If I wanted to go for a walk, where might I find an umbrella?"

"*Sí*, we are in storm season, *señorita*." She shot me a quick look which told me she knew where I hid the bugs. "The umbrellas are by the front door on the ground floor. Please be careful where you walk, as the rain can flood areas quite quickly here." I nodded, and she fluffed a pillow then reached for the lap blanket and arranged it over the back of the chair and left.

After breakfast, I decided to act on my idea and see what would happen if I went from room to room. Would I be allowed to roam at will, or was I allowed only in certain areas? It was time to figure out what Bruno's game was.

The last time I stayed here was after Raúl and

Raphael were killed. That was the night I knew I played too close to the fire, and I blamed myself for their deaths. If I had taken Jack's advice and kept Bruno at a distance, he wouldn't have used people I cared about to control me.

Back then, Bruno wouldn't let me out of his sight and treated me like I was his own personal plaything. He knew I could report what I was going through to the media, so he made sure to let me know just what he could do to the people I held close.

I never breathed a word of that night to anyone, and neither did anyone else who was there.

My saving grace was Sully Sanchez. He was no angel, far from it, but he did care for me enough to try to figure out a way to get Bruno to let me go. He knew if I didn't get back to work soon, that people would start wondering. It took Sully a while to convince Bruno that Blackstone might get involved if I wasn't released. At the time, Blackstone wasn't as well-known, but Bruno certainly knew who they were.

"Do you think that was the signal?" I heard Armondo's voice and froze. I'd just come down a long hallway after walking through one of the back rooms. *Is he talking about me?* I was thankful I didn't have shoes on. "If so—" Armondo stopped talking, and as I peeked around the corner, I saw he was on the phone. "Get me any and all information."

"Like what you're hearing?" Bruno whispered from over my shoulder, and a cold chill raced up my spine. I spun around, and he grabbed a fistful of my hair and yanked me backward. "Always the reporter," he chuckled darkly, "sneaking around."

"And you're just a pathetic man who needs to keep a woman hostage in order for her to stay with you." I breathed fire at him. "How's the foot?"

He slammed me against the wall and pressed his nasty body into mine to pin me in place. "I've had just about enough of that mouth of yours."

"And yet here I am." I knew I flirted with his temper, but I never backed down from Bruno. I thought it was why I was still alive. He liked that I pushed him. It seemed to excite him. However, history had proven he'd take his anger out on others rather than me, and that was scarier. I never knew who he'd prey on next.

"And here you'll stay." His lips twisted into a sinister smile, and he licked his lips.

"For now." I swallowed back the fear that had crept up on me and gave a shrug. "Like always, it's only a matter of time."

"Bruno," Armondo broke our moment and glared at me when he made the connection I had been listening, "something's happened. We need to talk."

"To be continued, my love." He ran the back of his fingers down my face, and it made my skin inch away from his touch. He pushed off me and followed Armondo into the other room and shut the door. I sagged into the wall. Bruno ran hot and cold in the blink of an eye, and it was screwing with my head that he wasn't showing his true nature. I'd shot him in the foot, and I escaped with the child. *What am I missing? Why these mind games?* Did he know it would screw with me more?

Shoes squeaked on the tile floor, and I swiveled to see the American with his insanely white teeth standing in the hall. He screamed military from the way he stood right down to his crew cut and I wondered what his story was. He was nasty enough, but I wondered why he was here working with Bruno.

"Try anything and I'll know," he growled.

"Don't worry. Your glowing teeth will alert me you're in a six-mile radius," I snarled back with as much sarcasm as I could then turned and stomped off in the opposite direction.

When I entered another room, the tattooed maid came in behind me. "Oh, hello, *señorita*." She turned to the other maid. "Don't forget to water the *succulents*." She'd said in Spanish but turned and raised her brows at me.

"We did that yesterday," the girl reminded her, and I immediately knew she'd emphasized that word for me.

Without drawing too much attention to myself, I scanned the room looking for anything to do with succulents. I checked the bookshelf first, but Bruno apparently had more of a taste for classic cars than gardening. Then I looked through the coffee-table books and entertainment center but found nothing. I moved into another room and came up empty there as well. That was when I noticed *teeth* was watching me, so I strolled into the kitchen, snagged a bright red apple from the top of a bowl, and headed to the sink to wash it. It was there I spotted three succulents sitting on a shelf near the sink.

I washed my apple slowly and studied the little pots. I had to try to find the connection as to why she steered me to them. I wasn't getting it until I saw the way the plants were sitting. There was space for one more. In fact, there was a small water ring that proved there'd been four pots, not three.

I leaned back against the counter and tried to look casual as my mind started to spin. I spotted some loose soil that had fallen near the faucet. More soil could be seen on the counter. I bit into the apple and made a face when an awful taste hit my tongue. "Gross." I flipped open the trash lid to toss it in and saw a battered succulent inside. On top of it was a receipt. I bent over the trash, and as I pretended to gag, I reached out and pulled a tissue from a box on the counter. I took the moment to glance at the American standing there with a grin on his face.

"Next time, choose a better one." He slapped his leg and laughed like a hyena.

"Jerk," I spat back and wiped my mouth.

I leaned toward the can again and studied the receipt. It was placed face up, and I could read yesterday's date and saw a time stamp with a mountain time zone. I used the tip of my finger to move it and could make out the word *Smith's*.

Huh.

I looked at the apple where it lay beside the succulent and noticed a sticker on it. A half a lemon sitting in a grocery cart stared back at me, and I immediately connected the dots. Smith's Food and Drug store was a chain of stores in New Mexico. Had Bruno been there? I remembered the red stain on the bottom part of his cane and on his shoes. New Mexico had reddish brown dirt. Though so did a few other places in the US. My gaze moved back to the receipt; it must be something significant, or the maid wouldn't have drawn my attention to it.

Had I just found my starting point?

FIFTEEN

BRUNO

"Tell me what you know." I grew excited as one of my men filled me in on what he had discovered in North Carolina.

"It led to a dead end, but then how could a car just vanish like that? It's in the middle of the woods. One second, I was following taillights, and the next they were gone. I'm close to finding the house. I can taste it."

Heat surged like fire beneath my skin and awakened parts of me that I had suppressed for years.

But as fast as the joy went through, me it was replaced by a call from Mama.

Fuck.

"I'll call you back." I hung up and accepted the call. I tightly closed my eyes and wondered what in the world she wanted to yell at me for now.

"Mama—"

"I'm twenty minutes out. You better be at your place when I get there."

The call ended, and I whirled to Armondo. "Get everything out. Get Nicole out of here."

He pulled in his chin. "Where to?"

I thought for a moment. Mama was unpredictable, and I didn't trust she wouldn't leave someone to stay with me - to watch over me. She sounded very angry. No, I needed to play this out right. "Take her to the farm."

His face dropped. "Are you sure that's a wise idea?" I raised my head and shot him a careful look. "I just mean that's your headquarters for everything you have going on," he sputtered in Spanish. He saw my look and switched back to English. He held up his hands in apology. "It's just that it's your space now that your mother moved her business out of there. What if Nicole sees something she shouldn't?"

"She won't." I didn't have time to think everything through; I just knew Mama never went to the farm anymore. Since my uncle was killed, she said it held so many memories of her brother that it was too painful to return. "It's the last place Mama would ever think I'd take someone."

He hesitated, and I fought not to lose control. How dared he question my actions? "What?" I snapped. "You are very close to having your throat slit, Armondo, so speak carefully."

"I have only your best interests at heart." His

earnest expression delayed his death. "Every time that woman is involved, situations seem to go sideways. Maybe you should kill the bitch. Look what she's done already." He glanced at my foot. "And now she's back? You've killed for much less."

I licked my lips as anger swept through me again, but I pushed it down and forced myself to think. Against my better judgement, I decided to reveal my plan. "If I kill the bitch now, she won't live to see the one thing I want her to see. I have hurt her before, but it's not enough. I want the satisfaction of seeing her bleed."

"I understand, and that's what I'm trying to say. The bitch needs to—"

I held up my hand to stop him. Suddenly, I wanted him to see, as I did, my vision for her, for all she'd done. "I want her to see everything she cares about slip through her fingers. She sees herself as a savior to help the people and save Mexico. All those years of pain and sacrifice, I want her to see it gone." I snapped my fingers. "Like sand in the wind, her life's work will crumble and fall to nothing at her feet." I paused to let my words sink in. "I want her to stand next to me and watch the soldiers fall, the so-called saviors of the north, and then she'll see *me* rise from the ashes and claim my place at the top. All of Mexico will kneel to me, as she will. After I finish using her body, then I'll kill her." I could see it so clearly, and a thrill went through me. Then I focused on Armondo's open mouth and made a motion for him to speak.

"I understand." He swallowed hard.

"I hope you do, Armondo, I hope you do. Because if you want to live to be a part of this, you will not question me again." I slit my eyes in a warning.

"No, boss."

"Good," I snapped. "Now, go! Get the woman to the farm."

"Yes, boss. Right away." He turned to leave.

Then an engine roared, and its tires squealed. I jumped toward the window. "Shit! She's already here." I rubbed a hand over my face; it was just like her to trick me. "It's too late to go now. Keep Nicole upstairs and don't say anything to alert her something is happening. Just keep her quiet! At the first opportunity, take her out the back way."

He nodded and raced out.

"Archie!" I yelled. "Bring Mama to the study, straight through, no stops."

"Understood."

Christ, she was maddening. When did she get back? I thought she was away for the next few months, at least. She was such a control freak. I grabbed my cane and headed toward the study. God forbid I'd keep her waiting.

Mama stood looking out the window with her arms crossed. Her fucking pet, Rio, stood watching. I hated him and refused to glance his way. I knew she could see my reflection in the glass.

"You were always my favorite son." She kept her

back to me. "I could see great things in you, even as a child. Your father favored your brother, and look where that got him. I never let him live that down." Her arms fell to her sides as she turned to look at me.

Oh, shit, she had that look—cold and disconnected.

"You know I don't like to look the fool, Bruno."

"I know, Mama." *Where is this going?*

She clucked her tongue and moved to the bar to make herself a drink. "I gave you a direct order, and you disobeyed me." Clinking ice filled the dead silence as my stomach sank. She knew I had Nicole.

"Mama, let me—"

"You told me you wouldn't make a move until I said so." That made the words I was about to say dissolve from my tongue as I fought to keep up. "This is your mess." Her voice was acid as she put her hands on the back of a chair. "You're going to have to do damage control and rope your people back in line!" she screamed, and it made my whirling head instantly ache.

"Mama, please," I raised a hand in total confusion, "I'm not following you at all."

She slammed her glass down, and it broke, sending liquid everywhere. "How could you be so stu —" Her eyes suddenly widened, and the mood in the room shifted as she went still.

"What?"

"Shut up!" she snapped then plucked a little

black square from my pen holder. Her murderous gaze traveled to mine as we both realized what it was. A bug.

What the hell? How? Who was I going to have soak in gasoline and set on fire?

Mama used her broken glass to smash the device into the top of my desk. Rio looked smug as he reached to flip on my office scrambler. It only had a short range, but it would have to suffice. I needed the place swept, and fast.

Mama crossed the room, and before I was ready, she slapped me hard across the face. "You have disappointed me twice today. Do I need to stay home and take care of this side of the business?"

I licked around my mouth and tasted blood as I fought to control my temper. She was dangerously close to me pushing me to remind her who was younger and stronger.

"No, Mama, I have things covered."

Her laugh made my fists clench. "Do you?"

"Yes."

"You better think hard about who is in this house, who you can trust, and what you can see on your cameras." She ordered. "Come, Rio." He shot me a look as he trailed Mama out of the room. *I'd like to crush his face.*

I walked to the window to make sure she left, and as I watched the car leave, I wracked my brain about what had just happened. I thought back over the last day. Nicole and Chili had been cleared for bugs, so it wasn't them. Grim and I went back far too long. That only left the house staff and…

"You!" I pointed at one of the girls wearing rubber gloves. She jumped, and her eyes widened with surprise then terror as she froze in place. "You clean my office."

"*Sí.*"

"There was a bug in my office. Who planted it?"

"Bug?" Her brows pinched together. Christ, she was stupid.

"Listening device, a recorder."

She shook her head. "No, I just clean and listen to this." She held up an old tape player.

"*El señor,*" another maid stepped forward, "I don't know who would do this thing, but I saw the American man in your office this morning." I stared at her hard to see if she'd show a sign she was lying. She didn't blink, just held my gaze. I waved her off and knew I'd have to check the cameras. She gave me a small bow then hurried out.

"Hey!" I called to one of my soldiers. "Where's Armondo?"

"He's downstairs waiting for the woman. She's gathering her things."

"And the American, Archie?"

"Not sure, *señor.*"

"Find him," I ordered. He picked up his radio and began to speak.

My vision went red. "Turn on every scrambler we have!" I yelled.

PRESS

NICOLE

"Miss," the maid with the tattoo ran into my room where I'd been trying to find a way to delay going down to Armondo. I knew something was up, and it scared me. When she closed the door behind her and spilled a glass of red juice on the white carpet, I panicked.

"What the hell are you doing?" I hissed the last thing I needed was Armondo needing a reason to bring Bruno up to the room.

She ducked her head as she said. "They're coming for you," she whispered as she dropped to her knees and started to spray the stain in case someone watched on the camera. "Mr. Perez found the bug in his office. I'm so sorry. I only planted it a few hours ago." My stomach dropped. "Do you know they're moving you?"

"I knew something was happening, because Armondo told me to hurry and get my stuff. I don't know what he expects me to get. I only have the clothes I wore here."

I glanced toward the small table in my room where she'd planted a bug when she brought my food. I hoped to God the guys were getting this. I hadn't been able to share what I'd found out earlier in the trash.

"The scrambler machine is on. The signal is no good." She knew what I'd been hoping. "Listen, quickly, we don't have much time." She kept dabbing. I made the American, his name is Archie, go into Mr. Perez's office this morning." I threw her a look. "You never know when you might need a backup plan." She looked up briefly. "Look, I told Mr. Perez I saw him there. I hope he'll think it was him. You have to sell it to him."

The door burst open, and Armondo took in the scene.

"Sorry, sir, juice was spilled, but I'll get it clean." She rubbed the carpet like she was hurrying in case it set.

He held his head ever so slightly tilted to the side. I knew he was listening to someone. I wouldn't have caught it, but I'd seen it often with Paul and the guys.

"Get up!" He grabbed her arm and twisted it. She yelped, and I reached for him to make him stop, but he pulled his gun and shot her in the face.

What? Oh, my God!

"Why?" I cried in shock.

"Shut up. Why do you take so long?" He grabbed me, and I fought him. Everything had gone south so fast I couldn't keep up. I kicked, bucked, and bit Armondo, but he was entirely too strong.

"Let go of me!" I screamed as loud as I could with a tight grip on the headboard in the hope that maybe one of the bugs would pick it up. "Get your fucking hands off me!"

"I don't trust you or anyone else in this house." He locked his arms around me, and as he began to drag me out the door, Trigger's face popped into my head. In a last-ditch effort, I kicked the ceiling light on with my foot. Maybe, just maybe the light would be left on and make the Devil's Reach wonder if something was wrong.

I fought with all my might as he dragged me out of the house and stuffed me into a car. He slapped cuffs on my wrists and ankles, and once again a bag was jammed over my head. I felt someone get in on either side of me, and Armondo told them to watch me closely. The door slammed, and the engine started.

I'd seen the clock on the dash before they'd put the hood over my face and noted the time. I just hoped we weren't going too far.

I was wrong.

The sun moved across the fabric, and I felt the time tick by. My mind wandered back to the maid, and tears soaked the hood over my cheeks. I'd lived through so much senseless loss in my career, but it hurt my heart. Death came to so many who didn't deserve it. The poor woman had been there to help me.

The car slowed once, and I thought maybe we were there, wherever there was. But it was just a gas station, and before long, we were back on the road.

I wasn't offered a bathroom break or anything to eat, and I knew something big was happening. I realized at one point that Bruno was in the front seat. I heard him speak to someone, but they had turned on some music, and it drowned out most of what was said.

I fought the numb feeling that tried to take over my head to force myself to think, but for once in my life, I felt defeated. I hadn't been able to get anything useful and had risked my life and gotten that poor maid killed for nothing. The chance that the Devil's Reach would understand my message was slim to none. I doubted if anyone knew I'd been taken from the house.

Once again, my life might come down to a faceoff between me and Bruno Perez, only this time I had no Sully or anyone else to help me get out of the situation.

A smack to my face shocked me out of sleep, and the bag was pulled from my head. I blinked at the guy beside me who held up the fabric with a black-toothed smile on his ugly face. If only I had a hand free.

"Morning," Bruno chuckled from the front seat, "welcome to your new home."

I leaned forward to see out the front windshield. I noticed we were following a long, winding drive through lush trees. We went over a hill, and below us were rows and rows of avocado trees. Workers bent at the waist sorted the fruit in baskets. Horses roamed freely on the other side, and off in the distance was a barnyard scattered with chickens. Under different circumstances, I might have thought the place was like a dream, so incredibly beautiful, but when I went to flip my hair out of my face, the handcuffs gave me a rude awakening. The farmers more than likely worked under threat of death, and no doubt the horses had belonged to some other poor family who once owned the place.

Armondo appeared and nearly ripped my arm off as he pulled me out of the car. I was tired of his rough demeaner and thought I'd try a new tactic as I remembered the maid's words.

"Why can't you be more like him." I pointed my hands at the American, Archie. It turned out *Teeth* had been one of my seat companions. "His touch is much kinder than yours." I smiled when I saw Bruno scowl at Archie.

SEVENTEEN

PAUL

I leaned my head against the cool brick wall and listened to the silence that blanketed the room. After we left Nicole and Chili in New Mexico, we left for Fort Echo in Texas. This place would be our home base for the next six days. It was close to the border and had all the resources we might need for a possible emergency extraction. With Nicole as a willing participant, Frank had gotten us clearance for whatever might come. It was a desperate measure, but the US was in a losing battle with the Cartels, and desperate measures were all we had.

Mark leaned forward and rubbed his eyes. He'd been suffering from a massive migraine since we left Shadows. I knew that witnessing June's death had been a terrible blow to him. The doc had given him a shot, but nothing could touch the pain. I hated seeing him suffer so much. I knew somehow, he blamed himself.

Keith flipped his phone over with a huff then shook his head, and I knew we still had nothing. Whoever hit and killed June seemed to be a ghost in the wind. Thanks to Nicole's description of the bumper sticker with the tiger on it, the police were able to find it and link it to June's murder. The car had been found only a few miles away. It had been driven into a bunch of thick shrubs. It was wiped completely clean of prints, and so far, nothing had been found that could possibly give a DNA sample.

We already knew the license plate was fake; it had been registered to some guy long dead. Frank said the car was registered to a teacher at St. Augustine Elementary who had reported it missing an hour before the accident. Whoever the driver was, they knew what they were doing.

"This is so fucked up." Mark suddenly pushed to his feet and rushed out of the room.

Cole followed, and we let them be. June had been part of both their lives since they could use a slingshot. As Abigail's sister, she'd mothered them as if they were her own.

"Paul." Frank stuck his head inside the door and waved for me to join him. My stomach bottomed out, but I stood. John mirrored me.

"Not you, Black," Frank grunted, but John stood his ground.

"What you have to say to Paul you can say to all

of us." Frank had lost the trust of the guys since they found out the part he'd played in why I'd been in Mexico. Frankly, I didn't blame them.

Frank removed his glasses as he stepped into the room. "Remember your rank, John. You take orders from me." It was a shitty comment and didn't go unnoticed by the others. Their faces had hardened.

"You lost our trust long ago, Frank, and you sure as hell haven't done much to fix it," John growled.

Frank's white eyebrows pinched together as Cole moved closer. He glanced at John then at me.

"Is there a problem here, boys?"

"I don't know. Is there?" Frank looked at me. I'd put a hand on John's shoulder when Frank commented on his rank.

"No," I pulled John backward, "Frank just needed a word with me."

Mike slowly stood and moved to stand next to John.

"Tensions are high, boys, but save that fire to use out there and not in here." Cole's voice was a warning to stand down.

"Tensions have been high for a while, Colonel." John stepped back, but his posture told me he was pissed.

"John," I moved myself between him and Frank, "it's all good."

"Something's off. I can feel it." I nodded, because shit was definitely off.

"Let's get through this mission and we'll talk." I gave him my word.

His gaze moved to mine and he tried to read my mind. Normally, he could, but I fought to block him out. I had to.

"Paul, let's go," Frank ordered, and I gave John's shoulder a squeeze and followed him outside. "Black needs to—"

"Frank," I cut him off, "don't pit me against my family. You won't win." His mouth twisted, but to my surprise, he didn't put me in my place either. "And this will be the last time." I brushed past, leaving him to follow me.

"Hey, hold up," Frank called. He'd trailed me for a bit, but I wouldn't turn. "Paul, Steve from North Rock just called in." His breaths came in huffs, and I knew his advanced age made it hard for him to keep up with my pace. I stopped finally but wouldn't turn.

"What'd he want?"

"Said he was followed all the way across state lines to Tennessee. Once he shook the tail, he scanned his Jeep, and guess what he found." He waited, but I wouldn't bite. "A tracker with a lion's head on it."

I whirled as a cold feeling spread through my limbs. That was the same logo on the one I'd found on Nicole

"Yeah," he nodded, "now you see why I need you. We're close, Paul, but we need to be closer. This is the only way." I cursed under my breath. "Nicole is planted deep, and she's good, so let her dig there," he pointed to the left, "while you dig over here." He pointed in the opposite direction. "It's a smart play, the only play, and you know it."

Do I know it?

"Does Cole know?"

His eyes went down then back up. "The fewer involved, the better. You know this."

"Fuck." I couldn't believe what I was hearing. "And when he notices I'm gone?"

"He'll be fine. Besides, you need to go. The chopper's waiting. I've got you covered."

"Of course you do." I spun back around and walked away from my brothers and toward everything I'd worked so damn hard to forget.

I refused to think of my son; the pain was too much.

***

"You must be Paul." A man stood as I entered the room and offered me a hand. I looked around and saw the box next to him. "I've been hired to—"

"I know who you are." I glared at him. "Let's get this shit over with."

Since I'd left Frank, I'd gone over the plan about nine different times in my head and couldn't see a way out of it.

Once the guy was finished with me, I found my way to where Chili waited with the old pickup truck that had been arranged for us. I got in, and he started the engine. I stared at a small hole in the floor and wished I was anywhere but where I was.

"You okay, man?" Chili, who hadn't said much at all since he'd also been roped into this shit storm, rubbed the dust from his face. The truck didn't have AC, so the windows needed to be open for any kind of relief.

"Never better."

I leaned my head back against the headrest, still angry for breaking the biggest promise I'd made to myself. I knew I had to get past it and keep my head in the game. I wasn't doing myself or anyone else any favors by wallowing in it.

The phone in my pocket vibrated, and I pulled it out and squinted at the screen. The dust in their air made me cough.

"Frank?" Chili questioned.

"No. Pull over, fast." I jumped out and answered. "What is it?"

"Paul, we got a problem." Brick made a noise like he was inhaling smoke, and I spun around to look at Chili through the open door. Devil's Reach had been watching Bruno's place. "Her light's been on all night, fuckin' place is too quiet. No one coming or going. She knew the plan, an' I think she's tryin' to tell us something."

A pain exploded in my head.

"Can you," I cleared my throat, but the emotion was too strong, "can you send someone up there?"

"Rail's on the way back now. He went to see what

he could figure out. Just needed you to know some-thin' ain't right, man." There was a reason Trigger kept Brick so close; his intuition was normally dead on. I fought not to panic. I was trained for this, but it was Nicole we were talking about.

"Did you let Cole know?"

"Not yet. Figured you'd call the shots here."

I looked up at the sky. "Okay, loop Cole in, and text me the minute you know anything. Don't use names, keep the texts clean."

"Yeah." He hung up, and I got back in the truck.

"We good?"

"Not even close."

I filled Chili in as we drove and kept a close eye on my phone. Cole had men listening to the bugs the maid had planted, but apparently nothing infor-mative had come of it. I wondered where the maid had been able to plant them, because so far, they'd been useless. We knew Bruno's mother showed up, but then the signal had gone shitty. They were working on it, but I was worried they'd been compromised.

"Shit, Chili, I wonder if they jammed the signal."

"Just breathe, man, one problem at a time. We're here." He leaned out and pushed the button near the gate. "Just stick to our story, and if there's trouble, we've got our signal." He drove through, and I forced myself to breathe.

"Out." The soldier pointed an automatic rifle at us. "IDs."

Chili handed him our IDs. The soldier was young, barely past eighteen.

"Check your records, son. I've been cleared, and Bruno is expecting my visit," he snapped at the kid.

The kid studied me. "You carrying?" I raised my shirt to show him I wasn't.

"You're not on the list."

"Yeah, he is." Chili grabbed the clipboard and jammed his finger at it. The kid blinked at him, confused about what to do next. "See," Chili pointed, "EN." The kid reached for his radio, and Chili raised his arms like he was pissed. "Make us late, then. I'll let him know it was your fault."

"Go." The kid tossed the clipboard and waved his gun at the truck.

"Hey, kid?" I pulled out the toothpick I'd put between my lips and pointed at his gun. "Your safety's on."

He quickly turned the gun over as I rolled my eyes.

We climbed back in the truck, and Chili laughed as we drove off. "Just like old times."

"Those days are long gone now." I checked the mirrors and looked straight ahead.

"Fuck, Paul," he laughed, "what are the chances he'll buy this?" Chili smacked me on the back. "Yup, just like old times."

I refused to comment and shook my head at him as I got into character.

He parked, and I glanced at myself in the mirror. I hated that I looked like the past. "This is our only chance." I fixed my shirt and threaded a pair of sunglasses through my shaggy wig then stuck the toothpick back between my teeth. The beard that was glued to my face felt like I was suffocating. All signs of Agent Paul were gone. "For the record, I hate every second of this."

"I know, brother." Chili held up his hands as Armondo approached with a gun pointed in our direction.

"What the fuck is going on here, Chili?" he boomed then whistled for his men to get Bruno. "This was a meeting with you, not…" He squinted at me and his gun wavered. "Impossible."

I greeted him with a nod then was shoved from behind to start walking around the side of the house.

I'd been to the place a few times in the past but was never welcomed inside. To even get past the gates required an extensive background check. One of Frank's specialties. It was the Perez family's property. I knew it was where Bruno had been born and raised and I also knew it was his mother, Esmeralda's, main place of business. It was heavily protected and well patrolled by soldiers and attack dogs.

We were directed through to a room that led out to the back patio where Bruno Perez greeted us. His face registered shock as he set his eyes on me.

I expected it; after all, I was dead.

"Eric Noah?" He said my name like he couldn't believe it. "You're the last face I expected to see," he paused, "well, ever again." He quickly pulled a gun, and we heard the clicks as his men did the same. "You tried to kill me. What makes you think I shouldn't return the favor?"

I shook my head at Chili so he wouldn't speak. I knew it was me Bruno wanted to hear from.

"You can," I lifted a shoulder, "but something tells me you'd be more curious to hear about my sudden resurrection before you decide to splatter my brain over your patio."

Bruno might seem unpredictable to most, but not to me. I understood him. He thought of himself as a badass, but he was just a spoiled boy with a temper and a mother who loved to order him around. I knew he hated that his mother still had control. It was almost pathetic the way he stood there waving around his gold gun with its ivory handle. He was all show. Evil and dangerous, though, so I knew I'd have to handle him carefully.

"Sit." He pointed to the table with his weapon, and Chili and I took a seat. A beautiful humidor sat in the middle of the round marble top, and I leaned over slowly to raise the lid and took an appreciative sniff. If I was to appear the same man as before, I had to act the part.

"Cohiba Behike." Bruno nodded, and I reached in carefully and held one up to show Chili. "You have always had excellent taste, Eric." He nodded at me in appreciation. "When those were first released, they sold for eighteen hundred US dollars a box. That humidor was one of only one hundred sold and held forty cigars."

"Really? That's incredible." Chili blew out an amazed breath and leaned close to take a whiff, but he didn't dare touch it.

"You were always a man of incredible taste." I eyed Bruno. His chest puffed up as he accepted my compliment. We made ourselves seem comfortable. Hopefully, it would convince him to let his guard down.

"I enjoy only the very best." Bruno's cocky side showed, and I knew it was time to dive in. "Well?"

I gently replaced the cigar and closed the lid. To show appreciation was one thing, but helping myself to one would be going too far.

"So, Bruno, I want you to know I had no idea that when I ran up behind your vehicle someone had planted a bomb inside." I started with the betrayal first. Bruno was an emotional man, and his ego needed to be stroked some more. "I can't figure out who was behind that. Though I have heard rumors." I made a show of glancing at Armondo. "Interesting how you both were there but only one of you was burned." I stated that quietly for only him to hear. A flash of memory found me of when I attached the explosive under the vehicle and how it had let go on one side. Then it must have fallen to the ground before it ignited.

Bruno rested his hand on the table, but I noticed he still held his gun. "The full story."

"That night, I was being followed by Rafeal Cruz on Perez territory. I was coming to get you so we could circle around, trap him, and kill him for trespassing." I gave him a wicked grin. "You know like the old days." The crease in his jacket around his shoulder smoothed out as he visibly relaxed at my comment. "Only I didn't get the chance." I pushed up the short sleeve on my shirt to show him where my fake burn started and traveled down to my hand. We had made sure the cosmetic scars covered the length of my arm in order to conceal my tattooed sleeve. "You weren't the only one who was left with a reminder of that terrible day."

He studied the ugly grooves and, without thinking, touched his own. My eyes shifted to Chili, and he gave me a slight tilt of the head that he'd seen too.

"I had every intention of finding you after the blast, but Rio got to me first."

"Rio?" he interrupted, and I swore I saw Chili's lips twitch. Bruno loathed his mother's right-hand man. He knew he'd never measure up to him.

"After your car exploded, I woke up in the back of Rio's car. My arm was bandaged, and they'd drugged me up with something for the pain. The stuff knocked me out for hours. Now I know the reason."

"Which was?"

"Well, after the fog from the drug wore off, I realized your mother had joined us in the car. She said you were alive, but things were going to be different." I knew the next part would raise his temper. "She thought our plan for Talya wasn't being handled correctly."

"Of course she did," he muttered more to himself. "What did she say?"

"She thought it would be a good idea for you to pretend to stay dead and for me to keep working our angle with Talya."

He cursed and shook his head. "She wanted me out of the way, you mean."

"No, look," I leaned my elbows on the table and lowered my voice, "you and me, we had come up with the perfect plan. We had the Canos daughter betray her own blood to work with us!" I added a level of excitement to my voice. "She was feeding us information, and we were actively stepping in and blocking their drug runs. We were making a dent, but your mother saw the writing on the wall and wanted in on it. Can you imagine if shit hadn't gone sideways?" I shook my head with a sly grin. "They would never have seen that coming."

"I know it was a great plan, because it was *my* idea," he said through a clenched jaw. "What else did my mother have to do with this?"

"Everything." I didn't miss a beat. "After the attack on you, she wanted you to lay low, so the Canoses thought you were out of the picture. Maybe she thought the Canoses suspected you or something." I went in for another dig at Esmerelda. "You know your mother, she hardly ever shares her plans. Anyway," I waved and let that sink in, "not long afterward, Jerry started to suspect something between *me* and Talya, even though she'd worked hard to keep Grim as her cover. So that day, when the soldiers from the north showed up and attacked Martin's house, your mom ordered me to fake my own death." I cleared my throat and scowled to show I didn't agree with it. "You know Esmerelda; you don't say no."

"Mm."

"But there was so much shit from the explosion, it was logical to think I'd get killed in the process, and from what I know, no one since has questioned my death."

His mouth sagged open. "My mother has known all along that you are alive?"

"Yes." I lied so easily. "Talya found me a few months later. Distraught about her parents' decisions and the direction they were taking their business." I kept this part vague because fewer details were better with a lie. "She decided she was leaving but gave me a parting gift." I wiggled my brows at him.

He leaned forward with interest. "Which was?"

I carefully reached for the USB stick in my shirt pocket. "Financial reports, drop-off and pick-up locations, and how the Canoses were using my fucking tunnel to transfer money. I didn't come to you until now because I needed to see it for myself, and guess what? It's true. I have the proof."

"You have all this?"

"Yes, enough to set up the American soldiers and have them take out the Canoses, and just when they think they've won," I looked excited, "we strike and end them!" I smacked my knee then set the USB stick down between us.

His eyes locked on it, like Gollum as he stared at the golden ring. I could practically see his obsession with ending Blackstone once and for all. His hand jerked forward, and he snatched it up and held it closer to his face. He flicked his wrist at his men. "Chili, give us a moment." Armondo stepped forward and avoided eye contact with me as he motioned at Chili to leave.

"Of course." Chili walked with Armondo across the patio, out of hearing range.

Bruno pocketed the USB. "Did Chili know any of this?"

"No. I didn't think it was wise at the time, but he knows everything now. I filled him in yesterday and asked him to find a way for me to see you."

"Chili stayed to work your tunnel after what happened with my uncle. Do you think he has any loyalty to the Canos family?"

"No," I held his stare, "he's loyal to a fault. I trust him with my life, as I do you." Bruno loved when I played *we were brothers*. He hated his own, so I often used that angle on him.

Bruno let out a long breath. "You slept with Talya?"

I gave a sleezy smirk, channeling the darker part of Eric. "That was a product of too much tequila, an empty bar, and, well, a gorgeous woman who wanted it as badly as I did."

"I understand that." He gave a wide smile. "A man needs release, and why not with a beautiful woman, ah?" He patted his crotch and looked up. I followed his line of sight, and my stomach dropped as I spotted Nicole up on a balcony.

Fuck!

I turned to stone. Lungs, heart, stomach, and brain frozen in time. No. That isn't happening. Not here, not now, it's impossible. I knew I couldn't let her see me, not as Eric. Even though I doubted she'd recognize me, I knew someday she'd have to find out. I didn't want her to have the mental image in her head.

"So, the kid is yours?" I barely heard his words and had to replay them twice to form an answer. *Focus.*

"Not sure, but for the sake of letting the Canoses panic, yes." I turned my back to the window with my mind still reeling. I had to ground myself to fight the panic. "If I am, then so be it. I'll only believe it once I get tested."

"Do you have the boy?"

"No," I squinted as if confused, "the last I heard, you had won the bid with Rafael."

Bruno looked up at the balcony again, and I dared a quick glance. She was gone. "Things did not go as they should have, but it won't be long before I'll have the child. In the meantime, I'm dealing with it."

All I had to do was jerk forward, grab the gun he left so carelessly on the table, and drive a bullet through his sweaty forehead. The world would be such a better place.

"All right," he pulled me from my murderous thoughts, "so, what do you propose to do?"

"I want to finish what we started."

"I want to trust you, Eric. Give me something more."

I pulled out a photo of Jerry Canos, courtesy of Mike's Photoshop skills. The one thing about Bruno was he was dumber than dumb when it came to technology. "And?"

"This was taken two days ago, and look who's he's talking to." He squinted to see Archie Kidd, all smiles as he stood behind Jerry. He looked completely at ease in the presence of the Canos family. "You have a mole, but before you plant a bullet in his head, I think we can use this."

He scratched his upper lip as he flipped the photo over as if it offended him. He was pissed. "How?"

"Let's just say I've been watching the Canos family, and that's how I got it. Bruno, I'm tired of all our best laid plans going sideways, and I bet you've had enough of stepping back until your mama says when it's time. Let's take control ourselves." Whether he meant to or not, his interest showed. I could see it in the way his skin tightened around his eyes and mouth. "Let's use Archie to lure Jerry out, then we start swinging and wipe the Canoses off the map. We'll take back the land, you take your Uncle Martin's spot at the top where you belong, and we go back to doing what we were meant to. Money, control, and power will be our reward."

He couldn't hold it back anymore. His lips stretched wide, and his teeth bared. He stood, and I did the same. "Now, that sounds like the perfect plan." He clapped me on the back, then we made arrangements to meet the next day to work out the details. I sweated every moment, as I desperately needed to get out of there without Nicole seeing me.

I breathed a sigh of relief when I found Chili and waved him toward the truck. Neither of us said a word until we were a few miles away from the place.

"Chili, pull over!"

Before the truck had completely stopped, I jumped out and pressed my palms flat against the truck's hood.

"Wanna fill me in?" Chili sounded worried, but I needed a minute to stop the magnetic pull that was trying to suck me back there. "Hey? You okay?"

"Give me a sec," I gritted as I dug my cell phone out from under the seat. I tapped on John's name and waited for him to answer.

"You're on speaker. Where are you?" He sounded pissed.

"She's at the farm, boys. He took her to the fucking farm."

"Farm?" John sounded confused. "That sounds like it means something?"

I wanted to scream with frustration. "It means getting Nicole the fuck out just became ten times harder."

PRESS

EIGHTEEN

NICOLE

I felt like I was stuck in a nightmare where two different versions of evil had found their way back together. I pressed my back flat against the wall and let the fear creep in like a fog, silent and thick enough to choke any air left inside me.

He's alive. I knew it. Eric Noah, here in the flesh. I'd seen him with my own eyes from the balcony, and I knew he and Bruno had to be planning something Godawful.

How was I going to let Blackstone know? They had no idea where I was. I had to tell them the man who'd trafficked women for a decade, who killed without a thought, was here in this house.

I had nothing. The room was stripped of anything worth turning into a weapon, and the ankle bracelet made sounds and sent off flashes of red lights when I traveled toward any part of the west wing of the house. The rational part of me said to stick it out and something would show itself, but the reporter side of me demanded action. It said I had to get creative because time might not be on my side. I had no plans of staying here more than the six planned days, with or without Blackstone's help.

Chase's face came into my head, and his sweet smile helped the panic subside. I could hear his little cries as he reached for me, and even though I'd never be his mama, there was something incredibly touching having a child trust you enough to be their person. A tear escaped and ran down my cheek. I would get back to him as soon as I could. I wasn't going to let him think I'd leave him the way his mother had.

"There you are." Bruno was suddenly in the room, and all the thoughts inside my head fled. "I was hoping you'd have dinner with me." The way he asked rather than demanded meant the old Bruno was back. He had often fantasized that he was a gentleman asking a lady to join him. In this role, he seemed to need to know he was someone a woman would want to be with. I knew this game, but I also knew he could switch tactics like a viper and strike without warning.

I fantasized about driving my hand straight through his heart, but I knew I had to play.

"All right," I whispered and brushed a hand down over the skirt of the white dress. I saw his eyebrows go up and his tongue as it went to his upper lip. He smiled.

I followed him downstairs to the main floor and out to the kitchen. Archie stood there, and sadly, his body was between me and the steak knives. I wanted desperately to kill him, but the maid had set him up for me, and her last idea before she died deserved to be set in motion, and I planned on using it.

Torches stood like soldiers along the edge of the patio, their flames swaying in the cool breeze. They flickered long, wavy shadows as if carefully placed to mark my confinement. They didn't light the space around me so much as they lit the prison I was in.

"Hungry?" He pointed toward the table that was set just a few steps up from the pool. The white table-cloth glowed in the firelight. "And if I wasn't?"

He grinned. "I can think of something else to fill our evening."

"Dinner it is." I slowly walked by him and up the stone steps. The long rectangular table held a spread of food that piqued my appetite. I lifted a brow and glanced at him. I waited for him to pull out the chair since he was determined to continue to play the role of a gentleman. As I sat, I placed the rose-colored napkin on my lap and waited for him to speak. I wondered when he'd drop the façade and show me what he was going to do to me.

"You will learn to love it here, Nicole." *Here it comes.* He placed his own napkin on his lap and looked out at the night. But when I didn't comment, he simply snapped his fingers like he was some kind of royalty, and a waiter placed a plate in front of me while a second waiter simultaneously served him. A lobster stared up at me next to a side of shrimp ceviche. The lime wedges were shaped like flower heads. At any other time, I'd be excited by such a beautiful meal.

"What are you thinking?"

I just couldn't hold back any longer. Waiting for him to show the side he was trying to hide was wearing thin. "I was thinking how you just ruined lobster for me." I reached for the wine glass and took a long sip while I studied his sour expression.

He speared a shrimp. "As I said, you will learn to love this place. You will enjoy it here as much as I do."

"I doubt that."

He rested his arm on the table, and I knew I was getting under his skin. Why did I continue to hasten my demise? "This is your home, Nicole, our home." Wow, the man was insane. "These will be our evenings. Yours and mine. You can fight it all you want, but you're not going anywhere. I enjoy having you by my side."

"Time will tell." I set my glass down. "I have escaped you before."

He licked his lips, and I saw his effort to restrain himself. "This property spans many miles. We have horses, goats, chickens, and donkeys. We grow avocados, peaches, lemons, and nuts." He smiled like I should be impressed.

"Yes, and all by using enslaved workers. The life of the Cartel getting rich off the backs of your own people."

"The poor, you mean. Who do you think gives them work so they can feed their families? They would have nothing if it wasn't for people like me." He waved a hand to dismiss the topic. "This is where I spent much of my childhood. It holds a special place in my heart, and I know in time it will for you too."

That was laughable. "Bruno, I shot you in the foot, helped get that child you wanted out of Mexico, and yet I'm sitting here at dinner with you. You've never gone back on your word. You said you were going to kill me, so why aren't I dead?" That certainly addressed the elephant in the room.

"You continue to push me Nicole," he hissed but raised a hand when Armondo stepped toward me.

"Down, boy." I smirked at him, and Armondo shot me a warning look. Suddenly, it came to me. I remembered the conversation Bruno had with Eric Noah and how he said something about Armondo that had made them both look at him. There was something there. I sensed Eric wasn't a fan of Armondo either. *Huh.* Archie wasn't the only one I was going to go after.

Anger flashed over Bruno's face, then it was replaced by a sinister look. "I thought about killing you," he cut into his lobster meat, "but what I have in store for the northern soldiers will be much more enjoyable to watch along with you."

I thought about how I should react and what he wanted from me, so of course I did the opposite. I held up my wine glass in a toast. "To the epic downfall," I stopped talking until he picked up his own glass to tap mine, "of the Perez family." His face fell at that, and I knew I was testing how important it was to him to keep me alive for whatever he had planned.

He glanced at one of the soldiers, who had cleared his throat at my comment. The man instantly looked down at his boots. "Your life is now mine now, Nicole. There's nowhere to run, nowhere to hide where I can't find you."

"Because of this?" I slid my leg out and showed off my tracking bracelet.

"Because of that, and the cameras, security, electric fences, etcetera."

I chuckled darkly. "If you have all of that, then why the ankle bracelet?"

"Think of it as a collar around my precious bitch's neck." He grinned behind his wine glass, and I felt sickened by that.

I moved my attention beyond the torches to the open stretch of land I'd hoped would, in time, hold some sort of escape, but the flames reminded me of an invisible wall, a fence of heat like a cage without bars.

The snap of his lobster shell brought my gaze back to the table. He'd gone back to concentrating on his food. I pushed mine around the plate, feeling nause-ated. My mind went to the mission. I was here to gain information, and I couldn't lose sight of that.

Blackstone were smart enough to track me down. I just needed to give them a direction to look some-how. I knew the Perez territory expanded over hundreds of acres of Mexico. It would be highly unlikely that Blackstone could narrow down where I was within six days without something to go on. I needed to focus.

I pushed that problem aside for the moment and decided to do what I could with the rest of the evening. I needed to do what I did best. I needed to trip him up. Bruno was reckless with his temper. He wasn't quick in the head. I decided to ask him a few questions to try to change direction.

"You said you spent a lot of time here as a boy. Was that with both of your parents or just with your mom?"

He looked out at the property beyond the torches. A clap of thunder boomed above us, and he answered as he studied the sky. "Just my mama."

"Why can't I go to the west wing of the house?" I threw that in quickly.

He paused. "Because its off limits."

"Is there anywhere else I can't go?"

"No, but you'll never be on your own, so don't worry about boundaries." He pointed to his men. "They'll set you straight."

"You mentioned horses. Do you ride?"

He glanced up at my change of topic and went back to eating.

I watched the sky behind his head and saw how angry it looked toward the mountains. Maybe Mother Nature could help me out.

"Yes," he decided to reply.

"I never knew how to ride. That was something I always wished I'd been taught." His men started to move like something was about to happen, but I kept talking, hoping to fill his brain with nonsense before I took a strike. "There was this one horse. He was brown and white and had all these beautiful markings. He was such a sweet thing with a white nose and a long, gorgeous mane." Armondo signaled something to Bruno, and he squinted over my shoulder. "He loved to run toward me and then stop really fast." I laughed lightly as my eyes darted to follow where Bruno looked. "I knew he'd never hurt me. It was just as a game like—will your mother be joining us here?"

"No, she's staying in the States." I stilled as I digested that tidbit. He didn't seem to notice what he'd said. His attention was totally on his men.

Then, in the blink of an eye, they all left. I was suddenly alone with Archie. At least I could use the glare from his teeth to see if I couldn't find a flashlight.

"Was it something I said?" I joked and gained a glare from him as I sipped my wine.

Holy shit, Esmeralda was staying in the States. As

far as I knew, that woman never crossed the border, not in all the years that I worked in Mexico. *Why now?* I needed to find out where she'd gone. It had to be connected to the realtor and the lawyer. What the hell was she up to?

Rain started to fall and made a soothing noise as it bounced off the stone patio. Archie stepped forward, grabbed my arm, and yanked me out of the chair.

"You're finished. Up to your room."

I pulled away and rubbed my arm as we headed inside with him tight on my heels. He walked me to my bedroom, then I turned and hoped there wasn't a camera in my room, but if there was, my idea could still work.

"Wait," I stepped forward, "my window won't close, and my guess would be that Bruno wouldn't want a flood on his guestroom floor. Can you shut it for me, please?" I held out my hands like I'd hated to impose. He scrunched his nose as he thought about what I asked. To my delight, he marched into the room and slammed the window shut. I needed him in there for another moment. "Any chance I could get the rest of that wine? In fairness, I wasn't finished yet."

"No." He left, and I smiled as he went. I really hoped the cameras had caught all that. Regardless, Buno wouldn't've wanted him in my room.

"Well, good night, then," I called after him. There was nothing more I could do but settle in for the night. I only hoped I wouldn't have a visit from Bruno. I shuddered at the thought and wondered again what he was up to.

The next morning, I begrudgingly changed into yet another of the white cotton dresses Bruno liked. The one that hung in the closet for me tied tightly like a corset up the front but at least it wasn't so snug I couldn't breathe. I detested having to wear what he wanted, but it was either that or a bedsheet. I wondered what kind of fetish he suffered from that made him want me to dress this way. *Yuck.* I quickly forced the thought from my brain.

The house was quiet as I made my way through the sunroom and into the kitchen where I snagged an orange from a bowl. I could see a few soldiers way out on the property with their rifles slung over their backs as they stood guard. They chatted then laughed when one of them said something. I grabbed a grocery bag that sat in the corner, hooked it on my wrist, and headed outside to peel my orange. I took a seat in the morning sun and began to drop the peelings into the bag. My hopes went up as I wondered if Blackstone could possibly be close and that was why Bruno and his men had left. I wondered if they were still gone. One could dream.

A snore nearly made me jump right out of my skin. I thought I was alone. Archie was passed out in the chair in the far corner. I spotted an empty wine bottle upside down between his feet.

I looked away and rolled my eyes. This was

perfect. Bruno would kill him if he caught the only person he'd left to watch me drunk on the job. Which meant…I shaded my eyes and pretended to scan the grounds when, really, I studied the area around where he slept. It had to be a dead zone for cameras. *Yes!*

I stood and continued to peel my orange as I made my way toward him. I pretended to fumble with the peel, then silently acted like there was a bee. I tossed the peels in a fake attempt to bat at the non-existent insect and sent them toward Archie. Reaching for my chest like I was terrified I laughed and started to clean up my mess. I should have gotten an Emmy for that performance. I drew closer to the open-mouthed idiot and spotted his flip phone. I prayed I was right, and no camera could see me as I leaned close and saw it was clipped to his belt like it was still the early 2000s. I breathed out through my mouth slowly, then in, and with steady hands and my breath still in my lungs, I unclasped the magnetic latch and inched the phone free. He jerked his arm, and I froze, waiting for his eyes to open, but he just snorted and fell back to sleep. I tossed it in the bag with the peelings and walked calmly back to where I'd been sitting.

I made sure all evidence of my orange was gone before I slowly walked outside. I made my way around the side of the house, looking about as if enjoying the view.

"Is the girl awake yet?" a man said in Spanish. He was out of sight around the corner I was about to step around, so I changed course and headed toward the avocado trees instead. My hands shook as I tried to remain calm. I knew I'd have a very short window to use the phone. Once Archie woke up and realized it was gone, he'd back the cameras up, and unless he was a complete idiot, he'd make the connection it was me who took it.

Finally, I found a spot and reached inside the bag and pulled out the phone. Only, as I dialed, the reception was bad.

Damn!

I hurried through the trees toward a nearby hill. My flat shoes gave me very little traction as I climbed the bank. The rain from the previous night had made the soil like clay, and it was slippery. It also stained the shoes from creamy white to brown, and I knew that was going to be bad. With each step, I watched to see if the ankle bracelet would flash red and alert Bruno I was running.

Finally, I got a set of bars at the top of the screen, and my heart soared.

A text message popped up, and I clicked on it.

> Bruno: Chili back tomorrow.
> Separate him and Nicole. Kill Chili.

No! I quickly dialed the number Savanah told me to remember if I ever got into trouble. I pressed the button and hoped they'd answer

"This is Daniel, leave your name, number, and the

reason you called." I felt defeated when the beep came.

"Daniel, it's Nicole. I'm at the house that Chili is about to visit. Don't send Chili. They're going to kill him. Eric Noah's alive, and Esmeralda is staying somewhere in the States. I found evidence about –" A noise made me freeze as I looked up into the face of a farm worker. He was an older gentleman, his skin weathered by the sun, with hands that showed years of working in the fields.

"Shhh." He placed a finger over his lips and head-pointed. I saw a guard approaching us. The farmer made a motion for me to get down behind his massive bag of avocados. I didn't hesitate and made myself as small as I could. My heart pounded so loudly I thought it might out my location, and my knees threatened to buckle.

"He's gone," the man whispered in Spanish, "but they are everywhere. You should go back to the house."

He was right. I had gotten out my message and said what I needed to, and the rest could wait. I realized I hadn't ended the call and wondered how long it had continued to record. I quickly deleted the number, and the text Bruno sent about Chili. I stood and felt lightheaded. The man studied my face then seemed to make a decision.

"There are no cameras inside the barn, and they cannot see you if you head southeast toward the forest."

"How do you know that?" If he worked with the avocado trees, he wouldn't necessarily work with the animals.

"My wife, Camila, she cleans the security room. If you ever get a chance to leave, don't hesitate, run."

His kind smile showed some of his own pain. I could only imagine what he'd lived through in his own captivity on Perez land.

"Here." I held out the phone.

He refused it. "No use for me. Drop it somewhere you can get the owner in trouble." He winked, and I liked the way he thought.

"Thank you." I squeezed his arm.

"No, thank you, Ms. Winter."

"You know who I am?" I figured he wouldn't have access to a TV in this place.

He nodded then patted his heart. "You bring hope, and hope is all we have."

"I won't forget that," I promised. It continually amazed me that so many knew my face, but the power of technology was a double-edged sword.

I turned off the phone and was about to put it back in the bag but changed my mind and tucked it into my bra. I knew it was the only place the soldiers wouldn't spot it right away and made my way down the hillside. I could see the entourage of vehicles driving up toward the house and wondered what shit-storm I was about to be greeted with once I got back.

"Why are you here?" Someone's voice made me whirl around. I had almost made it to the house and hoped I could slip back inside without anyone the wiser. The voice belonged to a rather handsome man in a dark blue jacket. He held some papers and looked very surprised to see me. A cigarette dangled from behind his cauliflower-shaped ear. He looked to be a mix of Hispanic and Caucasian, but given his accent, I'd guess he'd spent time in the US. A bag hung from his arm, and I recognized the same logo as the one from before, a half a lemon sitting in a grocery cart. *Interesting.*

"Why are you?" I shot back. I didn't need some new person to figure out. I could feel the phone that burned its existence against my chest.

He swung his arm up so fast I didn't have time to react, and he stuck his phone in my face. He tapped the screen. "This is too good not to get on camera."

"My eyes were probably closed." I snickered. "Let me give you another try." I held up my middle finger then turned my back to him and continued on my way. Never would I act so rude in front of a camera—or anyone, really—but I was at my max with this place and my job. Giving a shit about my professional persona was long gone. If I didn't act strong, I'd be swallowed whole.

"Be ready, Ms. Winter, because she wants you dead," he called, and I knew then exactly who he referred to. Esmeralda. I dropped the bag with the peelings in it in the trash by the door and slipped inside.

I heard voices at the front of the house and

could tell Bruno was panicked about something. I headed for his office but smacked right into Armondo, causing him to drop the handful of things he carried. Stuff went flying, and so did Archie's phone. *Shit!* I scrambled around like I was trying to help and saw two phones that looked identical. Damn. One had to be Armondo's. I took a guess and swatted at one of them and sent it through Bruno's open office door. I saw it slide under the desk and breathed a sigh of relief, but it was short lived because I was hauled to my feet in Armondo's nasty grip.

"Ow! I didn't see you. Let go!" I screamed, and seconds later, Bruno was in his face.

He shoved Armondo back with a puzzled look and then glared at me. "Where were you?" He made a show of looking at my shoes.

"I went for a walk."

"Where?"

"To see the avocado orchard."

"Why?"

"Why not?" I made a show of rubbing my arm like it hurt. "What else am I supposed to do with my time?"

"Where's Archie?"

I stepped back. "The last I saw of him, he was in my room making a pass at me." His jaw flexed. "Don't believe me, check the tapes."

"Armondo, check them," he ordered. "Did he hurt you?"

"Depends on what you mean by hurt." I looked away for a beat. "Physically, I'm fine."

I saw Bruno react as someone came up behind me. "Archie," he shouted, "take Nicole downstairs."

"Yes, Bruno." He headed toward me, and I pretended to cower toward Bruno. I still needed to play the part.

"I'll deal with you later, but for now, get her downstairs and keep her there until I say otherwise." Then he reached out and shoved his gun up under Archie's chin. "If you touch her, I'll skin you alive."

"Understood."

When he went for my arm, I jerked it back. "Don't touch me! I'll follow you." He glanced at Bruno then began to walk.

"Everyone out," Bruno ordered his men. "That means everyone. Outside, go!"

What is happening?

We headed to the bottom floor and then through a door that was flush with the wall. Inside was a cold room full of canned goods. I glanced at the pickles, onions, pears, and pepper sauce that were all stored neatly in sealed jars. The labels were all easy to read; someone had very neat printing. It reminded me of the cold room the sisters had at the orphanage where I'd grown up. I was often sent down there to get things for the sisters when they cooked. I loved to open those jars and help with the cooking.

Archie leaned against the wall and rubbed his head. I wondered if he was suffering from a hangover.

I hoped so. I spotted a metal chair and table, and I hooked the back of the chair and pulled it so it scraped across the concrete floor. It sounded like nails on a chalkboard, and he grabbed his head. Instantly, something dark came over me, and I saw my opportunity. I leaned my hip into the table, and when it scraped against the floor, his eyes flicked to it, and I lifted the chair and swung it at his head with all my might. He screamed in pain, and I swung it back and rammed the leg of it straight into the top of his head. The vibration of the impact made the pieces of orange in my stomach try to come back up. I might fantasize about killing the men who hurt me in life, but it was a completely different thing *actually* taking a life.

"Oh, my God." My fingers released from the chair as it fell, still impaled in his head. His lifeless body twitched, and I gagged. It had happened so fast; it wasn't planned. I just saw the moment and reacted.

"Okay, okay," I repeated and tried to control my freakout. I couldn't afford to lose myself just yet. I knew the cameras would catch me, and I would only have a few moments to make my escape.

"Where is she, Bruno?"

I ducked by the stairs at the sound of Esmeralda's voice. My skin prickled like my nerves were being dragged over broken glass. I feared Bruno because I knew what he was capable of, but I also knew he was attracted to me, and it gave me an advantage. But I was downright terrified of his mother because she just wanted me dead. She was smart enough to sense me as a threat. She might realize I could be close to discovering something.

"Don't make me search this place inch by inch."

"Why aren't you back in the States?" Bruno's voice was tight.

"Because I know you can't handle anything on your own. Now I'm having to manage you, and both projects. Give her to me."

"Mama, like I told you yesterday and I'm repeating today, she is not here. Whoever is feeding you this trash is lying." Bruno was a pretty good actor himself. "Did you really come all this way for her, or is there something else going on that you're not telling *me* about?"

"If I find out you're lying, I'll send you to join your father and brother in Mexico City."

"Mama," Bruno snapped, "I'd appreciate some respect and—"

"You'll get respect when you've earned it!" There was a pause, and I pressed my chest a little closer to the wall and caught a glimpse of the sleeve on Esmeralda's blouse. "I heard Eric Noah was back."

"Yes, he is."

"Why did he come and see you?" she demanded.

"How do you know that?" Bruno sounded suspicious. "Where are you getting your information?"

"Does it matter? Why did he come to see you?"

Bruno's shoes squeaked as he moved on the stairs, and I desperately scanned the room for a way out. "I noticed you're not surprised that he's still alive, Mama."

"Nothing surprises me anymore." She sounded even more annoyed, and I knew I had to get out of there before she decided she'd had enough of her reckless son. I took off my shoes and moved down the hallway with them in my hand. I slipped inside a room and saw it had a set of sliding glass doors that led to the outside. I saw the barn in the distance. The only problem was to reach it I'd have to get past all the parked cars. What choice did I have?

Slowly, I opened the doors, slipped on my shoes, and dashed across the small patio and through a succulent garden. I waited for the two soldiers up by the pool to turn the other way then raced between two SUVs and ducked down.

I heard a man's voice very close to where I had hunkered down. "Her breasts were like ripe peaches." Another man laughed and made a rude comment. They were only a few feet from me. I lay flat on the ground and inched my way under the vehicle then carefully moved across the sharp rocks that scraped and scratched at my skin.

Boom! A crack of thunder shook the ground so hard that I had to force the scream that wanted to erupt back down my throat. Seconds later, it was as if someone opened the gate to a dam as water poured down all around me. I saw feet run by me, and the two men raced for cover. I hurried out from under the car and jumped to my feet. With my back flat to one of the cars, I looked at the house. It was now or never. *Wait, what?* I spotted what could only be Esmeralda's purse inside the car. It was open on the front seat.

I quietly opened the door a little, reached around blindly, and grabbed whatever I could from inside the purse. I saw it was a plastic bag with stuff inside it. I wrapped it up as tightly as I could and raced off with it toward the barn while the rain pelted painfully against my bare skin. I heard some people yell, and I picked up the pace and flung myself around the corner and tore open the door.

Once inside, I dropped to my knees to catch my breath, but it was short lived when I heard voices outside. I scrambled to my feet again and moved toward some horse stalls and hid behind a stack of hay. Peeling my wet dress from my legs, I hiked it up and tucked the stuff from Esmeralda's purse into the corset part of the dress.

"You go that way, I'll check here!" a man yelled, and a tremor started in my fingers and traveled through my body. There was no way out that I could see, and chances were he'd check every inch of the place before he'd move on. I needed a weapon, but before I could find anything, the door opened, and with that suction of air, I heard a rattle from behind me. I turned and felt along the panel next to me. It was loose. Someone was watching over me. With a look at the man who slowly moved past a small pen of bleating goats, I took a deep breath and pushed the panel back and ducked outside. I shut it behind me, thankful for the sound of the rain. I remembered what the older man said and headed what I hoped was southeast toward the open forest.

Everywhere was Cartel territory, and it went against my instincts to simply run blind, but there was nothing I could do but go for it.

Someone shouted, "There she is!" just as I slipped into some dense terrain. I gasped for air as my chest pounded in terror. My head screamed at me to run, but my body felt like lead as I squeezed my eyes shut like a child playing hide and seek. I knew someone was behind me. I could feel him. Then a hand latched onto my shoulder and yanked me off my feet, and I was tossed against a tree. His dark eyes glinted, and I knew exactly what he wanted to do to me.

"I haven't been with a woman in years." He grinned, and I saw his black tooth. Holy shit, it was the same guy from the car when I was brought here. "You got my brother Nando killed, and for that, *chica*, you'll pay." His rough hand shoved up my wet dress as I clawed at his chest, but he was too strong.

"No!" I hissed. The fear of adding more men to the moment was enough for me to hold back any screams. "Get off of me!"

He hooked his nasty fingers into my panties, and I had to turn my head to the side as his nasty breath found me. My mind started to shut down as he pressed his disgusting body against mine. He ran his tongue down my cheek, and I kicked into survival mode. I tore at him like a wild thing. Tears of terror burned down my cheeks and mixed with the rain. *This isn't happening, I won't be a victim, I can't do this.*

Suddenly, the weight of the man left me as a pair of hands wrapped around his neck, and a loud snap made me stop fighting as he was flung to the side. I desperately pulled my dress down and scrambled back to see Paul standing in front of me in his fatigues.

"Paul?"

NINETEEN

Forty Minutes Earlier

PAUL

"Anything?" Chili switched his polo and reached for a dress shirt. He was about to get dressed in the clothes he often wore when he played the part of a high-class businessman in the horrific world of human trafficking.

I leaned over the steering wheel to get a better look at the house. We'd spent the night in the woods after we left Bruno's property. We'd been escorted for several miles, but once they turned away, we doubled back. "Nothing yet." I blinked to clear my vision and spotted Nicole going back into the house. Her dark hair was heightened by the stark white dress she wore. "Just got a visual on Nicole."

"Does she look all right?"

"Yeah."

Bruno had called a meeting with Chili that morning, and every red flag was raised. Why wasn't Eric included?

We'd known something wasn't right. It was confirmed when my phone buzzed, and I got a text.

> Daniel: Thought you might want to hear this. We'll talk about what was said when you get back. For the record, I'm not pleased, but it will stay between us for now.

I had pressed on the attachment and played it for Chili to hear as well.

"Daniel, it's Nicole." My gaze swung to Chili's face. The reception was spotty and there was a sentence missing. "Don't send Chili-plan-kill-him." I knew it. "Eric-alive—" My stomach sank when I realized she'd friggin' seen me at the house. "-meralda- in the States." Then there were some muffled sounds like someone talking to her, but she didn't seem scared. Nothing could be understood.

"Oh, shit, Chili," I looked at him, "they've got company!"

"Plan B, it is." He threw the business shirt in the back and began to pull on his fatigues as I started the engine. I drove down the mountain to get a better view of who was there.

Five minutes later, Chili held up the binoculars

from where he lay next to me behind a rock and gave a grunt. "Fuck. It's Esmeralda."

"We need to get Nicole out. This is getting worse by the second." I fought the rough terrain as we drove and hoped we wouldn't get hung up on an axel.

"There's a good spot." Chili pointed just as a loud crack of thunder shook the area around us. "At least if the rain comes," just as he said it, the heavens opened and the rain poured so hard it almost deafened us, "they won't hear us coming," he shouted.

"Look." I saw a flash of white from behind the SUV Esmeralda had been in. "That Nicole?"

Chili rolled his window down to get a better look. "What the hell is she doing?"

"Only one way to find out." I grabbed my weapon. "I'll head southeast, see if I can intercept her. I'll radio you my coordinates. Stand by."

"Copy that." He slid over the console as I hopped out. "Be safe."

"Copy that." I raced through the trees and fought to see against the rain. I cursed as I ran. This area of Mexico was known for this; when it rained, it came on fast and hard. When I made it three quarters of the way down, I spotted Nicole's dress as she crawled out of a hole in the barn wall and dashed across the field into the woods. I picked up speed and almost lost my footing as I tripped over a root.

I stopped for a moment and focused on where to cut her off, and as I got close, I could hear a scuffle.

"No!" Her soft cries told me she fought someone,

and my chest tightened. I cleared my mind of everything and muted my rapid heartbeat. "Don't touch me!" She was at my ten o'clock. I pivoted in that direction and whipped through the branches, thankful for my army jacket.

I ducked behind a tree and saw a man trying to tear her clothes off.

Rage boiled through me, and I shot forward, grabbed his head, and twisted with all my might, snapping the man's neck. I tossed him to the ground and stared down at Nicole's terrified face as she pushed her dress down.

"Paul?" Her chin quivered as rain streamed down her face. The nightmare of what just happened showed in her eyes. She lunged forward and wrapped herself around my body and shook as I held her close. We both knew what would have happened if I'd been only few minutes later.

"I got you," I whispered against her frozen skin. "You're safe." I heard a snap of a twig and knew we were about to have company. "We need to move. That white dress is a damn beacon, but we don't have time." I grabbed her hand and pulled her along behind me as she hung on and tried to keep pace. The pelting rain helped cover our sounds, but in turn made it tricky to get good footing on the slope of the hill.

I reached up and squeezed the button on the radio strapped to my chest. "I got the mark," my voice just above a whisper, "continuing southeast."

"Copy that, Stonewall One, heading southeast" Chili repeated to me. "I will intercept your location in one-point-five miles."

"Copy that." I dropped to the ground when someone raced across the path not more than ten feet from where we were. I signaled for Nicole to stay low. She pointed to her eyes then to the left and held up two fingers. Indicating that she could see two men through the thick leaves. I grinned inside; I forgot she was trained by soldiers. The woman constantly surprised me. I nodded and quickly assessed the situation. One of her hands moved to my back as she stabilized herself. Her hand was like ice, and that made me look back at her again.

Shit. That damn white dress practically glowed in the dark, and she also looked frozen. I pulled her to her feet and moved her along a bit farther then handed her my weapon.

"I'm not using this," she whispered as she held it like a grenade about to go off. "It weighs more than me."

"Just hold it." I undid my tactical vest and unzipped my jacket then pulled it out from under and yanked it free. "Put this on. That dress is going to out our position."

"Okay." She took the jacket and awkwardly handed me back my weapon. Once it was on, she wrapped her arms around herself. "It's so warm," she sighed. Then her eyes went to my t-shirt. It stuck to me like a second skin. She shook her head and bit her lip but didn't comment. "I sure hope this rain lets up soon." She kept her voice quiet and looked around. She shivered again, so the jacket had only brought temporary relief.

"No, but we can use it to our advantage." I looked her over and realized a lot of the white dress still showed, but there wasn't much we could do about it. She could tie it up around her waist, but it was also her only barrier from the sharp scrub brush we traveled through. "We need to move. Stay at my six and keep your hand on my back. Whatever I do, you do."

"Copy that." She smiled, but I saw her eyes dart around, and I knew she was trying to keep it together. I respected the hell out of that.

"If you see something, tap whichever side they're on." I showed her with my hands.

"Got it."

I held the scope of the gun up to my eye and waited until I felt her hand on my back, then I started to move forward. She kept her hand there and stayed with me without hesitation.

I was thankful my ball hat provided a shield from the rain. With every step, I scanned the trees and was glad there wasn't any wind.

I wondered where the two men Nicole had spotted had gone. I figured they couldn't be very far and kept my ears open for any sound as we moved steadily through the trees. I tuned in to my senses and repeatedly scanned around us to pick up on anything

I might miss with my hearing as the rain pounded around us.

I used my gun to pull back the branches as we went then eased my body past it. Nicole reached out with her free hand and took each one and let it settle behind us as we kept a steady pace. Where I stepped, she stepped, and when I looked one way, I felt her hand curl in the opposite. She had me covered, and I thought about how impressed Cole would be to see her in action. She handled it like a pro.

I froze when I sensed something, and she did likewise. I smelled smoke. Then the familiar scent of tobacco hit my nose. It was too close. Way too close for me to move.

She tapped my right side, and I slowly looked in that direction. I eased my head back a little and could just make out a man with his hand cupped around a cigarette. He fumbled with his lighter, and I realized he was having trouble keeping it lit in the rain. I was thankful his attention was focused on his smoke, but I knew he was going to be a problem.

I held up a fist then motioned for her to stay put. My mind raced as I tried to come up with a plan. There were only a few feet between where we were and the Perez soldier. Rain or not, he'd soon spot us. It wasn't good. Then I felt my jacket slide to the ground behind my feet. *What the hell?* I managed to look around to see Nicole moving her hand to tell me to circle around behind him while she'd distracted him. Before I could protest, she started to move, but I grabbed her wrist.

"No!" I shook my head. She lifted her shoulders and indicated we had little choice. She had a point. We didn't have time to go around, and if I fired my weapon, we'd give away our location to every soldier in the vicinity. I slowly let go, and she nodded then stepped through the trees. As soon as she knew he'd seen her she moved into the woods across from him and flapped her arms and looked around like a crazy person. I snatched up my jacket and circled around the other side.

"Hey!" I heard the man call. My feet slipped in the mud, and branches clawed at me as I made my way as fast as I could around them all the while I prayed, he wouldn't hear me. As I got close, I jammed my jacket under my vest then pulled my knife from my belt. I began to inch closer behind the guy. The last thing I needed was for him to sense I was there and fire his weapon.

"What are you gonna' do, big guy?" Nicole yelled and jumped back and forth on her feet as if deciding which way to run. I knew she could see me and wanted to keep his attention on her. The guy laughed at her then swung his gun around his back as if she didn't pose a threat.

"You think you can get away from me?" He laughed again then suddenly lunged forward. She dodged him, but he grabbed her by the hair and slammed her to the ground. In that moment, I dove at the guy and tackled him. He was fast and managed to get in a few punches. I swung my legs around his neck and got him in a headlock. He continued to punch and kick, but I felt nothing thanks to adrenaline and the fact that my jacket was stuffed between him and his fists and helped cushion the blows. I used all my might and continued to squeeze, and he fought me hard for another few minutes, then he finally relaxed, and I let him roll to the side.

I got to my feet and immediately looked for Nicole. She lay on the ground, not moving. *Shit!* "Nicole," I forced myself to be calm as I bent and felt her pulse. He must have knocked the wind out of her, and she'd fainted. Normally, if it was one of the guys, I'd slap them to draw them back to the land of the living, but I couldn't bring myself to be rough with her. Instead, I pressed my thumb down on the side of her hip, which I knew would bring her a dull pain that would increase with each second. When she suddenly jolted awake, I covered her mouth and released my hold. When I removed my hand, she pulled her chin in and rubbed where I'd hurt her.

"Ouch!" She looked angrily at me as I pulled her to her feet, then she dipped to the side as vertigo came over her, and I pulled her into me and hugged her.

"Let me give the orders next time," I warned. She nodded then huffed a small sob. "There isn't much farther to go, so hang in there with me, okay? You're doing great." She didn't answer, and when I handed her my jacket, she didn't take it. I took her face in my hands and studied her. I could see she was struggling and wondered if that trick she'd pulled back there had drained her. I forced her arms through the sleeves and wrapped the jacket around her small body. "We're going to be okay. We're almost through this. No more playing the hero, you hear?" I grinned at her in hopes she'd show some of that spunk she had. "Okay, let's get out of here." I was happy to see her nod and tucked her behind me again.

We moved in unison again. A few times we stopped to let her catch a breath or when we came across more soldiers. They were everywhere. Bruno had activated his entire army to hunt for her, and navigating through such difficult terrain was taking a toll on Nicole. At least the rain had stopped. I knew this place was going to be next to impossible to escape, and it was why my stomach sank when I knew she was being held here. Bruno had the place locked down hard. The only reason we'd made it this far was because his focus had been on the arrival of his mother. That, and they weren't expecting me to be so close by.

I glanced at the compass on my watch to make sure I kept on course. I picked up the pace and stopped when I finally saw the dirt road. I knew they'd have men watching, so we stayed in the tree line. I got out my binoculars and scanned along the rough woodland road for Chili's truck. I spotted it just out of sight in the trees.

"I have visual on you." I kept my voice low and crisp into the radio. "We'll be at your nine. Start moving now, but slow."

"Copy that." I watched him pull out of the trees then reach back and open the door behind him.

I lowered the binoculars then turned to meet Nicole's pale face. Her jaw bounced and her lips were blue with cold. She was near exhaustion. "Chili's not far away with the truck." She nodded and looked around as if she could spot it. "He's our ride out of here. We'll go a little farther staying in these trees, then you see that clearing up there?" I pointed. "We just need to get across that to the road. I don't see any soldiers, but they're around."

"Okay," she said and nodded again.

"I'm going to go first, then once I get across, if it's safe, and Chili's close, I'll wave you over. I'll cover you, but you need to run straight to the truck as fast as you can. Do you understand me?" She nodded. "I need to hear you say it."

"I do."

"Good." I turned and hurried her along then stopped next to a tree. I saw the truck slowly approaching. "Okay, are you ready?"

"Yes." Her head bobbed.

I raced across the clearing, hoping to draw any fire. I stopped on the other side and looked back at Nicole. My heart lurched, and all the wind went out of me.

Rio, Esmeralda's right-hand man, stood with Nicole in his arms and a knife to her neck.

"No." The word dropped from my mouth as the realization hit hard that I might not be able to save her from this. Who knew fear could feel this heavy?

I walked slowly back across the clearing until I was just a few feet from them. I heard the truck stop behind me.

"Well, isn't this perfect?" He chuckled.

"Rio," I used his name to show I knew exactly who he was, "do you know who I am?"

He stared at me and tilted his head. I could see him try to connect the dots.

"Think," I said as I stepped closer, and he stepped backward. "I'm Blackstone. I'm the one you guys want, not her. Take me and let her go with Chili."

"Why do I know you?" He was so close to saying it. I knew it was a risk to potentially out myself to Nicole as Eric Noah, but at that moment, I knew I would rather have her alive and know it than face the death that was only moments away.

"I'll tell you when you give me the girl." I reached towards him as I made eye contact with Nicole. She looked done. Worse, she looked resigned. "Nic," I used her nickname in hopes I could get through to her, "Chase needs you to keep your head on straight." She blinked, and I saw a tear leak down her cheek. *Good.*

"Don't come any closer." Rio shifted his hold on her, and I knew I needed to let him know who I was.

I changed my accent to reflect Eric's and went with a saying I hoped he'd recognize. I had used it before when portraying my alter ego. "In a world of illusions, you stay alive by being honest—"

His eyes widened. "You stay alive by being one step ahead of the liars." I locked eyes with him and gave him a small tilt of the head. "Holy shit, you're—" *Bang!* I shot him straight in the shoulder before he could say it. His grip on Nicole went slack. I lunged forward and caught her then scooped her up and raced for the truck. I tossed her in the back seat and jumped in next to her.

"Go! Go! Go!" I shouted at Chili, and he took off so hard we flew backward.

I wished I'd killed Rio, and I should have, but she had seen the dark side of me back there. When I flipped between two head spaces. Killing as Paul was one thing, but killing as Eric Noah was something I never wanted her to witness.

I reached over and buckled Nicole's seatbelt. The way she reached for my hand made me breathe a sigh of relief that she hadn't understood what had happened back there. I pulled out my handgun and scanned through the back window for company. I was sure the gunshot would have them running like cockroaches toward the sound. The engine screamed as we bounced around, and I wondered how Chili could even follow the old road. We took a good beating from branches and shrubs that had overgrown it. Nicole leaned forward, covered her head, and stayed down. Whether she realized it or not, her training was still there protecting her. We swung out onto the main road, and things grew quiet. There wasn't a car in sight. It concerned me that there wasn't even a roadblock or anyone waiting for us.

"Clear." I squinted as I looked around, then finally took a deep breath. Nicole was still huddled over. "Hey," I touched her arm, and she yelped. "It's me." She shook her head and wrapped her arms around herself and leaned her head back. Her eyes were closed.

Chili caught my attention in the mirror, and I shrugged. She was beyond exhausted, and I let her be.

"Let's get the fuck out of here, Chili," I huffed.

"Happy to oblige. Glad you didn't die back there." His eyes crinkled in the mirror when I nodded.

After we made it through the border and on US soil, Chili pulled over and parked around the back of a diner. "I'll give you some time with…" he nodded at Nicole, "and I'll order something warm to go. I'll be back." He flipped up the collar on his jacket and headed out into the rainy evening.

Nicole had opened her eyes and sat up when the truck stopped. The day's events were very much the elephant in the room, and I wondered how to navigate it.

"You want to talk about it?"

"No," she said softly.

"Do you want to eat?"

"No."

I cleared my throat. "What can I do to help?"

She leaned forward and put a hand over her mouth.

"Let me help you." I felt so helpless.

She leaned back and took a few short breaths then turned toward me. "You want to help?" I nodded. "Help me get this," she rubbed her chest, "feeling of pent-up panic out of me." I went by instinct and grabbed her waist and lifted her onto my lap before she could say anything then slammed my lips to hers. I forced my tongue inside her mouth and kissed her until she squeaked for air. When I released her, she didn't waste any time pulling up her dress, then I had my belt undone and my button and fly down, ready for her.

She put both hands on my shoulders, and I lifted us to free my now aching erection. Her icy hand wrapped around the base of me as she eased herself down onto my tip. My head flopped back with how great it felt. She was tight, warm, and velvety-soft. She hovered there, and I looked up at her.

"Thank you," her lips brushed against mine, "for saving me back there." She slid me inside a little farther. "If you hadn't come, that monster would have been inside me." The fear in her voice told me that moment back there scared her. *How can it not?*

I threaded my fingers through her hair and touched my forehead to hers. "No one is going to be inside you but me." I thrust upward from the bottom until I hit my base. "You're mine, Nicole, and I'm not letting you go." I thrust into her again to drive my point home. "Ever."

She moaned into my neck, and I felt even more deliriously protective. "Yours," she panted and kissed my neck, and I felt my need to take all I could from this woman. "Paul." My head spun at the mention of my name. "Paul, I need more."

I couldn't think straight. I needed more too. I flipped her around, so her knees were on the seat, and she faced the back window. I folded myself over her and took her from behind. I silently thanked the powers that be for building such a large truck. I reached around and laced my fingers through hers as I pumped against her.

"Yes!" she screamed with a deep gasp. "It's so good."

I moved my lips to her ear. "I don't want to be anywhere but here," I confessed while my hips moved in a steady rhythm, "deep inside you. I can't get enough." I pulled a hand from hers to reach down and touch just above where we were joined and felt her fall apart beneath me. She shook and moaned as she released, and all thoughts left my head as I followed her into oblivion.

We both panted as I withdrew from her and turned her around. Our chests heaved against each as I fought to regain some sort of logical thought. The windows were steamed up, and I rubbed a spot clean to see nothing but smeared lights as the rain ran down the glass.

I felt her relax against me then tense for a moment, and it made me wonder if she was thinking back over what we'd been through. She reached for something.

"What is it?"

"Something I stole from Esmeralda's purse." She leaned back and arched herself up a little, and I moved over so she could get at it. She struggled a bit then pulled something from inside her dress.

"What is it?" I took the small plastic bag from her and saw it contained some paper.

"I don't know, but I'm hoping it'll be something useful."

I opened it and looked inside. "Holy shit."

TWENTY

BRUNO

"Bruno, you're coming with me to the States. I need to focus, and I can keep an eye on you there. Things are moving fast, and we'll have our first shipment through in two days."

Mama's mouth moved, but I wasn't paying attention. Something had caused my men to disperse in different directions. I had a bad feeling, an almost physical slap. The sudden internal silence alerted me that my world was about to buckle.

"Excuse," Armondo approached and leaned into my ear, "we have a problem. Archie is dead, and Nicole escaped."

Rage ripped through me like a chainsaw.

Mama gave a dramatic sigh. "Are you even listening?"

"No," I barked and spun on my heel and headed

toward my office. Rio blocked my path, and my gaze landed on his bloody shoulder. His face was pale and sweaty.

"Do you know?" he gasped and glared at me with such intensity I could physically feel it.

"Know what?" Mama's voice cut through what little sanity I had left. "Rio," she rushed to his side, "what happened to you? Have you been shot?" Her voice was full of concern.

Rio struggled to speak. "I'm nowhere near all right. Your son has been a hiding a secret."

I couldn't deal with the two of them; I needed to get to my cameras. "I'm not in the mood for you right now." I moved around him, but he dared to grab my arm, and I saw red. I jammed two fingers straight into his wound and felt the satisfaction as he dropped to the floor.

"Bruno, stop!" Mama cried and reached down to help Rio to his feet.

Rio groaned like the little bitch he was as he held his shoulder and leaned into her. "Tell her or I will!" Saliva flew from his lips. "Tell her how you let the enemy into our lives. Into our world!"

I rubbed my face and pulled my gun and pointed it at him. "I don't have time for this!" My voice boomed across the room. "Say what you mean or get the fuck out of my house!"

"Eric Noah. He's a fucking Blackstone soldier!"

I jerked back as I took in his words. My mind spun as I thought about all the times Eric and I had done business together. I'd seen him shoot people point blank in the face, he trafficked women, and had been close with my uncle Martin.

"What have you done?" My mother's eyes were dark, round pits. Her voice scraped my brain.

"You're a fool, Rio. That's a total lie." I seethed at him. I knew Eric. He was friends with Grim Gates and Trigger. There was no way he could be what Rio was saying…unless I was being played… by Rio.

Things started to click in place. Rio was always coming at me. He had Mama's full attention. I looked at her hand on his arm. He had her in his pocket. Of course!

"Get the fuck out of my house!" I screamed at him. When he didn't move, I shot over his shoulder, shattering the window. Men quickly came inside with their guns drawn.

"That's enough!" Mama demanded. Then she whistled for one of her men. "Take Rio. He needs medical help."

"Wait," Rio looked at her, "do you want to know who Eric is protecting? It's that reporter, the woman who he claims isn't here." Mama's face went to stone as he turned to look at me and sneered. "She got away, in case you were wondering."

"Rio, that's enough. You need to get that shoulder looked at. I can't have you out of commission." Mama waved him off, and he nodded and started to limp away like it was his leg that was shot and not his shoulder. I didn't wait around for her reprimand and headed up the stairs toward my office. I'd get my men to look at the cameras. I was wasting time dealing with all these lies.

"Where do I even begin?" She had followed me.

"You can start by leaving," I shouted over my shoulder.

I heard her come up the stairs behind me. "You don't walk away from me, boy. I am your mama. I say when you leave! How could you let this happen? How could you be so blind? I'm pulling your position in this family. I'm stripping you of the Perez name altogether."

I expected to snap, but instead everything fused together and seemed to make perfect sense. I turned to her.

"I'm more of a Perez than you, Mama. Need I remind you that you're a Castillo, and last I checked, that blood line ends with you." Her mouth dropped open, and before I saw it coming, her hand made contact with my cheek.

I chuckled at the sting, then I sprang forward and wrapped my hands around her neck and squeezed with all my might. Her eyes bugged out, and I watched dispassionately as her mind tried to understand what was happening. All the white noise that came with her started to dissolve. She had seconds left when I let go. She put a hand to the wall as she sucked in deep, gasping breaths which then turned into nasty sobs.

"You tried to kill me," she croaked.

"No Mama, I did kill you." I lashed out with my foot and kicked her in the chest and watched as she toppled down the stairs. Her legs flipped over her head as she summersaulted a few times, then her head hit the floor below. Her limbs were spread out in all directions.

Silence.

I leaned over the banister and studied the pool of blood that trickled out from beneath her head.

Armondo stood at the bottom of the stairs, and he looked up at me.

I straightened my jacket. "Do you have anything to report?"

"Not yet, but Marcel said to check the back-road camera."

I nodded then took one last look down at the woman who had made my life a living hell. She wouldn't stand in the way of my plans anymore.

"Get that cleaned up."

I marched to my office and flicked on the computer monitor then placed my finger on the pad to bypass all the logins.

Armondo's phone rang with that ridiculous sound he insisted on using for work. "Once you get rid of Mama, deal with Archie." When he didn't answer, I looked up and saw he wasn't there. His phone rang again.

"What the hell?" I searched for the sound and had to pull my chair out to find it. *When had Armondo been in my office, and why?* I quickly silenced the call and sat it on my desk.

Then my own phone alerted me to a text, and I pulled it out from my coat pocket. I scrolled down and stopped on the message where my informant had written me about what border Nicole and the child were going to cross. It still bothered me that the other Cartel families were there too. I had my suspicions about who shared that information, but I'd deal with him later. One shit storm at a time. I kept scrolling to the last message.

J: See attachment.

My excitement bloomed as I read the words, "You're invited…"

I opened a group message.

Bruno: Green light. Every sleeper has the green light. ATTACK.

TWENTY-ONE

PAUL

Once we finally got back to the base, Nicole was approached by Daniel with a hug and an explanation that he needed to debrief her of any information she could provide. She hesitated, and Daniel apologized but explained it was necessary. It was obvious she was sleep deprived and emotionally wrung out, but being the professional she was, she agreed.

"You're not leaving the base, right?" Her words made me want to hug her, but I just nodded.

"Not without you," I assured her. Her teeth caught her bottom lip, then she followed Daniel. I watched until they turned the corner then headed to get cleaned up. I met John's hard stare as he leaned against a wall outside the room. "Jesus." I nearly ran into him.

"I've known you the longest out of everyone in there," he pointed to the room where I was headed, "and when you left here, after all that shit went down with Frank, I was pissed because I knew you were holding something from me."

"Yeah, I know," I admitted. It killed me I was in the position I was in.

"Okay," he stared at me, "I wanted to tear you a new asshole and remind you that you're still in the doghouse."

"I know."

"But what I also saw was that Cole was out of the loop on where you went as well. I felt maybe Frank was up to his old tricks and maybe he has you doing things you don't want to be doing but you're under orders." I couldn't answer, but I didn't break eye contact. "And now you're back covered in the same mud and dirt as Nicole. Now, as I understand it, and correct me if I'm wrong, that woman wasn't supposed to be extracted for another few days." He stepped forward so we were inches apart. "So, I know you can't answer, but look me in the eye when I ask this." I didn't flinch. "Did you go back under cover as Eric Noah?"

I hated that I was filled with shame when I heard the name. I'd never asked for any of it. I'd been fed a false promise that I had served my team, and I'd never have to go back to such a dark place. My mind twisted around itself, but I reined it in because what choice did I have? I was under orders.

"I'll never lie to you." I held his gaze.

His jaw ticked. "Copy that, brother."

"Hey," Cole came up behind me, "Frank said you had something?" He stopped when he caught our body language. "Is there a problem here?"

"No," John stepped back, "we were just discussing the trip." Cole knew better but wisely let it go.

I held up the paperwork in the bag Nicole had given me and handed it to him. "Nicole managed to take this from Esmerelda's purse before she ran. I went through it, and there's mail in there with an address in New Mexico. There's a contract with the same lawyer Nicole mentioned before. Looks like she's interested in some land in the area around that address. There's also an invoice for two SUVs that have been upgraded to military level protection. There's some other stuff, but that's all I got through."

"Sounds like you got through a lot." His face was bright with interest.

"Yeah, and I forgot, that bag is from Smith's food store and still has a receipt inside for some snacks. It's time-stamped three days ago. Nicole said she saw fruit with the same logo in Bruno's house before she was transferred to the avocado farm."

"Christ, this is huge." He grinned. "I'll get the guys on this and see what else we find. You get a shower and something to eat. We ship out in two hours."

"Copy that."

John took a deep exaggerated breath before he

walked away. Just as he did, Frank came around the corner.

"Good, just the man I needed to see." I brushed past him, opened the door to the bunk room, then slammed it shut. I'd probably get reprimanded for my behavior, but I didn't give a fuck.

Nicole and I slept most of the way back to Shadows. She was beat, and I needed to be alone with my head. A few times, I caught John's stare, but I knew he wasn't mad anymore, just concerned.

I knew Frank was being forced into retirement and was determined to have one more big win before he left. Only he'd almost dragged me down with him while doing it. I was below him in rank, so I couldn't go against his orders no matter how much he bent the rules.

My eyes popped open when Nicole's hand touched my arm. "We're here."

I didn't even know we had landed. The others were already off the chopper, so we hurried down to meet everyone.

After the wives greeted their husbands, they went straight for Nicole to make sure she was all right. Abby came out with Chase, who wiggled with excitement when he spotted her. She wrapped him up in a huge hug and buried her face in his neck.

I stood back and watched as warmth spread through me. She loved my son, and he loved her. She smiled and took his hand to wave at me. I joined them, and as I did, he reached out for me. I dropped my bag and scooped him up and held him high while I made my chopper noises. He laughed and gave me the sweetest smile.

"Seems someone got past his nerves." She beamed at us. "He trusts you, Paul. We both do. That's something to be proud of." She stood on her tiptoes and kissed my cheek, and that instantly caught Savannah's attention. Damn woman never missed a thing. Chase nosedived back into Nicole's arms, and they headed inside the house while I stood there and tried to wipe the silly grin from my face.

"You need to tell her, man." John came up next to me, and all the joy I was just filled with was sucked away, as I knew he was right. "She's falling for you and is head over heels in love with your son."

"I know." He may be right, but I couldn't imagine how.

"Come on, we have a lot to celebrate, so everything else can wait a few days." He started to walk then turned back to face me with his face all serious. "Just so it's said, you're out of the doghouse."

"My boy is off the couch." Mark wrapped an arm around me with a grin. "Look at you two making up."

I shoved him off and headed inside.

The next day, we had a celebration of life for June, in the same spot we had it for Lexi. It was hard to process that we still had no answers for what happened, but the one thing Doc Roberts drove home was that she had lived a full, beautiful life. One that most only could dream of living, and that was what we needed to hang on to.

The following week, things seemed to fall back to normal. The pain of June was still there, but acceptance of her loss started to take hold. Nicole worked tirelessly with us, filling in as many gaps as she could with her resources.

"Son of a bitch," Cole said as he hung up his phone and walked into the conference room. We were watching drone footage that Dark Water had taken of the Canos Cartel. "Mark, bring up the map." He pointed at the property Esmerelda had bought. "We can't touch it. There's legal paperwork in place that protects it."

"What do you mean? What's it filed under?" I asked.

"It's under a privatized community project for, of all things, a religious group."

Mike looked around. "Meaning?"

"Shit," I rubbed my head, "it makes it damn near impossible for federal agents or the military to legally raid the area. At least without extreme justification."

"Is this not extreme justification?" John huffed.

I pointed to the map. "Even if we could storm it, they'd have time to get rid of evidence. We'd need to know exactly what they're up to, and we'd need someone willing to cut corners for us."

"We need to bring the Feds into this." Daniel pulled out his phone. "Let me make some calls, see what I can do. For now, we watch. Thanks to Nicole, we're a step ahead of them."

"Excuse me," Savannah was in the doorway, and Cole's face lit up, "I know you're all busy, but Olivia is ready to leave for Zack's, and I'd rather not have her friends wait."

The heaviness from work evaporated, and we all jumped to our feet. Olivia's birthday that year had been a bust because of a mission, and her father promised her a redo. He even bent a little and agreed to have it at Zack's so she could invite some of her friends. She was over the moon excited and hadn't talked about anything else since we got back.

"Ready?" I came up behind Nicole as she struggled to get Chase's mittens on. He looked like a starfish stuffed in his snowsuit.

"We are." She handed him to me, and we headed outside to join the others. Cole had decided to add a few more guys from the safe house for extra eyes. With how bad things were getting, we couldn't be too careful. Travis was a good friend of Keith's, and he was leading the new team assigned to us. "How was the meeting?"

"Good. I'll fill you in tonight."

We joined the others as they piled into the vehicles that would take us to Redstone. I shot Cole a look in the mirror when Olivia finally stopped talking and took her first breath on the way there.

The place was full of balloons and streamers. Kids ran around like it was a frickin' Chuck E. Cheese.

Thank God, Zack had closed down part of the restaurant for us because no one would want to sit through this if they didn't love the kids to death.

I caught Mark's smile as he spotted Liza. She'd shown up. She was still making an effort with Keith, and that meant a lot to us.

"So, this is a kid's birthday?" Nicole laughed and rubbed my back. "I think I need a drink."

I wrapped an arm around her waist. "Let's get doubles."

My ears rang from all the yelling and from some of the topics of boys I wished I'd never heard as I held the door open. The silence that blanketed us thanks to the snow was just what I needed. Nicole held Chase by the hand as she carefully walked him down the steps.

Easton yelled as he ran with Liam right on his heels. "Uncle Paul, help!" He laughed. "He's trying to eat me!"

Mia huffed as she went by me down the steps. She had a tight hold on the hood of Tabby's jacket. "I get why they say only have two kids. I've only got two hands!"

I scooped up Tabby and flung her over my shoulder. "That's why there's uncles." I grinned and raced down the stairs as she shrieked with laughter. Keith grinned at me as the two little beasts, Easton and Reagan, both grabbed an ankle and sat on my feet when I stopped for a breath. They wanted a ride, too.

"You little monsters, get off!" I pretended to struggle as I hauled them toward the vehicles.

Easton yanked on my pants. "Faster!" I kicked my foot out to try to send him into the air, but the hyena stayed on like glue. "Again!"

"Hey, Tabs?" I whispered in her ear. "Ready for your next mission?"

"Yes, sir!" Her tongue slipped through the space where her two front teeth had been.

"I'm going to toss the ankle biters in the snow, so when I lean down you jump off and run to your dad as fast as you can." She giggled with excitement.

"Okay!"

"Okay, one," I swung Easton so he wouldn't predict my motive, "two," I swung Reagan next, "three!" I dipped down, Tabby jumped off, and I plowed the two little buggers into a giant drift. The snow from the night before had left enough soft powder for them to shoot through the other side like the Kool-Aid man coming through a wall.

"We got you!" Tabby screamed from the protection of her father. Easton wiggled out of his jacket with a laugh, and Reagan just sat there spitting out snow. I grabbed them both by their waists and pulled them over to their parents.

"Your children fell into a snowbank. They really need to be more careful." I dropped Easton next to Cole's feet in another pile of snow. I really did love my role as an uncle. "Oh, buddy, did you slip?" I grinned at him.

"Just wait!" he yelped, and Cole grabbed him by the shoulder with a laugh.

"You want to ride with Grandpa or Mom and me?"

"Grandpa!" He jumped with excitement, and I saw Daniel step out of the vehicle and scoop the kid up in his arms.

"No, Dad, it was Uncle Paul who tossed us in." Reagan outed me, and I shot her an innocent look.

I put my hands on my face. "I tripped, Reagan." I pretended to be hurt. "Do you think I'd ever toss you in the snow like that?"

"Lies!" She pointed her mitten hand at me. "Dad!" He lifted her into the car as she kept talking. "I think I need a hot cocoa to get over this."

"You do, do you?" He buckled her in as she added things to her hot cocoa order.

I looked for Nicole and saw her with Chase in her arms as she bent to get into the SUV at the front of the convoy. Sue was in the passenger seat. I could hear her calling to Daniel to put Easton down. He ignored her and kept swinging him around. He probably was trying to wear off a little of the kid's endless energy before the car ride. Abby tapped her boots together and climbed in behind Sue.

Okay, that was it for that vehicle. I did a quick scan of the others. Savannah was helping Cat get little Gabby settled as John and Sloane packed the trunk with all the leftovers.

"Uncle Paul?" Olivia called, "Can you come

here?" I spotted her by the snowbank where I'd tossed the boys. I chuckled darkly at the cutouts from where they'd gone through the drift and was excited to plan my next attack on the littles.

I waved at her and started to jog toward her. Out of the corner of my eye, I saw Nicole get out of the vehicle with Chase. She looked over at me, and I sighed. It was like gathering hens trying to get everyone settled. I shook my head at Travis as I trotted by him.

"Hard to round 'em all up." He grinned.

I heard Easton's laughter ring out in the clear air as I got to Liv. "Hey, kiddo, what's up?"

"What's this?" She had Easton's jacket in one hand as she lifted her other toward me. My stomach hit rock bottom. A silver coin with a lion's head stared back at me from her small palm.

"Where'd you get this?"

"Easton's jacket."

I swung around to the line of vehicles and saw Easton being flung into the sky. "Grandpa! Again!" Just as he disappeared from my view…BOOM!

Heat.

Flames.

Screams.

That was the moment I knew our lives had changed forever.

The End

MESSAGE FROM THE AUTHOR

I know.
I know.
I can hear your screams from where I live!

Don't toss your Kindle or paperback, I got you…
keep reading, and I'll give you a little peek at Book 3.

PAUL

I was in a battle zone. In the split second of the blast, I'd thrown my body over Olivia's. The explosion hit us like a wall of fire. It was blistering and deafening all at once. The heat had been instant, unforgiving, and merciless. It crawled over us like a living thing.

I tried to keep my weight off Liv as I rolled us onto our sides. We both gasped for air that wasn't there. The oxygen had been sucked away, along with any sound. The ringing in my ears was intense, and I fought to block it out. It wasn't the first time I'd been through a blast like that, and I knew my ears would bother me for a while. My vision was spotty, but I blinked to see Olivia and quickly patted her down to make sure she was okay. My eyes kept going to the vehicles, but I had to check her out first.

She was like a zombie, and I knew she was in

shock. I pressed a hand to her shoulder and made the motion to stay down. I had to assess the situation. I spotted the tracker Liv had handed me where it lay on the ground. I rammed my fist into the face of the lion then stood and used my heel to crush it. Staying low, I moved quickly in the direction of the SUVs.

Holy shit. It might be a war zone, but this one included everyone I loved.

Chase! Nicole! Their faces pushed through my mind as I began to run. I looked for the guys and saw, like me, they'd transformed from husbands and fathers to combat soldiers. They moved swiftly about in the chaos. As I got close, I saw their faces were white with pain and shock as they tried to get everyone away from the still-burning vehicle. We all knew more could be coming.

What the hell had happened? How could this happen here?

Cries and shouts from our loved ones intermingled with the sounds of people as they arrived on the scene to help.

There was so much distraction, I couldn't even fathom that Nicole and Chase's SUV was the one that had been blown up.

John and Travis were quickly herding the wives and children to Zack's entrance. Sloane raced past me, headed for Olivia. "I've got her." Her voice sounded strangled and her face was pale.

Then I saw Savannah. Cat was at her side pulling

her arm desperately to try to get her to move with the others toward the safety of Zack's restaurant.

"Savi!" Zack appeared out of nowhere and sounded a mile away. He shook her shoulders, and she blinked out of the trace she was in. "Olivia!" she screamed.

"She's over there. She's okay." He pointed to the stairs where Sloane half-carried Olivia up the restaurant steps. Savannah sobbed and ran for her daughter.

I quickly veered around to head toward the inferno. I needed to see. I had to know. *My son.*

"No!" Mike's voice boomed, and I whirled to see him intercept Cole as he hurled himself at the burning vehicle. "You don't want to see that! Cole, stop!"

I raced around them. I felt weightless and heavy all at the same time. Tears formed but didn't fall as I stared at Sue's and Abby's black and burning bodies. I couldn't see Nicole or Chase. But they'd been in there. Hadn't they? I reached desperately for the lava-hot back door handle when someone slammed my hand away.

"No, Paul!" Keith grabbed my shoulders and turned me around. I saw Cole's expression as he stood with Mark and Mike on either side. They held him tightly. Nothing could be done.

"Easton!" The break in his voice was enough to tear my heart in two as he tried to fling himself at the door.

"No! Cole!" Mark yelled, and he and Mike

yanked him backward. "Dad," he yelled again, and I pulled myself away from Keith, dropped to my knees and ripped off my jacket to protect my hands. I had to see inside. I yanked the door open.

My eyes went everywhere, but there was no sign of them. There was only an empty seat next to poor Abby. I sobbed. *Oh, my God, where are they?* We were trained in such situations, but it all went out of my head. I wanted nothing in that moment but to see my son and *her*.

"Everyone inside!" Travis yelled. His team ran toward us. They were still trying to clear the area, and as the emergency vehicles began to arrive, they set up a line of protection around us.

"Paul." Keith's voice made me look up, and he pointed to something. Cole also looked. "Oh, my God, Dad!" Cole cried. We all ran together to where Daniel lay face down on the ground. I pushed through and used my jacket, and with the utmost respect, Keith and I lifted Daniel's charred, lifeless body off Easton. My stomach violently rolled as Daniel's eyes stared up at me. Mike handed us his own jacket to put over him and gave me a nod to keep going. I glanced up at Cole, who now stood in frozen silence.

"Medic!" Mark yelled.

Easton was covered head to toe in blood. He had some burns, and a huge piece of metal was wedged right below his knee. "Oh, my God, my boy!" I heard Cole's cries, and it broke me. "Is he—" He went down on one knee next to us and reached out his hand.

"Cole," I stopped him, "let me do it." His eyes were so frightened and in so much pain. He gave me a small nod, and I leaned forward. With a shaky hand, I gently pressed two fingers to the little guy's neck and waited.

We were taught to believe in a higher power. Whether that was God, something else, or someone else entirely, we had to believe, and it was that belief that carried us. It existed for moments exactly like this. There had to be a line between good and evil, and we needed that higher power to stand with us.

Then I felt it, like Easton himself had tapped me to say *I'm still here*. A tiny pulse. I looked over at Cole and gave him a weak smile and saw the relief wash over him.

"Barely, but there." I smiled up at the guys. Then, before we could think, we were shoved aside by paramedics. They went to work and got Easton on a gurney and ran with him. Another stretcher arrived for Daniel.

"Paul!"

"Nicole?" I jumped up and looked around.

"Paul!" I heard it again. Keith pointed. Nicole was running straight toward me with Chase in her arms. My heart pounded with pure joy as I went toward her.

Zip! Zip! Zip! Zip!

Bullets rained down as screams erupted around

us. I grabbed her and pulled her to the ground with me. I took Chase from her and tucked him under us as I desperately looked around for the source.

"Get 'em inside!" Keith yelled over the roar of confusion.

I pulled Nicole to her feet, and we started to run as pieces of pavement sprayed up in front of us. I pulled her behind a car.

"Two o'clock!" Mike huffed as he joined us. He slid me a weapon, and I grabbed it, pressed my back to the tire, and prepared to kill the fuckers who had taken out three of our own and left a little boy clinging to life.

They wanted a war, they'd get one.

COMING 2026

ACKNOWLEDGMENTS

To my mother, for always plotting, scheming, and gasping at the cliffhangers like we're caught inside our own murder mystery. I wouldn't want to conspire with anyone else the way we do!

Veronica and Kasey, for always having time to read and give feedback on my stories.

To Rachel and Lyle Womack, for always being there day or night.

To my beta readers,
Rachel Womack, Maggie Savarese Rro, Kasey Griffin, Veronica "Vern" Nelson, Deb Peach, and I'm sure there are more!

To my editor Lori Whitwam for going above and beyond with anything I need edited.

To my street team and fact-finding group, for help with all my random questions.

To my reader group, I just love you all!

To anyone who has taken a chance to read my
books, I
thank you!

J.L. Drake, born and raised in Nova Scotia, Canada, later moving to Southern California. Though she loves the weather in Cali, she would sell her left kidney for a good rainstorm. Jodi's love of the seasons back home in Canada definitely appear in her books.

When she's not writing, you can often find her sitting somewhere along the coast of Huntington Beach, reading, or at home curled up on a couch with her two children and husband, binge watching a good movie.

AUTHORJLDRAKE.COM

FOLLOW ME ON SOCIAL MEDIA

facebook.com/JLDrakeauthor
x.com/jodildrake_j
instagram.com/j.l.drake
tiktok.com/@authorjldrake
bookbub.com/profile/j-l-drake

BROKEN TRILOGY

Broken

Shattered

Mended

BLACKSTONE SERIES

Honor

Escape

Freedom

Courage

DEVIL'S REACH TRILOGY

Trigger

Demons

Unleashed

QUIET MAFIA SERIES

Quiet Wealth

Quiet Secrets

Quiet Power

Quiet Empire

DARK WATER SERIES

Shadows

Whiskey

Alpha

Tango

HAVOC OF SINS

Grim

Havoc

Sins

DARKNESS SERIES

Darkness Lurks

Darkness Follows

Darkness Falls

STONEWALL SERIES

Extraction

Embedded

Breached (Coming 2026)

STANDALONE BOOKS

Behind My Words

Christmas At The Cabin

Omerta

For the suggested reading order, please scan the QR code:

www.ingramcontent.com/pod-product-compliance
Lightning Source LLC
Chambersburg PA
CBHW021407310726
48971CB00005B/1234